THE PERKS OF LOVING A VISCOUNT

The Strongs of Shadowcrest
Book Two

Alexa Aston

Text by Alexa Aston
Cover by Dar Albert

Dragonblade Publishing, Inc. is an imprint of Kathryn Le Veque Novels, Inc.
P.O. Box 23
Moreno Valley, CA 92556
ceo@dragonbladepublishing.com

Produced in the United States of America

First Edition March 2024
Trade Paperback Edition

Dearest Reader;

Thank you for your support of a small press. At Dragonblade Publishing, we strive to bring you the highest quality Historical Romance from some of the best authors in the business. Without your support, there is no 'us', so we sincerely hope you adore these stories and find some new favorite authors along the way.

Happy Reading!

CEO, Dragonblade Publishing

Additional Dragonblade books by Author Alexa Aston

The Strongs of Shadowcrest Series
The Duke's Unexpected Love (Book 1)
The Perks of Loving a Viscount (Book 2)

Suddenly a Duke Series
Portrait of the Duke (Book 1)
Music for the Duke (Book 2)
Polishing the Duke (Book 3)
Designs on the Duke (Book 4)
Fashioning the Duke (Book 5)
Love Blooms with the Duke (Book 6)
Training the Duke (Book 7)
Investigating the Duke (Book 8)

Second Sons of London Series
Educated By The Earl (Book 1)
Debating With The Duke (Book 2)
Empowered By The Earl (Book 3)
Made for the Marquess (Book 4)
Dubious about the Duke (Book 5)
Valued by the Viscount (Book 6)
Meant for the Marquess (Book 7)

Dukes Done Wrong Series
Discouraging the Duke (Book 1)
Deflecting the Duke (Book 2)
Disrupting the Duke (Book 3)
Delighting the Duke (Book 4)
Destiny with a Duke (Book 5)

Dukes of Distinction Series

Duke of Renown (Book 1)
Duke of Charm (Book 2)
Duke of Disrepute (Book 3)
Duke of Arrogance (Book 4)
Duke of Honor (Book 5)
The Duke That I Want (Book 6)

The St. Clairs Series
Devoted to the Duke (Book 1)
Midnight with the Marquess (Book 2)
Embracing the Earl (Book 3)
Defending the Duke (Book 4)
Suddenly a St. Clair (Book 5)
Starlight Night (Novella)
The Twelve Days of Love (Novella)

Soldiers & Soulmates Series
To Heal an Earl (Book 1)
To Tame a Rogue (Book 2)
To Trust a Duke (Book 3)
To Save a Love (Book 4)
To Win a Widow (Book 5)
Yuletide at Gillingham (Novella)

King's Cousins Series
The Pawn (Book 1)
The Heir (Book 2)
The Bastard (Book 3)

Medieval Runaway Wives
Song of the Heart (Book 1)
A Promise of Tomorrow (Book 2)
Destined for Love (Book 3)

Knights of Honor Series
Word of Honor (Book 1)
Marked by Honor (Book 2)
Code of Honor (Book 3)
Journey to Honor (Book 4)

Heart of Honor (Book 5)
Bold in Honor (Book 6)
Love and Honor (Book 7)
Gift of Honor (Book 8)
Path to Honor (Book 9)
Return to Honor (Book 10)

The Lyon's Den Series
The Lyon's Lady Love

Pirates of Britannia Series
God of the Seas

De Wolfe Pack: The Series
Rise of de Wolfe

The de Wolfes of Esterley Castle
Diana
Derek
Thea

Also from Alexa Aston
The Bridge to Love (Novella)
One Magic Night

PROLOGUE

London—August 1790

"HOLD STILL, SETH," his father admonished as he tied the cravat around Seth's neck. "There. That will do nicely."

Seth reached for the small hand mirror and held it up, seeing the cravat perfectly knotted. He also wore a new coat, a little too large for him, but his father always purchased his son's clothes with plenty of room so that Seth would be able to take his time growing into them and wear them for a good, long while.

They were going to visit Lord Hopewell today, a man who was Seth's uncle. Father said Hopewell had seen Seth shortly after his birth, having come to the funeral of Seth's mother, who died giving birth to her firstborn. Father said the viscount rarely came to London, and so this was a special occasion, getting to meet his uncle.

Father finished dressing himself, and then they set out for Mayfair, a part of London which was quite exclusive. Father and son walked all areas of town because his father enjoyed getting out and seeing people. He worked long hours at a solicitor's office, coming home extremely tired, but saying that walking and being with Seth energized him.

Seth vowed never to work in an office. He enjoyed the outdoors and was happiest when his school day ended, and he was able to walk home each day. Many days, he walked down to London's waterfront area, watching the great sailing ships come in from around the world. He could think of no life better than one lived outdoors, especially as a sailor on the seas.

Father hailed a hansom cab, surprising Seth. They rarely rode in one, saving their coin and walking everywhere. Even at eight years of age, he understood that his father wanted them to look their best when they arrived at Lord Hopewell's townhouse.

Seth only knew bits and pieces about his father's family and nothing of his mother's. He knew this uncle they visited today was a viscount, which meant people addressed him as *my lord*, and he had received property and money when his own father died. The other three sons in the family had to make their own way in the world. One uncle was in the military. Another was a vicar in the country. Father constantly reminded Seth that he would also need to earn a living, encouraging him to work hard in school. Father had told him if he did so, there would be a place for him at Mr. Peabody's office. Seth merely smiled, knowing he would never want to be a clerk and toil at a desk over papers every day.

They reached Mayfair, and the hansom cab pulled up in front of a beautiful stone townhouse. Several carriages sat nearby, lining the street, their coachmen waiting for the passengers to return.

As they disembarked from the vehicle, Father reminded Seth, "You will bow to Hopewell. Always address him as my lord—and never uncle. He may extend his hand and if he does so, shake it firmly but briefly."

His eyes looked over the large townhouse. "He lives here all by himself?"

"Hopewell resides in the country. In Kent. He rarely comes to town, but when he does, he stays here at the Atwell townhouse. It belongs to whoever is the current viscount. Because he comes to town so infrequently, most of the furniture will be covered in sheets to keep away the dust. Only a skeleton staff operates it. In fact, it wouldn't surprise me if Hopewell has chosen to keep no servants at the townhouse and merely brings a few from the country with him on the rare occasions he is in town."

Father ruffled Seth's hair. "You will be fine, my boy. Do not speak unless spoken to. I doubt we will be here for very long. Just remember that it is a great honor to have been invited."

A butler admitted them, and Seth gazed about in wonder at the grandeur of the foyer. They were encouraged to mount the stairs, where a footman escorted them to a drawing room. He had never seen such a large room in his entire life and marveled that a handful of people lived this way since he and Father lived in two small rooms.

The room currently held about two dozen guests, and Father nudged him along to what he called a receiving line. Seth could see a tall, lean man greeting his guests. As they moved up in the line, it struck him at how sad this man appeared. To think he was a viscount and possessed wealth and a house large enough for dozens of families to live in, and yet he looked so very unhappy.

They reached the head of the line, and Father bowed, as did Seth.

"Hopewell, it is good to see you again. This is my boy. Seth."

The viscount shook hands with his brother and then turned his attention to Seth, giving him a sad smile. "I last saw you when you were but a few days old. How old are you now?"

"I am eight years of age, my lord. It is good to see you again, even if I don't remember the last time."

The remark caused Hopewell to chuckle, and Seth felt good he had made the viscount laugh.

"We will talk later," Hopewell said abruptly, and he understood that meant they were to move on so the viscount could greet his other guests.

He and his father strolled about the room, Father talking to a few people and introducing Seth, who grew increasingly bored. He wandered away, moving to the window and looking outside.

He glanced around, seeing his father engaged in conversation, and decided that he might explore just a little bit of the house. He doubted his father would miss him. Father never got to spend time with adults other than at work and never went to social affairs. He seemed to be enjoying himself.

Seth slipped out the door and wandered along the corridor. He opened several doors, entering the rooms, seeing furniture covered. The vast rooms seemed a bit forlorn, much as their owner was.

One room was lined with shelves of books, and he stepped inside, closing the door behind him, eager to see what lay on those shelves. He ran his fingertip along the spines of books, amazed that one man would have so many books gathered in one place. For his birthday each year, Seth received a book from his father since he loved to read. Father had taught him books were expensive and should be treasured.

He roamed the room, and near the window stood a large globe. Seth began turning it, his finger tracing different countries, faraway places that he vowed to visit one day.

Lost in thought, he didn't realize someone else had entered the room until he felt a presence beside him and glanced up.

Hopewell smiled down at him. "You enjoy geography, Seth? Are you good at your studies?"

He nodded enthusiastically. "I like geography and history, and I'm very good at maths. What I don't like is having to sit at a desk so long each day."

He turned back to the globe, running his finger along the broad Atlantic Ocean. "Someday, I'm going to sail the Seven Seas. I love Father, but I don't want to be a clerk as he is. I prefer being outside when I can."

"So, you fancy yourself a sailor?" asked the viscount.

"I do," he said. "One day, I'll sign on to a ship's crew and travel the world. There are so many places I want to see, my lord. I wish to feel the heat of India on my back. Scale a mountain. See the Great Pyramids."

Seth's enthusiasm took over. "I go down to the harbor and watch the great ships come in. I thought I could join the navy one day and fight for England on the waters."

Hopewell grew thoughtful and then said, "If you truly wish to go to sea, Seth, you should go now, while you are young, and learn all you can."

He frowned. "And leave my studies? Father would never approve."

"You already know how to read and write," the viscount pointed out. "You have told me you are good with numbers. Any learning beyond that, you can do on your own. If you truly wish to go to sea, I can make that happen for you. I invest in numerous businesses, and one of them is a shipping line. Strong Shipping. We could see about getting you onboard as a cabin boy."

Excitement rippled through him. "Would you really do that for me, my lord?" Then his face fell. "Father would never allow it."

"I think I might be able to talk him into it." Hopewell winked. "After all, I am a viscount. I am also the oldest of the four brothers and have always held sway over my younger siblings."

"Could you, my lord? I would be forever grateful."

The door opened, and Father rushed in. "There you are, Seth. You vanished, and I have been looking all over for you."

Father bowed again to Lord Hopewell. "I apologize for my son wandering about, my lord. It was not for you to chase him down."

"I did not go looking for Seth," the viscount admitted. "I was merely wishing to escape from all those guests. You know I am not good with people, Atwell, but your son and I have had a most interesting conversation. One thing he told me? He wishes to go away to sea."

His father frowned deeply. "Seth has talked such nonsense before, but he must stay in school if he is to make anything of himself."

"The boy has no interest in being like you, Brother,"

Hopewell said. "He enjoys the outdoors and has a love for the sea. I have told him he knows how to read and write. Any additional education beyond that would be his dedication to his own learning. Pursuing what interests him and developing those interests. I can arrange for Seth to be a cabin boy. It is well within my grasp to do so."

Hopewell paused, his gaze searching his brother's. "You know how unhappy I have been my entire life. Being saddled as the heir apparent and then Viscount Hopewell. Don't let your son be as miserable as I have been all these years. Allow him to follow his heart's desire and go to sea."

Hope spring within Seth as he saw his father consider the idea.

Father placed his hands on Seth's shoulders. "Is this truly something you wish for, Seth?"

"It is, Father!" he exclaimed. "I want to seek adventure. Travel to new lands. Get to know all kinds of people and learn about their cultures."

"All right, Hopewell. Arrange it. I would see my boy happy."

Seth threw his arms around his father, hugging him tightly. "Thank you, Father. Thank you so much."

He released his hold and gazed up at his uncle. "And thank you, my lord, for making this happen."

"All I ask is that you do as your captain says and learn as much as you can. Not just from the other sailors but from books that I will send to you. You will read these books, and we will correspond about them."

"Yes, my lord," Seth agreed enthusiastically, knowing his love of reading would always be a part of him and that he would be happy to read whatever books his uncle gave to him.

"I will send word to you when the arrangements have been made," the viscount told his brother. "Thank you for coming today. I know these are not your people, so feel free to leave now."

They took their leave, walking to Hyde Park. Occasionally,

his father brought Seth here to sail a toy boat along the Serpentine. Today, they merely walked the path beside it.

"I will miss you, Seth," Father said. "But you have that sense of adventure which your mother had." He smiled gently. "Her spirit was one of the things I loved most about her. I see so much of her in you."

"Do you miss her, Father?"

"Every minute of every day," Father said quietly.

Having never known a mother, Seth could only guess at what it might be like to lose someone you loved. He realized that in a way, his father would also be losing him now—to the sea.

"If you don't wish me to go away, Father, I will stay with you in London. I don't want you to be lonely."

His father smoothed Seth's hair. "I would not keep you from your dreams, my dear boy. More than anything, you should follow your heart. Your mother would want that for you." He gave Seth a bright smile. "And you can always come and visit me when your ship returns each time."

"I promise I will do so, Father. Every single time. And I will write to you, so you will know everywhere I have gone or will be going."

"I will cherish each and every letter from you, Seth."

Two days later, a message arrived from Lord Hopewell. It asked for Seth and his father to be at the docks early the next morning, where Seth would be sailing on his first voyage.

He barely slept because of his excitement.

They arrived at the docks, having indulged in the luxury of hiring a hansom cab. Seth had a haversack holding his clothes and a few books which had accompanied yesterday's message, books which Lord Hopewell wanted him to read while he was at sea.

Surprisingly, the viscount himself was standing next to the ship, and they made their way to him. The pair bowed to the viscount and then shook hands with Hopewell.

"You must complete this voyage in its entirety, Seth," his uncle told him. "The ship will be gone close to two years. By then, you should have a good idea whether you want to remain at sea or not. If you decide the life is not for you, you have only to tell the captain, and we can see you return to school. If you choose to stay a sailor, that will be your decision and no one else's."

"Can we go aboard so I might see where he will live?" his father asked.

Hopewell chuckled. "I thought you might ask that. The captain has given us permission to board. We will use this gangplank." The viscount indicated a wide length of board which men were going up and down.

They boarded the ship, and Lord Hopewell introduced them to the captain. He seemed a bit gruff, but Seth supposed all men in charge must act that way and keep their distance, not wanting to get too close to their men.

The time came for him to say goodbye, and Seth hugged his father tightly.

"Be a good boy," Father said. "Do everything your captain and those above ask of you."

It surprised him when Lord Hopewell also hugged him briefly. "Read those books and write to me, Nephew."

He handed Seth a slip of paper with an address on it in Kent.

"I will write to both of you," he promised.

The brothers walked down the gangplank. Once they were back on the docks, two sailors hoisted up the gangplank, returning it to the ship. The ship became busy with activity as it prepared to leave port. Seth had been given no instructions yet, so he stood out of the way, watching everything happen, excitement growing within him.

The sails were raised and the anchor lifted, and the ship began to move. He turned and waved to his father and uncle for as long as he could see them, London receding from view.

Then a sailor appeared before him.

"Come along, Atwell. It's time to start your duties." The sailor slapped Seth on the back. "Welcome to the Seven Seas, lad."

CHAPTER ONE

London—Late October 1809

CAPTAIN SETH ATWELL'S belly churned uncomfortably, causing him to wonder if he would even keep down his most recent meal. It had been so ever since they left Bristol a few days ago.

He would be bringing in *Odyssey* for the second time as a captain. All his life, Seth had envisioned himself in charge of a great sailing vessel, and it had finally come to pass. He had risen through the ranks for two decades as he sailed for Strong Shipping Lines, finally attaining his current position.

But how long would he hold it?

News had awaited him when they landed in Bristol to unload a portion of their cargo. His father had known of that stop, and Seth was not surprised to find a letter waiting for him upon his arrival. When he had opened it, however, it had rocked his world.

Seth removed that letter from his inner coat pocket, unfolding it once more, wishing its contents could be magically changed. Unfolding it, he glanced at the familiar handwriting and read through it for what had to be the hundredth time.

My dearest son Seth –

Something incredible has come to pass, an event which has changed my life—and yours.

Hopewell is dead. I know that news will jar you since you and he have grown close over the many years you have corresponded. From what I have learned, he did not suffer. He went quietly in his sleep, simply not opening his eyes one morning.

What is so remarkable about his death is that it will mean a new life for the both of us.

You see, Seth, my other two brothers are also gone, one lost in the war with the Little Corporal, and the other passing from a bad heart. Both those deaths came close together, only a week apart. In fact, it was Hopewell who wrote to me of them, asking if I might come to Hopewood for their burials.

I did so, seeing my brother for a last time, observing how thin and weary he appeared, but never guessing he would soon be dead himself.

I returned to town and received news of Hopewell's death less than a week later. You know what that means now, Seth.

I am Viscount Hopewell.

As I write to you of this news, I am about to forever leave the two rooms I have spent so many years living in, the rooms I brought my lovely bride to. I regret that you never knew your mother, Seth. She looked at everything in life with such gusto, and she could find happiness in even the direst situation. I only hope we shall be reunited when I pass from this life into the next.

Of course, this means a change of life for me. I have spent my last hour at Mr. Peabody's office, making copies of wills and marriage contracts. I will never again have to carefully watch each farthing. I can once more dress as a gentleman and move among the ton because I am a part of it again.

I know you will be home soon from your latest voyage,

and we will have much to discuss. The sea claimed you long ago, Seth, but she has had you two decades now. You will need to prepare for a different kind of life, one of ease and freedom. I came from it and know it well, but I will have much to teach you until it is time for you to take on the mantle of Viscount Hopewell yourself.

I will meet Odyssey when it sails into London, the first time I will have had the luxury of being on the docks when you arrive.

Take care, my wonderful boy. A new and exciting life awaits you.

With much love,
Father

Seth resisted the urge to tear the letter into a thousand pieces. He did not want to leave the life he had built for himself. His father may have missed being a part of Polite Society, but Seth had never been a member of it. He would have to find a way to refuse this eventual title and all that came with it. It would be imperative to quickly seek out a clever solicitor to learn what steps he must take in order for the title and estates to pass from his father to some other relative. The problem was, he knew of no other such relatives.

Years ago, he had finally met his uncle, a second son, who at that time was a colonel in the British army. The last he knew, his uncle had worked his way up to the rank of major-general and had never wed. His other uncle, playing out the role of a typical third son, had become a country vicar whose wife had died giving birth to their first child, and he had never married again, telling Seth's father he could not be disloyal to his loving wife's memory.

Seth would have to find a way to locate some relative and see how he could have the title skip over him and be awarded to some other male in the Atwell family. If no relative could be found to take it on, then perhaps both title and lands could revert to the crown. With Britain at war with France, he thought the royal treasury would appreciate gaining back the wealth and could put it to good use.

His temper under control now, Seth refolded the letter and slipped it into his coat pocket once more. He had always been nothing but honest with his father, but he believed he would need to seek a remedy to this problem and not involve his father in it until a solution had been found. It would greatly disappoint the new viscount that his son wanted to wash his hands of being an heir apparent. He could only imagine how proud Father was, a fourth son finally holding the title of Viscount Hopewell, and wanting to pass it on to his only son.

As far as Seth was concerned, though, he wanted no part of a system which favored only sons to begin with and only the eldest one, at that. Why should a man inherit wealth, lands, and a lofty title, while his siblings had to work for their living? He believed things should be earned by hard work, not due to the whim of birth order.

He entered a final entry into his captain's log and then made his way up to the deck. They were on the Thames now, and London soon came into view. He could put a smile on his face because he would be happy to see his father again after a long couple of years at sea. *Odyssey* would need a few repairs done before she could be taken out again, but Seth planned to be the captain who did so. He would not be giving up anything because he was supposed to inherit some worthless title, and he was far too active to become a gentleman of leisure.

He gave several orders as they approached London's waterfront, and men scurried about the deck. They pulled into a slip owned by Strong Shipping Lines and dropped anchor, lowering their sails. Seth scanned the wharf, looking for his father and not seeing him. He turned and spoke to his first mate, relaying a few more instructions, and then went downstairs to claim his captain's log to turn over after he went to the Strong Shipping offices to report in on *Odyssey's* time at sea.

By the time he arrived on deck again, the gangplank had been lowered, and cargo was already being unloaded from *Odyssey*. Descending the gangplank, Seth saw the supervisor of Strong's warehouse, stopping to visit with him for a minute.

"A good trip, Captain?" the man asked genially.

"Everything was smooth sailing," he shared. "It is nice to set foot upon British soil again, however. I am headed to the Strong offices now."

"During your absence, there have been some changes, Captain Atwell. The Strong heir turned up. He was none other than a ship's captain for Neptune Shipping."

"What?" he asked, having been familiar with the story of the Duke of Seaton's heir apparent vanishing at London's waterfront years ago, never to be heard from again.

"No one knows the full story, Captain, but apparently the boy was taken and sailed on Neptune ships all these years, working his way up to captain."

"How did Josiah Grant react?" Seth asked, referring to the owner of Neptune Shipping, Strong's chief rival.

"Grant passed away in his offices back in August. Mrs. Grant took over in his stead."

That did not surprise him, knowing that Mrs. Grant had been running Neptune Shipping alongside her husband since their marriage several years ago.

"I'm sorry to hear of his passing, but Mrs. Grant should do a fine job. I have heard she is a most clever woman."

"Clever enough to have snagged a duke," the supervisor said. "She is supposed to wed the former captain of *Vesta*. The announcement was in the newspapers this week. I suppose it will mean that Strong and Neptune will merge into one line."

Seth rubbed his chin in thought. "You're most likely right. The duke will control Neptune once the vows are spoken. It would only make sense to fold Mrs. Grant's shipping line into that of Strong. Thanks for letting me know of the situation. Good seeing you."

He turned and headed in the direction of Strong Shipping,

which was but a short distance from the Thames. Then someone called his name.

"Captain Atwell? Captain Atwell? Is that you?"

He found a stranger standing there, a nondescript man in his mid-twenties, with brown hair and brown eyes, dressed much as Seth's own father had dressed as a clerk.

"Yes, I'm Captain Atwell."

The man handed him a letter. "This is for you, sir."

"All right," he said, accepting it, starting to slip the letter into his coat's pocket.

"Mr. Peabody said for you to read it immediately, Captain," the man said nervously.

Peabody was the solicitor Seth's father had worked for all these years.

"You work for Peabody?"

"I do." The clerk paused. "Good day, Captain." He scurried from sight.

His curiosity raised, he broke the seal on the letter and opened it, glancing to the bottom and seeing Peabody's signature there. His eyes drifted to the top, and he began reading.

Dear Captain Atwell –

I regret to inform you of the passing of Viscount Hopewell. I know this will be a surprise to you, and I am most sorry for your loss.

If you will go with my clerk, he will bring you to my offices, where we can discuss the matter further.

Sincerely yours,
Arthur Peabody

Confusion filled Seth. Why would Peabody wish to speak to him about his uncle's death—unless he had served as Hopewell's attorney. Then again, he and Hopewell had grown close over the years, their correspondence covering a wide variety of topics, ranging from politics to history to literature. Seth had never seen his uncle again in person once he went to sea since Hopewell had been such a recluse and was never in London. Still, they had a close relationship and a deep respect for one another, achieved through two decades of correspondence. Perhaps his uncle had left Seth something in his will, a small item in which to remember him by.

He folded the letter and glanced up, seeing the clerk hovering nearby.

"I have a hansom cab waiting for us," the man said. "If you will come with me."

He looked about the docks a final time, not seeing his father, thinking he must had been delayed or called to the country and had not been able to greet Seth upon *Odyssey's* arrival. He supposed it would all be sorted out soon. He would see this solicitor first and then go to the Hopewell townhouse in Mayfair.

Neither man spoke during the ride to Mr. Peabody's offices, which suited him. Seth had been a small boy when he had last visited the premises, but things seemed remarkably the same as they entered the office and he looked about. The clerk asked him to wait a moment, and within a minute, Mr. Peabody himself appeared.

Offering his hand, the solicitor said, "It has been many years, my lord. You have grown into a man, a fine man, according to your father. Then again, that does not surprise me, knowing what a good soul he was. Would you accompany me to my office?" Peabody asked.

He hated already being addressed as my lord and supposed the heir to the viscountcy held some minor title. It made him all the more determined to seek a remedy to this nonsense.

Seth followed the older man, and he took the seat indicated. Peabody went behind his desk and sat, moving a few papers around.

"This is Lord Hopewell's will. It was written recently, as you might guess."

Seth had no clue why that would be the case, but he merely

nodded.

"I know you have limited knowledge of the properties held by Lord Hopewell since you have been away at sea. I will be more than happy to go over everything with you, my lord. I know this must be a very difficult time for you."

He froze, understanding washing over him. "You . . . you are referring to my father, aren't you?"

"Why, yes, I am. Did you not read the letter I sent? I instructed my clerk to have you read it the moment you came ashore."

Shaking his head in denial, he said, "You talked of . . . you wrote of Lord Hopewell's death. I thought you meant . . . my uncle."

"No, my lord," the solicitor said quietly. "I referred to your father, the Mr. Atwell whom I employed for many years. Didn't you receive his letter when you came ashore at Bristol? Lord Hopewell told me he was writing to you, breaking the news before you saw him here in London."

Tears welled in Seth's eyes. "Yes, Mr. Peabody. I did receive that letter. Father said he would meet my ship on the docks today. When I didn't see him, I merely thought he'd been delayed. I had no idea when I read your letter that you referred to my own father's death. I supposed you had been my uncle's solicitor, and that he had left me something to remember him by."

"I regret I did not make that clear to you in my brief note, my lord. I didn't wish to elaborate on something so personal, thinking it better to visit with you in person regarding the passing of your father."

"How did Father die?" he asked, removing his handkerchief and mopping his eyes.

"It was remarkably similar to the previous viscount's passing," Peabody said. "Your father had taken up residence in the Atwell townhouse in Mayfair. He and I had spent two full days together, going over what he, as Viscount Hopewell, now owned. We were to meet again for a third and final day when I received word yesterday morning that Lord Hopewell had passed away in his sleep. Knowing you would be home in the next day or so, no burial arrangements have been made. However, all three of your uncles are buried at Crestview, the nearest village to Hopewood, the country seat of your family. It is in Kent."

Sympathy filled the solicitor's eyes. "I am sorry to be the bearer of such bad news, my lord."

Hearing himself continually addressed in such a manner riled Seth. "I have no wish to be a viscount. I don't want the title. Or Hopewood. Give it to someone else. Find my closest relative, Peabody. I will see Father buried alongside his siblings, but I plan to take *Odyssey* back to sea as soon as possible."

Peabody shook his head. "Things do not work that way, my lord. There is no rejecting the title and passing it on to someone else. Like it or not, *you* are—and will be—Lord Hopewell until your own death. You have a townhouse in Mayfair, as well as Hopewood in the country and all its tenants, which you are now responsible for. Hopewood is entailed, so there can be no selling of it. It is meant for your son, the next Viscount Hopewell. You also have investments in several companies, and I will be glad to share all that with you. The fact remains, my lord, that you will always be Viscount Hopewell. Until your death."

Seth felt as if he'd been laid flat with the blows. First, learning of his father's recent death. Second, hearing he was permanently saddled with a title he never wished for, and not one but *two* places to live. He would have too many people depending upon him. He must take up the mantle of responsibility, one which he had never wished to hold.

To think he'd spent his last voyage at sea and not known it almost caused him to break down, especially knowing he would never sail the seven seas again as a captain for Strong Shipping. In the blink of an eye, his life had forever changed.

And not for the better.

"I must see Father properly buried, Mr. Peabody. Would you accompany me to Kent for this? Then I will need to learn everything I can from you."

"I would be happy to accompany you to Hopewood, my lord. Simply tell your staff you wish to leave for the country tomorrow morning, and they will make it happen. I can ride down in the carriage with you if you wish. It should take about three hours to reach your new home."

Home was the water. Not land. And certainly not a large estate. Home wasn't Polite Society. It was his crew.

Worse, he would now have to shackle himself to some emptyheaded woman and produce an heir, forcing his oldest son into a life Seth didn't want to be a part of and would never care about.

"I must meet with the head of Strong Shipping and let him know I will no longer be in their service," he said stoically. "Can you be at my . . . townhouse tomorrow morning? We can ride down to Hopewood together then. After breakfast."

"Of course," Peabody agreed. He rose. "I will see you in the morning, my lord."

Seth left the solicitor's office without a word. He couldn't speak, his voice thick with emotion.

He was now Viscount Hopewell. No wonder his uncle had appeared to be so unhappy, stuck in a role he never asked for, tied to an estate.

And now Seth shared that unhappiness.

CHAPTER TWO

Shadowcrest—Kent

PHILIPPA STRONG AWOKE, feeling Georgie snuggled next to her. Her twin snored slightly. It was the only thing wrong with Georgina. Her sister had a sweet nature and was very feminine. Georgie never rushed in doing anything, preferring to be methodical. While both girls were the same height and had dark brown hair and the cornflower blue Strong eyes, Georgie had ample breasts and wider hips.

Though Pippa thought her sister's figure beautiful, she preferred her own—long and lean, with small breasts. Aunt Matty had always called Pippa a tomboy, not simply because she enjoyed riding and swimming, but because Pippa liked to dress as a boy whenever they resided in the country. She preferred the freedom that came from wearing breeches and shirts, and she really liked wearing an oversized man's coat. It was much warmer than what women wore, and dressing in that manner allowed her to roam about Shadowcrest feeling comfortable, no matter what the weather.

She was grateful to finally have returned to the country after three long years of living in London. The usual pattern had been for her family to go to town each spring for the Season and then return to Shadowcrest when it ended. That had changed when Papa had grown ill. Mama called it apoplexy. Pippa only knew that her mean Uncle Adolphus and his sneaky son, Theo, had moved into their London townhouse, changing everything. They bossed the servants about and told Mama and her daughters what they could and could not do. Her two cousins, Lyric and Allegra, already lived with the duke and duchess most of the year, simply because Uncle Adolphus didn't like having females about.

It was her uncle who had forbid them from seeing Papa. No one dared go against those orders, especially after Aunt Matty did and was banished to the country. None of the duke's daughters was particularly close to him, but Pippa thought it unfair of her uncle to demand they stay away.

All that had changed when her half-brother had returned. James had been gone seventeen years, vanishing as a boy when Pippa and Georgie were still in leading strings. James had come home finally. She still wasn't quite clear on all the particulars, but James was now the Duke of Seaton and head of their family since Papa had recently passed. At least she and her sisters had been allowed to see Papa once James returned and took charge of the household. Uncle Adolphus and Cousin Theo had left, and no one had seen—or missed—them.

James had also married the nicest woman three days ago in the Shadowcrest chapel. Sophie was beautiful and intelligent and very different from any woman Pippa had ever met in the *ton*. She had been married before, to a much older man, and he had left his shipping business to her. Sophie ran it—and would continue to do so, thanks to James being generous and allowing it in the marriage settlements. Frankly, Pippa couldn't think of one man in Polite Society who might have allowed his new wife to run any business, much less a shipping empire. And Neptune Shipping was Strong Shipping Lines' competitor, which made it all the more delicious.

Sophie had become Pippa's new idol. She liked that Sophie used her brain. Maybe her new sister-in-law would help teach

Pippa about business so that she, too, might run a company someday.

She snickered. Georgie would laugh at that. Her sister would never have thought such outrageous things. While she adored her twin, Georgie was a typical young woman of the *ton*, eager to have her first Season next spring and find a husband.

Pippa didn't want a husband.

She had never liked anyone telling her what to do, and that seemed to be what husbands did best. They bossed about their wives. Their children. Their servants. She had no tolerance for that.

What if she refused to make her come-out?

It would be unheard of, for a duke's daughter to not make her debut into Polite Society. But if anyone might understand her feelings, it would be Sophie and James.

She glanced at Georgie, who still slept blissfully. Her twin would be upset if Pippa didn't join her for the Season next spring. Yet they couldn't always be together. Yes, they had been conceived and grown together in Mama's womb, born within a few minutes of one another. They had always slept together in the same bed. Shared clothes until their bodies began changing a few years ago. She and Georgie were not only sisters, but also good friends.

Having a husband would change all that, however. A husband told you where and when to go. Georgie might wed someone who lived a hundred miles from Kent. Upon her marriage, Georgie would have to leave Shadowcrest and be with her husband and raise their family. Even if Pippa were to agree to wed some gentleman, his country estate might be at the opposite side of England from her twin's new home. That would mean the sisters would only see one another during the few months of the Season.

Or worse. What if one of them wed a Scotsman? She had heard sometimes titled lords from Scotland came to London, seeking a bride, and then once they had her?

They stayed home in Scotland!

That would never do. It would be better if Pippa didn't marry at all. She would be free to come and go as she pleased in a few more years. She could be the kind aunt to Georgie's children, who spoiled them terribly, just as Aunt Matty was to all the Strong girls.

How was she to tell Georgie, though, that she didn't want a Season—or a husband? Her sister would never understand that. It might even drive a wedge between them, which was the last thing Pippa wanted to do.

"Oh, bother!" she said aloud, causing Georgie to stir, but she did not awaken. The Second Coming would occur, with trumpets blaring, and Georgie would sleep through it.

Pippa slipped from the bed, sensing it was still early, but her thoughts were swirling. An idea was already forming. She knew she would never fall asleep. Instead, she gathered her clothes, which had been laid out the previous evening at bedtime. The six girls shared two maids, who helped them to dress and bathe and took care of their clothes. She rang and hoped one of them would be up and about to help her dress. Instead of a shirt and trousers, she would dress in a gown, hoping her attire might soften the blow.

It was Kitty who appeared, quietly entering the room, carrying a jug to fill the basin with fresh water.

"Couldn't sleep, Lady Philippa?" she whispered.

"No. Would you help me dress, Kitty?"

"Of course, my lady."

The maid helped Pippa into her layers of clothing and then brushed her hair until it shone, winding it into a chignon.

"Thank you, Kitty. And I am sorry if I roused you too soon."

"You weren't too early. I was heading this way to light the fire anyway."

"Go ahead and do so. Georgie should be up soon."

She went downstairs to the breakfast room, finding Aunt Matty already there, buttering toast points.

"Good morning, Pippa, my dear," her aunt said, as one footman seated Pippa and another poured tea for her.

"How are you this morning, Aunt?"

"My knees are creaking a bit more than usual. Other than that, I am fit as a fiddle."

Pippa asked for eggs and toast and then asked, "Did you do a Season?"

"Oh, my. What a question." Aunt Matty fell silent, a wistful look on her face.

She watched her aunt, having never seen such a tender look in her eyes. "Aunt Matty?"

Blinking away tears, the older woman cleared her throat. "The answer to your question is yes, I made my come-out at eight and ten. Oh, so many years ago. I was quite the dancer, you know, graceful and light on my feet. And I fell hopelessly in love."

"You did?" she asked. "I have never heard you talk of this."

The older woman smiled ruefully. "Because I never have. Until now."

Her aunt flicked her wrist, and the footmen and butler quickly vacated the breakfast room.

"You see, he was in the military. Or was about to be. His father had already purchased the commission. As a second son, he had little choice. But he had just completed university, and his mother thought attending a few events of the Season would put a bit of polish on him. Make him a better officer."

Aunt Matty sighed. "He caught my eye right away, as did I his. When we danced together, it was as if we were made for one another. We had many things in common. The only problem was that he would be leaving England soon, with his regiment, bound for the American colonies. Trouble had been brewing with some of the native tribes in the Great Lakes region, led by a chief named Pontiac. I had always been interested in current affairs and read the newspapers voraciously, so I knew what my beloved was being sent to."

When her aunt didn't speak, Pippa prompted, "What?"

Tears filled the old woman's eyes. "War is brutal, Pippa, my dear. English forts were being attacked, along with settlements. Hundreds of colonists were killed or captured. In a desperate attempt to gain an advantage, British officers tried to infect their enemies with smallpox by using blankets which had been exposed to the virus."

Aunt Matty shuddered. "My beloved left England, bound for the colonies to fight in this rebellion. He refused to offer for me, saying life as a soldier's wife was no life for a duke's daughter. I told him that I did not care. That I loved him. But he was firm. He told me he would not write. That I should go on and live my life, merely holding fond memories of him."

Pippa found herself growing emotional at this tale. "Did you ever see him again, Aunt Matty? Or hear from him?"

"I did," Aunt Matty confirmed. "My beloved had another officer write to me as he lay on his deathbed, his wounds too severe to survive. He told me that he loved me. He had not done so before because he was afraid I would wait for him." She wiped away her tears. "And he was right. No man ever caught my interest. I could not give another my heart when I had already given it to him."

Her aunt fingered the locket she always wore. "I have a lock of his hair inside this. I have never taken it off, not in forty-four years. He is the reason why I never wed."

Pippa reached and squeezed her aunt's hand. "Do you regret that decision?"

"No. I have had all you girls to keep me company. You have been more than enough."

She rose and embraced her aunt. "I am sorry."

"Don't be, my sweet. Some women are never lucky enough to find love. I did for a brief time—and I have held it in my heart all these years."

She seated herself again. "I do not wish to do a Season," she blurted out. "I cannot think about wedding a man."

Aunt Matty looked at her thoughtfully. "Are you worried

about the physical intimacy of the marriage bed?"

"No. Not really. I merely want to do what *I* want to do. I do not need a husband hovering over me, telling me what to do. I have so many siblings and cousins, I can get my fill of children by being a good aunt to them, the same as you have been to us."

"You are only eight and ten, Pippa," Aunt Matty reminded her. "You might change your mind. I have always thought you to be intelligent. This idea of remaining unwed might pass." She chuckled. "You might even find that rare gentleman such as James. Look at how he has given Sophie such freedom. Why, it is unheard of to allow a woman to keep everything she owned before a marriage, particularly a widow. And yet here is James allowing Sophie to run an entire business. Why, if there is one man such as James, there could be more in the *ton*."

"I doubt it," Pippa said. "Realistically speaking, Aunt Matty, James isn't from the *ton*. Being a sailor all his life, he simply doesn't carry the same prejudices against women that other men in Polite Society do."

"Perhaps you should find a seafaring man yourself then," her aunt advised, smiling at Pippa.

"Would you help me talk to Mama about this?" she pleaded.

"No," her aunt responded, surprising Pippa. "If you feel this strongly, you must be the one to discuss it with her. My advice, however, is to tell her you wish to delay your come-out. That you simply need more time. If you change your mind, you can still do so. If you don't? Cross that bridge when you come to it."

Pippa stood and embraced her aunt again. "Thank you, Aunt Matty. I will talk to Mama today. And Seaton, I think. After all, he is the head of the family. He will likely have a say in this matter."

"Be sure Sophie is present at this meeting," Aunt Matty said. "If anyone will support this decision, it would be the new duchess."

"Sage advice, Aunt," Pippa said, smiling. "I will most certainly take it."

They allowed the servants back in and finished breakfasting, and as she left the breakfast room, she went to their butler.

"May I have a word, Forrester?" Pippa motioned for him to follow her into the corridor.

"Yes, my lady?" he asked.

"I need to speak to my mother and the duke and duchess together. Just the four of us. Do you know what His Grace's plans are?"

The butler's color rose on his cheeks. "I will check with His Grace's valet, my lady."

"I'll be in the library."

She realized why the servant had blushed. After the wedding breakfast three days ago, James and Sophie had disappeared to the duke's rooms, staying there most of the day. She knew whatever they were doing were the things married couples did. Mama had promised to tell her and Georgie more about that once they had received an offer of marriage. Mama said she wanted her girls to be prepared. If Pippa didn't wed, she might not ever learn about those things.

No, Georgie would tell her. They told one another everything.

Except this. What would her twin think about Pippa skipping the Season?

Going to the library, she lost herself in a book. While she enjoyed the outdoors, she could also be happy for hours with a good book and a cup of tea.

It startled her when she heard a voice. "There you are, Pippa, darling."

Glancing up, she saw Mama wasn't alone. James and Sophie accompanied her. Suddenly, nerves filled her, causing her to grow lightheaded. Aunt Matty was right, though. If she felt so strongly about not participating in the upcoming Season, then she needed to be the one to address the matter.

Pippa bounced to her feet and dipped into a curtsey. "Good morning, Your Graces. Mama."

"Oh, you do not have to do that," Sophie chided gently. "Not in the house. It makes me feel so odd."

"You are a duchess now," Pippa reminded her sister-in-law. "You must get used to it."

"From others, but not my own family." Sophie hugged Pippa. "I have told you how thrilled I am to have a family. I feel as if all you girls are my new sisters."

She knew Sophie had no siblings and that her father had died several years ago, her mother even before that.

"Would you all please have a seat?" she asked formally. "I have something to talk over with you. Something of great importance to me."

Her brother cocked one eyebrow, looking amused, but said nothing. He laced his fingers through his wife's and pulled her to a settee. Mama sat in a chair.

Pippa decided to stand.

"I have a request of you. It is something I feel quite strongly about." She paused, seeing she had their interest, and plunged ahead. "I am not ready to do a Season come spring."

"Why not?" Mama demanded. "You are of age, Pippa, dearest. Some girls make their come-outs when they are even younger than you."

"Are you nervous about doing so?" Sophie asked, which Pippa thought was a good question.

"No." She decided to fudge a bit. "I simply am not ready to settle down. Georgie is. She's ready to be wed and have babes and run a household. I . . . want a little bit more time to myself."

James spoke up. "You want your freedom a while longer. I can see where marriage could seem restrictive to a woman." He glanced to his new wife, raising their joined hands and kissing her fingers. "But if you find the right one, Pippa, marriage can be liberating in itself."

"You do not have to wed after your first Season, Pippa," Mama said. "Some girls do two. Even three. They enjoy the social activities before settling down."

So much for trying to skirt the issue.

"Honestly, Mama? I do not want to be social. I have never cared for dressing up. I am awkward when I dance. Our dance master has told me that I possess no rhythm. I would prefer staying at Shadowcrest and riding and walking. Just having time to myself."

"I see," Mama said, frowning. "Have you talked to Georgina about this?"

"No," she admitted. "She is so ready for us to make our come-outs. I did not want to disappoint her. We have done everything together our entire lives, but I understand that Georgie will wed and go live with her husband."

"Are you trying to pull away some now to assert your own independence?" Sophie asked. "So that you will not miss Georgina as much when the times comes for you to part?"

"Perhaps. I haven't thought of it that way. Frankly, I am not certain I even wish to wed."

"There is the truth," Mama said. "You have never liked anyone telling you what to do. That is the root of this discussion."

"Yes, Mama, you are right," Pippa confirmed. "Men always tell women what to do and what to say and what to think. That would drive me mad!"

"I don't tell Sophie what to do," her brother pointed out.

"But you aren't like others, Seaton," she said. "You did not grow up in this world. You actually believe a woman has a mind of her own and can think for herself."

"Surely, I am not the only man in England who believes this way," he said.

"Amongst the *ton*? I am betting that you are," Pippa declared. She looked pleadingly at her mother. "Oh, Mama, let me simply postpone my come-out for a year. Have a year here at Shadowcrest, to do as I please."

"You mean you wish to run around in your breeches," Mama admonished.

"I will do that sometimes," she admitted.

"She is eight and teen, Dinah," James said. "Old enough to

know her own mind. She shouldn't be rushed into marriage as you and Sophie were."

Her mother flushed. "I would never force any of my girls to wed."

Pippa took her mother's hand. "I know that, Mama. We all do. We know how you wed Papa when you were very young. He was a duke, and your parents encouraged that." She looked to Sophie. "I assume your papa told you to wed Mr. Grant."

"He did. I did not even make my come-out. I was wed before the Season even began," Sophie told her.

Turning back to her mother, Pippa said, "Please, Mama? You already have Georgie, Mirella, Allegra, and Lyric to worry about. Four come-outs. *Four!* I am certain Madame Dumas would be grateful to have one less wardrobe to sew for this upcoming Season. She'll be doing theirs, yours, and Sophie's, as it is."

"You would stay here the entire Season? I would miss you, Pippa," her mother said, tears brimming in her eyes. "The entire family would be in town and you here."

"I could come and visit," she said. "It is not far."

"I think that would be a good compromise," Sophie said. "And it would give you time to focus on four rather than five girls, Dinah. You have to admit that is a huge bite of apple you have bitten off, with so many come-outs happening in one Season."

Mama nodded. "That is true. All right, Pippa. We will delay your come-out for a year. But only a year."

Embracing her mother, she said, "Oh, thank you, Mama."

Mama pulled away. "Now, you must go and inform Georgina of your decision."

Pippa left the room, walking slowly, as if she headed to the gallows—and death.

CHAPTER THREE

USUALLY AFTER BREAKFAST, Georgie went to practice the pianoforte. Pippa headed to the music room and heard the strains of Mozart coming through the doors. She stood in the doorway a moment, listening to her twin playing effortlessly. Georgina Strong did everything—except sing—with ease and charm. Pippa couldn't help but wonder if perhaps that was the reason she had decided not to do a Season. Because she would be compared so unfavorably to her beloved twin. The girls favored one another in the face, but Georgie was more feminine and moved with a grace which Pippa would never possess.

Steeling herself for their encounter, she sailed through the open doors, waving at her twin as she did so.

She went and stood next to Georgie, asking, "Shall I turn the pages for you?"

Georgie chuckled, continuing to play. "You can, but I am already three pages ahead of what is in front of me. This is the fifth number I have worked upon since we returned to Shadowcrest. I prefer memorizing the music. That way, I feel it more in my soul."

Her sister played for a few more minutes, finishing the piece, and then she lifted her fingers from the keyboard, folding her hands and placing them in her lap.

"Can we talk, Georgie?"

"Of course," her sister replied, rising and moving to the nearest settee.

Pippa took a seat next to her, wondering how to begin the conversation.

"You don't want to do our Season, do you?" Georgie asked out of the blue.

Her jaw dropped. "How did you know?"

Georgie shrugged. "How do we know anything about one another? It is innate. Sometimes, Pippa, I feel as if I know you better than I know myself." She paused. "The only thing I do not understand is why. Can you explain it to me?"

"I really do like who I am,' she began. "Yes, I will admit that I am a bit hardheaded at times. I do like things my own way."

Her twin chuckled. "You and Effie both. Why, Effie is so strong-willed, I believe she could run Parliament on her own if she wished to do so. But back to you, Pippa. Talk to me. Tell me what is in your heart. I love you and want to understand."

Sudden tears welled in her eyes, taking her by surprise. Georgie reached for her sister's hand and squeezed it encouragingly.

"I am most comfortable in the country," Pippa said. "I enjoy pursuits here. You know I am not one to go dressing up. I could try to be feminine all day, but it is simply not me, Georgie. *You* are the epitome of feminine beauty. You have a grace about you which is most appealing. I know you will easily have half a dozen offers of marriage by Season's end."

"And you think to compare yourself to me?" her twin demanded. "You think you need to be like me? Nonsense, Pippa. Though we favor one another quite a bit, we are each vastly different once people get to know us. Yes, I may look and act more like the duke's daughter which I am, but you are your own person. You will blaze your own trail through Polite Society and do things your way. You will attract a man who will appreciate your high spirts and individuality."

"I told Mama—and James and Sophie—that I did not want to participate in the upcoming Season this spring," she admitted. "I do not believe I am ready for it, Georgie. Frankly, I think I would be lost in the Strong shuffle. Think about it. Mama would be bringing out five girls. Five! The two of us. Mirella. And our cousins. I am a quieter sort. More introspective. I would vanish in the chaos of our household. You, on the other hand, will shine above them all. You will be the envy of every girl making her come-out. You will draw attention as a moth is drawn to a flame. I do not want that attention, Georgie, and I hate to say this—but I do not want to be compared to you or any other Strong making her come-out."

Georgie embraced Pippa, and the twins held tightly to one another.

"Are you postponing your come-out—or will you ever make one?"

"I cannot say," Pippa said truthfully. "I have never dreamed of my come-out, as you have. I have never pictured myself with a husband or children, while you have yearned for both."

"I do want to have a family, one very different from ours. We rarely saw Papa. Mama, with help from Miss Feathers, is the one who raised us. I may be searching for the impossible, but I wish for a husband who wants children. Not just an heir and a spare, but daughters, too. I need a man who would be involved in our children's upbringing and openly show them—and me—love. Whether I find that or not amongst the gentlemen in the *ton* remains to be seen. Do not think I will wed by Season's end, Pippa. I plan to be most particular. If I cannot find a gentleman who suits me, then I will not wed simply to be married. I want more than what Mama had with Papa. I long for happiness. I need love."

Pippa cradled her twin's cheek. "I hope you find everything you desire, Georgie."

"Are you worried about us being separated?" Georgie asked, her voice quivering. "Because I am."

"That might be part of my dilemma," Pippa shared. "We have done everything together since before we were born. If you wed, your first allegiance must be to your husband and the family you create. Not me. If I never wed, I would be free to come and go. I could remain at Shadowcrest, and yet I could still come and visit you wherever you are. If I had a husband, I would be stuck with him at his estate."

Georgie clasped Pippa's hands tightly. "Do not ever say the word *stuck*. If you choose to wed, Pippa, it will be because you have found someone you cannot live without. A man whom you love and who will love you in return. I do not want either of us to marry men who would keep us from one another."

"Georgie, it could happen. You could marry someone whose estate is far from Kent. They could live in Cornwall or Northumberland. At least if I remain unmarried, I could be the doting aunt who travels to visit her nieces and nephews often."

"No decisions need to be made yet," Georgie said in her practical fashion. "We should not borrow any kind of trouble. I will do this first Season—without you—and I will either find a fellow who suits me or not. You can have that time to yourself. To grow. To mature. To think. You might change your mind about a Season and marriage, or you may confirm you wish to maintain your freedom. Nothing has to be decided at this very moment, Pippa. Only know that I love you more than anyone in the world. Nothing will ever see us parted."

They hugged again, and Pippa felt better, having told her twin what was in her heart.

Pulling away, she said, "I am going to go change. I need to walk and think."

Georgie grinned at her. "You wore a gown when you talked to Mama, thinking that would help your case, didn't you?"

"I might have," she said loftily, returning her sister's grin. "If I am going to tramp around Shadowcrest now, I would rather be wearing my breeches and boots." She paused, her eyes misting over. "Thank you, Georgie. For knowing me. For always being here for me."

Pippa left the music room, passing Mirella, who had come for her turn at the pianoforte, telling her hello. She went to her room and rang for a maid. This time, Millie answered the call. The servant was one of two maids Sophie had brought to Shadowcrest with her. Her new sister-in-law had kept Libby as her lady's maid and given Kitty relief by assigning Millie to help with all six girls in the household and their needs.

The maid greeted her with a knowing look in her eyes. "Ready to change into your usual attire, Lady Philippa?"

"I am. I plan to go and walk about the estate."

As Millie helped her undress, the servant said, "You aren't the only one in breeches today. Miss Lyric is working in the gardens in her breeches. And Lady Euphemia has gone for a ride about the estate with Mr. Strong in hers."

Effie, being the youngest of the duke's four daughters, had followed her three older sisters about since she was in leading strings, but Effie had attached herself to Pippa early on. For her part, Pippa had taught Effie how to ride, hunt, and fish. You were just as likely to find Effie in breeches as a gown, the same as Pippa herself. She knew Effie had missed being able to dress in such a fashion, and she had grown close to Caleb since their recent return to Shadowcrest.

With Caleb now the Shadowcrest steward, Pippa believed James would give their cousin wide latitude in managing the estate. Being a former ship's captain, James did not know much about crops or livestock, whereas her cousin had managed Shadowcrest for the past three years. Since Sophie still owned and ran Neptune Shipping, Pippa thought the couple might return to town soon.

Donning her male clothing, she felt utterly comfortable as she headed out on the estate. She had wandered aimlessly about it since she was a child and knew all the tenants on their land. It had been good to visit them after their long absence.

She had also been friendly with Lord Hopewell, their neighbor to the north, since she had been a young girl. The viscount was a bit of a recluse, rarely leaving Hopewood or socializing with his peers. He, too, liked to be out and about on his estate, however, and the two of them had often met at the lake which separated their properties. She and Lord Hopewell had fished for many hours in companionable silence, no conversation necessary.

Unfortunately, the viscount had recently passed. Pippa had only seen him once since her family had returned to Kent after their three-year imposed stay in London. When she had seen Hopewell out riding, he looked thinner and sadder than usual. She had joined him, explaining why she and her sisters had been absent from Shadowcrest for so long.

Lord Hopewell had expressed his sympathies at her father's recent death and told her that he was glad she was back in the neighborhood. They had made plans to go fishing the next day, but he had not shown up. News soon arrived that the viscount had passed away in his sleep sometime the previous night.

It saddened her to have lost her special friend, and she doubted she would become friendly with the new Lord Hopewell. Through listening to servants' gossip, she had heard he was a fourth son who surprisingly had inherited his brother's title. She wondered when he would be coming to Hopewood, having learned he was a longtime widower with a son, who was a sea captain as James had been. Pippa thought that would have to change because heir apparents simply weren't sea captains, James being an exception to that rule.

She crossed the long lawn in front of the house and continued around it, heading north. Pausing in the gardens, she chatted with Lyric briefly. Her cousin had a way with plants and flowers and was happiest when she was digging in the dirt.

Pippa ran across a few of the tenants mending a fence and stopped to chat with them as they worked. She had missed these long walks in the country during her time in town. While London had much to offer, a young lady simply couldn't go about town without an escort. Miss Feathers had usually served as their chaperone, but here at Shadowcrest, Pippa was free to come and go as she pleased.

Finally, she made her way down to the lake, walking along its shore until she reached the halfway point, the invisible boundary between Shadowcrest and Hopewood. Lord Hopewell had a bench placed at this juncture, and he and Pippa had sat on it many a time, having lovely conversations about a variety of topics. It was too bad Lord Hopewell had been so much older than she was. She could have envisioned herself wedding a man similar to him, one who appreciated Pippa for her mind and did not try to squash her opinions. Rather, the viscount had encouraged her in them.

It made her curious as to what his brother was like.

She placed her palms flat on the bench's seat, leaning back and raising her face. The day was cool and crisp but quite sunny, and she basked in the ray's warmth and the peace which Shadowcrest offered her.

She wondered what it would be like to live here by herself once her family returned to town for the Season. While she would miss her sisters and cousins, Pippa was eager to see what it would be like to be on her own. She hoped to come to learn more about herself and understand herself better than she did now. Maybe Mama and Georgie were right. What if she actually found that one unique man in the *ton* who might accept her for who she was? A man who might give her the opportunity to have children and still be herself.

Her thoughts meandered until she sensed a presence nearby. She remained stock-still until someone cleared his throat and said, "Good morning."

Opening her eyes, Pippa sucked in a quick breath. The man before her was, without a doubt, simply the most handsome man she had ever seen. He was a few inches over six feet, with black, curly hair and clear blue eyes that seemed to look deeply into her. He was all muscle, easy to see thanks to his fitted coat and tight breeches.

Pippa came to her feet. "Good morning," she said, not being able to curtsey because of the breeches she wore.

She felt awkward, having no one to introduce them, but remembered this was how she had meet Viscount Hopewell many years ago.

Offering the man her hand, she said, "I am Lady Philippa Strong."

The stranger smiled, causing Pippa's heart to hammer in her chest. "Oh, you are the new owner of this fishing rod."

Chapter Four

SETH SAT AS Tompkins shaved him.

What grown man let another man do such a thing?

Yet that is exactly what his life had become during the past few days, one in which servants waited upon him, doing for him things he had done for himself his entire life. The valet cleaned and pressed Seth's garments. He shaved and dressed Seth. Tompkins had even attempted to scrub Seth during his bath, but he had drawn the line at that.

Peabody had been the one to tell him this was how things were if one became a peer of the realm. The solicitor had given Seth an intense, thorough set of information of life as a titled gentleman in the three hours it had taken them to journey from London to Kent, where Hopewood was located. Though the solicitor held no title himself, most of his clients did, and Peabody had learned a great deal about the *ton* over his years of service to its members.

The hours spent in the Hopewell carriage had proven vital to Seth. By the time they reached his new country estate, he had a good idea how things were run. Peabody had also given him a firm grasp of his finances, estimating the amount of income the estate brought in, and telling Seth of various investments he held.

Apparently, the investments were unusual for a member of

Polite Society. Most gentlemen lived off the income from their country estates. Peabody had said only a handful—though it was a growing handful—invested in companies. His uncle had been one of them. Seth realized that from long ago when the viscount had used his connections at Strong Shipping to land his nephew a job as cabin boy aboard a sailing vessel.

A wave of sadness washed over him. He would never go to sea again. Never see his father. Never receive another letter from his uncle. He now had an enormous country house, which sat upon a large estate, and he would eat all his meals in solitude. At least Peabody had offered some company, but he would be leaving after breakfast this morning.

Then Seth would truly be alone.

"How is that, my lord?" his valet asked, holding the hand mirror so that Seth might inspect the closeness of the shave.

"A fine job, Tompkins," Seth said.

He had learned as a ship's captain to praise his crew members when he could and call them by name often. That personal connection encouraged them to work harder and inspired loyalty. He supposed the same principles would apply to his own staff in town and here at Hopewood.

The valet smiled, obviously appreciating the compliment. Though Seth would prefer to maintain his privacy, he realized this man earned his living by being a valet. As Viscount Hopewell, Seth employed a good number of people in his household. He understood it took a great deal of others to keep a place such as Hopewood running.

After dressing with Tompkins' help, Seth went to the breakfast room, finding Peabody already present.

"Good morning, my lord," said the older man.

"Good morning, Mr. Peabody," he replied, allowing a footman to pull out the chair for him.

Another footman offered him coffee or tea, and Seth chose coffee, which he had not gotten often on the ship.

"Coffee is my preference at breakfast," he told the footman, knowing the servant would remember and make certain the viscount received it without asking each morning.

"What might you want for breakfast, my lord?" his butler asked.

"Three poached eggs. A rasher of bacon. Several pieces of toast."

"Yes, my lord."

As he and Peabody ate, the solicitor said, "I forgot one unusual thing of note, my lord. Naturally, everything went to your father and then to you, upon his death, but your uncle did bequeath one small item to someone."

Curiosity filled him. "What item? Is it here at Hopewood?"

Peabody smiled. "It should be here. A fishing rod."

"What? Who receives this?"

"One of your neighbors is the recipient. To the south of Hopewood lies Shadowcrest. It belongs to the Duke of Seaton."

"My uncle never mentioned this duke, and we corresponded for almost two decades."

Peabody shrugged. "Lord Hopewell was not one who enjoyed Polite Society. Frankly, I have no idea if he ever meet His Grace, even if they were neighbors. The fishing rod goes to the duke's daughter, Lady Philippa Strong."

"A woman inheriting a fishing rod?" Seth had never heard something so odd. "Once again, I never heard mention of Seaton or this daughter."

"All I know is that your uncle willed the rod to Lady Philippa. Your father had yet to travel to Kent before his untimely death, but he told me he would see it delivered to the lady."

Seth turned to his butler, knowing he and the two footmen present had to have heard everything spoken.

"Robb, do you know of this fishing rod?"

"Yes, my lord," the butler replied. "It was Lord Hopewell's favorite, amongst several he kept. His lordship enjoyed being outdoors. Fishing was a passion of his."

"Do you know this Lady Philippa?"

Robb tried to suppress a smile—and failed. "Yes, my lord. Lady Philippa also enjoys the outdoors. She and your uncle frequently spent time together over the years, especially fishing at the lake that is shared by your family and hers. Lady Philippa and Lord Hopewell also rode together upon occasion."

Knowing how withdrawn his uncle had been, Lady Philippa must be a very special woman for his uncle to have spent so much time in her company. He wondered why the pair had not wed if they were so comfortable with one another and spent so much time together.

"Then I will hand deliver the item in question to her," he declared. "I surmise it would have great sentimental value for her."

He wished he had known of Lady Philippa because he could have sent word to her of his uncle's death. They had arrived with the former viscount's body yesterday at noon and buried him in the afternoon. Though women usually did not attend funerals, Seth would have sent a message to Lady Philippa to inform her of the death of Lord Hopewell.

They finished breakfast, and Seth escorted his solicitor outside. Peabody was taking the mail coach back to London. Seth had protested, telling the solicitor that his carriage could get him there more easily and quickly, but Peabody did not want to have to stop and change horses, as they had on their way down to Kent. The older man merely wished for a ride to the village, where the mail coach would be picking up travelers within the hour.

Offering his hand, Seth said, "Thank you for your sage advice, Mr. Peabody. Not just about my financial affairs, but all that I am now experiencing."

"It wouldn't hurt to get to know a few of your neighbors, my lord," the solicitor suggested. "Become friendly with other gentlemen in the neighborhood. You can learn a great deal simply by observing others. I am certain as a ship's captain, you had a discerning eye and paid attention to details."

"I have all my life," he agreed.

"My last suggestion? See a tailor. You cannot go about in your captain's clothes forever, Lord Hopewell. Most likely, there is one in the nearest village, but you will wish to have the bulk of your garments made up in town. I can suggest a few tailors to you."

"Write to me then, Peabody. Tell me all the things you forgot and think I need to know. I don't know when I'll next be in London. I want to learn as much about Hopewood as I can while I am here. I have arranged to speak to my steward later this afternoon."

"A fine idea, my lord," Peabody agreed.

"Thank you again for coming to Father's funeral with me yesterday."

"I was happy to accompany you, my lord."

The solicitor climbed into the carriage and gave a jaunty wave.

Seth watched the carriage head down the lane. He had been able to speak to Peabody more as an equal. Now that the solicitor was gone, he would have no one to talk to. He couldn't prattle on to his servants. Even he understood a certain distance must be maintained between a viscount and his staff.

Since the carriage would be gone for a while, he decided he would walk to this Shadowcrest. The exercise would do him good.

Returning inside the house, he asked Robb, "Where is this famous fishing rod?"

The butler nodded to a footman, who left the foyer. Robb said, "I had it retrieved after breakfast, my lord, knowing you would wish to take it to Lady Philippa."

"I will walk now to Shadowcrest with it."

The butler frowned. "You do not wish to wait for the carriage to return, my lord?"

"No, the day is a pretty one. Walking will do me good."

"It is several miles there, my lord, and then you must return."

Seth had nothing better to do between now and his midafternoon appointment with his steward.

"I enjoy walking."

"You could ride on horseback," Robb suggested. "It would be much quicker. The stables are full of mounts for your use."

"I have never been atop a horse," he admitted.

"Oh." The butler looked perplexed.

"Since I haven't been about on the estate yet, Robb, tell me the best way to reach Shadowcrest."

"The quickest way is going along the lake, my lord. Might I draw it for you?"

"Come to my study."

Seth led the servant to the room, one he could foresee spending a great deal of time in. He asked the butler to sit at the desk, and Robb took out parchment.

Watching him as he drew, the butler walked Seth through the crude map, saying, "The lake is the dividing point between the two properties. Both households have shared the use of it, for fishing or boating. Even swimming."

"Well, it is much too cold for swimming today," he said amiably, seeing the look of horror upon his butler's face, realizing he had overstepped. He needed to find that fine line between being friendly and not too cozy. He had learned the boundaries with his crew. He would need to practice them with his staff.

Accepting the map from the butler, he studied it a moment and then folded it, placing it inside his coat's pocket.

"Thank you, Robb."

They returned to the foyer, where a footman awaited them with the fishing rod. He handed it to Seth, who thanked him.

"I will be home in time for my meeting with Mr. Hunt," he told Robb, not knowing if he was supposed to inform his butler of such things but thinking it the polite, practical thing to do.

"Very good, my lord," Robb said solemnly.

He headed for the lake, based upon the map drawn by his butler. He was eager to explore his own estate but decided he wanted to get a clearer picture of it from his steward. He would likely strike out early tomorrow morning and see as much as he could in a day, hopefully meeting a few of his tenants along the way. For now, though, he merely enjoyed the autumn weather and the land he strode across, still finding it a bit hard to believe that everything he saw belonged to him.

Reaching the lake, he saw the far shore in the distance and set out along the path, glad he had some water near him. Perhaps he would take up fishing. He had never been involved with that aboard any of the ships he sailed upon, nor had he spent any time cooking food. He had learned about other aspects of sailing instead, from mending sails to navigation to weaponry.

When he reached approximately the midpoint, he came across a young man basking in the sun. He sprawled upon a bench, his booted feet turned outward, his face lifted to the sun. As Seth grew closer, however, he realized it wasn't what he first imagined.

The young man was a young woman.

A very pretty one, at that.

Approaching, he said, "Good morning," announcing his presence so as not to startle her.

She leaped to her feet and replied, "Good morning," hesitating a moment. Then she stuck out her hand, saying, "I am Lady Philippa Strong."

Ah, this was the mysterious Lady Philippa. Somehow, he had pictured her to be quite different, an old maid who had retired to the country.

Smiling, Seth said, "Oh, you are the new owner of this fishing rod."

He raised the rod he carried and thrust it toward her, seeing the delighted look on her face.

"Oh, Felix!" she cried. "You are mine!"

Her smile melted his heart. "Felix?" he asked.

"That is what Lord Hopewell and I decided to call the fishing rod," she explained. "You see, he was quite lucky in catching salmon and trout with it in this very lake. I suggested we give it a name in Latin. Since he seemed to have great fortune in catching fish with it, Felix became its name."

Then her joy fell away. "I am very sorry he is gone. I saw Lord Hopewell the day before his death. We made plans to meet at this very spot and fish. He even told me he might allow me to use Felix." She glanced at the rod in her hands. "And now he is gone. He was a kind, decent man."

The woman's gaze met his. "I have introduced myself. Might I know your name?"

"Captain Seth . . ." His voice trailed off. "That is, I am . . . Lord Hopewell. The new viscount."

Lady Philippa's brows knit together. "*You* are Hopewell? But I thought the viscount's younger brother had claimed the title."

He swallowed. "That would be my father. He was Viscount Hopewell for less than a week. Like his brother, he also went to sleep—and did not awaken."

Her mouth trembled. "Oh, I am very sorry for your loss, my lord." Then something obviously came to her. "You are Captain Atwell. Lord Hopewell's nephew. The one he helped send to sea."

"I am," he said. "How do you know this?"

"I was friends with your uncle for many years."

After having seen how young this woman was, he couldn't help but express his doubt, despite what Robb had said earlier. "You? Were friends? He wrote to me regularly for two decades and never mentioned you to me."

A hot blush stained her porcelain cheeks. He realized he had offended her.

"I am sorry, my lady."

She snorted. "Well, you should be, my lord. Insulting a lady is not the done thing. Yes, I do know about you because your uncle mentioned you from time to time. He was quite private, though, and he didn't give away too much about himself or you. Only that he was immensely proud of what you had made of yourself and how intelligent you were. What a leader you had become."

Lady Philippa frowned. "And why should he have mentioned me to you? I know he gave you books to read, and you discussed those through your correspondence. I was a small, insignificant part of his life. And we hadn't seen one another in almost three years before our last meeting."

This time it was Seth who frowned. "Why did you avoid him for so long? Or he you?"

She sighed, her exasperation with him clear. "Because I was stuck in town. My father became bedridden after an attack of apoplexy. My uncle took over the family and forced us to remain in our London townhouse. Once Papa passed, my brother became Seaton. He knew how much we all missed the country, and so we finally came home to Shadowcrest. That is why I had not seen the viscount in so long." Her eyes filled with tears. "I will miss him."

She looked at the fishing rod in her hands. "Oh, the beauties I will catch with this. I will ply Cook with fish weekly."

"You enjoy fishing?" he asked, trying to placate her after hurting her feelings.

"I learned to fish from an early age. Your uncle recommended Charles Bowlker's *Art of Angling* to me. You should read it. It is quite enlightening."

She ran her hand along the rod. "This is made from bamboo. It gives a rod much greater strength and flexibility. My two rods are made of Lancewood from the West Indies and Greenheart from South America." She smiled. "I am delighted to add Felix to my collection. He will be my favorite fishing rod. You see, Felix is a multiplier reel. That was invented in America less than a decade ago by watchmakers in a place called Kentucky. Felix is a complex reel. That means he . . ."

She cut herself off. "Forgive me, my lord. I get carried away discussing things I am passionate about. I could discuss the various worms and grasshoppers to use as bait for a good hour or so. I do not mean to take up your time, however. Thank you for bringing Felix to me. And my condolences regarding your own father's passing. Good day."

Lady Philippa whirled and strode off, her shapely derriere and long legs evident, thanks to the tight breeches she wore.

Seth wanted to call out to her, but she moved so quickly, he couldn't think of a thing to say to stop her.

But he would definitely take Peabody's advice and call upon his neighbors.

Starting with Lady Philippa and her family.

CHAPTER FIVE

SETH RETURNED ALONG the lakeshore to Hopewood. His idea of walking a good portion of the estate before he met with his steward this afternoon proved to be ridiculous. Most likely, he would not be able to see a quarter of the land if he walked for the next six hours. He was going to have to learn how to ride a horse in order to get about better in the country.

Returning to the main house, he decided his time would be better spent if he went into Crestview and saw its tailor.

When he arrived home, Robb greeted him, saying, "Mr. Hunt would like to speak with you, my lord. He has received a bit of bad news."

"Have him come to my study," Seth told the butler.

He went to the study, once again thinking this room would be his retreat from the world. He had yet to explore the vast library upstairs, but he could see himself pulling books from its shelves and bringing them to this study to read. The room possessed a large desk, and it also had an excellent view of the front lawn.

Taking a seat in one of the two chairs next to the window overlooking the lawn, he waited for his steward to appear.

Mr. Hunt arrived a few minutes later, looking a bit flustered. He had only met the man briefly before his father's funeral yesterday, and had arranged to spend a chunk of time with Hunt this afternoon.

Hunt crossed the room, and Seth willed himself to remain seated, knowing it was not appropriate for him to stand when his employee entered a room.

The steward bowed. "Thank you for seeing me on such short notice, my lord."

Seth indicated the chair nearby. "Have a seat, Mr. Hunt."

The steward appeared startled, and he realized he had broken some unwritten rule by inviting the man to sit. Rules be damned! He was the viscount now, and if he wished to show common courtesy to his staff and employees, he would do so.

"What troubles you, Mr. Hunt?" he asked once the steward had sat. "It is obvious you are distressed. Robb said you had received some bad news."

"My father is quite ill, my lord. He has been going downhill for some time now. He lives in Haselton, which is only two hours away by horseback. Lord Hopewell—your predecessor—allowed me one day off each month to go and visit Father, as well as the use of a horse from his stables." A shadow crossed the steward's face. "I received a message this morning, however, that it looks as if Father is near the end. I know we were supposed to meet this afternoon and begin discussing the estate, but I—"

"You will go at once to your father," Seth instructed. "I would have it no other way. I did not see my own father for the last two years while I was at sea, and he died the day before I sailed into London. I will carry regret in my heart until my own passing for not having made it home sooner."

He paused. "Family is everything, Hunt. Go to your father now. Stay as long as you need. A week. A month. I am sure you have run Hopewood with a steady hand, and it will not fall apart during your short absence."

Gratitude filled the steward's face. "Thank you, my lord. I cannot express my appreciation enough. Might I have a horse from the stables instead of waiting for the mail coach?"

"What I have is yours," he said simply. "Go, Mr. Hunt. Godspeed."

Both men rose, and he offered the steward his hand. They shook, and Hunt departed.

Seth realized the steward might be gone for a couple of weeks, possibly even longer. Hopewood would, as he had just stated, still be here. He would begin anew first thing tomorrow morning and walk as much of the estate as he could. For now, however, he would go into the village and see about a tailor. Peabody had encouraged Seth to meet his neighbors, and he was eager to call upon the Duke of Seaton before any of them. It would make a better impression if he were properly attired as a viscount and not a sea captain.

He would admit he was intrigued by Lady Philippa Strong. He was eager to spend some time with her. He also wanted to apologize again for being a bit dismissive of her in regard to her friendship with his uncle. She was young but seemed wise beyond her years.

Ringing for Robb, he asked for the carriage to be readied so he might go into the village and visit its tailor.

"I will do so at once, my lord," the butler told him. Hesitating a moment, Robb added, "Might you wish for Tompkins to go with you? He was with Lord Hopewell for many years and has remarkable taste. He might . . . guide some of your choices."

"Suggestion taken, Robb," he said, smiling at the butler. "Notify Tompkins of our trip to the village."

A few minutes later, Robb returned and told Seth the carriage awaited him. Stepping outside, he saw his valet sitting next to the coachman and realized that most likely, it would be inappropriate for the servant to ride within the carriage with a lord.

"We are going to the tailor's," he informed the driver. "Wherever he is located."

"Aye, my lord," the coachman replied. "That would be Mr. Crocker in Crestview."

Seth mounted the stairs and entered the coach. As he sat

inside the vehicle, it was still a bit hard to believe how the winds of fortune had changed for him. He now rode in luxury, a viscount in Polite Society. He would be received places a sea captain would never have been admitted, all as the same man, the only change being an arbitrary title. He was only sorry that his own father had not been able to hold the title longer and enjoy the change in his status after toiling so many years as a clerk in Peabody's office. Still, from all he knew of the solicitor, Peabody had been a fair employer. Seth felt fortunate that the man was now his own representative in all legal matters.

They reached Crestview after a short ride, and he and his valet entered the tailor's shop.

"I am Lord Hopewell," he told the man sitting behind a counter, a needle and thread in hand as he sewed the hem on a pair of trousers.

Immediately, the tailor sprang to his feet, setting aside his work and bowing. "My lord, I am blessed to have you enter my establishment. What might I do for you today?" he asked, eyeing Seth up and down. "Perhaps a new change of clothes might be needed?"

He recalled Peabody telling him to use the village's tailor sparingly, to add a few items to his wardrobe, saving the bulk for a London tailor.

"I have recently come into my title, Mr. Crocker. As you can see from my manner of dress, I was captain of a ship in my former life. I suppose I need to dress for my new station now."

He indicated his valet. "This is Tompkins. He was the previous Lord Hopewell's valet and will continue in that capacity for me. Tompkins has a discerning eye, and I would like him to assist the two of us in what I will need for the next few days. I will be seeing a London tailor once I return to town, but it would be nice to have a few things made up for while I am in Kent."

"I am honored to serve you, my lord," Crocker said. "Shall we look at some of the available cloth?"

They spent half an hour viewing bolts of material, Tompkins

and the tailor talking things over and deciding Seth's immediate needs. He nodded a few times and grunted a few more, happy to go along with whatever the two men suggested.

"How long will it take for you to finish up?" he asked.

"I can have you back in two days' time, my lord," he tailor said. "We can do our first fitting then. It will be another few days before you would have the clothes to wear."

Disappointment filled him, but Seth did not let it show. He understood this man was a craftsman and would not rush, especially when working for such an esteemed client.

Still, he would not let this delay keep him from visiting the Duke of Seaton's household.

"Please send word to Hopewood when you wish me to return to your shop. Tompkins will come along again to advise me."

"It is a pleasure to serve you, my lord," Crocker said.

Seth and his valet left the shop, and Tompkins said, "Thank you for including me on this visit to Mr. Crocker, my lord. Not many gentlemen would have done so, and I appreciate your faith in me."

"Nonsense, Tompkins. I may know what it takes to sail a ship around the world, but this viscount business is all new to me. I will depend upon others, such as yourself, to help me ease into my new role and become as good a man as my uncle was in this position. I'm grateful you decided to stay on and serve in my household."

They returned to Hopewood, and Seth went back to his study. He rummaged through a few drawers until he found what he was looking for—calling cards. Peabody had told him when he wished to call upon his neighbors, he was to present his card to the butler. Seth assumed his uncle would have a set of these in abundance since he stayed home most of his time. Sure enough, there was a decent sized stack with his title upon it and nothing else. He would use these when he visited others, thinking he would eventually have to have some of his own made up.

He had asked for the coachman to wait and returned outside again, telling the driver, "I want to call upon the Duke of Seaton."

"Ah, my lord, you wish to go to Shadowcrest."

"Yes, Shadowcrest."

Once more, Seth boarded his carriage and paid special attention on the journey to his closest neighbor's house. He understood now why it was easier to cut across his land and navigate around the lake because it took much longer to reach Shadowcrest by carriage.

He would be arriving at the estate about two o'clock. He hoped to see the duke and if he was lucky, be asked to stay to tea, where he might speak with Lady Philippa again.

His carriage came to a halt, and Seth bounded down the stairs the footman had placed. He knocked at the door and a footman answered.

"I am Viscount Hopewell, here to call upon His Grace," he said, presenting his card.

He watched the servant take in the new viscount's manner of dress and added, "I am new to my title and eager to meet my closest neighbor."

"Yes, my lord," the footman said smoothly. "Would you come and wait in the parlor? It is this way."

Seth followed the servant and took a seat. After a brief time, a young man who looked to be in his early twenties entered the room. He came toward Seth, who rose, and said as he bowed, "Good afternoon, Lord Hopewell. I am Mr. Strong, the steward here at Shadowcrest and cousin to His Grace."

He offered his hand, and the two men shook.

"His Grace is indisposed at the moment, but he will be joining us when he can. He asked that I entertain you until he arrived."

"As you can tell by my dress, I was not meant for the title I now bear. I was a captain for Strong Shipping."

"Is that so?" Mr. Strong remarked. "Then this will be quite a change for you, my lord."

"I know nothing about an estate, Strong. I have no idea what crops my tenants grow or what livestock they might raise."

"Then I suggest you meet with your own steward as soon as possible, my lord. You can learn a great deal from him."

"Unfortunately, my steward left earlier today. His father is on his deathbed, and I encouraged him to go and be with him. In the meantime, might I ask you a few questions? Things to help me get started in learning about my estate."

"I would be happy to talk in generalities with you, my lord."

The Shadowcrest steward launched into an overview about this area in Kent and what crops were usually grown. He explained the growing season, when it began and also when the harvest occurred. Strong told of what went on between plantings and harvesting, and Seth took it all in, saying, "This has been most helpful."

"After your visit with my cousin, I would be happy to show you some of our ledgers. You will wish to examine those at Hopewood, of course, but I can show you various things to look for while you do so."

"Your generosity knows no bounds, Mr. Strong."

The young steward smiled. "I had to learn most of this on my own. I took over my position at Shadowcrest three years ago, after spending a year at university. I am self-taught, but I am more than happy to share the knowledge I have acquired with you, my lord."

The door opened, and a tall, muscular man strode into the room, one whose size and air of confidence marked him the duke.

"Ah, thank you, Caleb, for entertaining our guest."

The duke came forward, and Seth rose, shaking the offered hand. "Thank you for meeting with me, Your Grace. I am Seth Atwell, now Viscount Hopewell."

"It is good to meet you, my lord. I am Seaton." He paused a moment, obviously thinking, and then said, "I know your name from having looked over records at Strong Shipping. You were captain of *Odyssey*, weren't you?"

"I was indeed, Your Grace. Until the recent death of my uncle. And my father."

"I am quite new to my title myself and will admit I feel like an imposter at times. A part of me still wants to escape to sea and leave all these new responsibilities far behind."

"I appreciate your honesty, Your Grace. I have only held the title a few days, and I already miss being at sea."

The duke slapped Seth on his back. "I have a feeling we are going to be good friends, Hopewell. We have something in common that most likely no other titled gentleman within the *ton* has. It is going to be hard to replace you as one of my captains. In fact, my duchess and I are leaving Shadowcrest tomorrow morning and returning to London. Town," he corrected himself. "Never call it London," he advised. "I am told Polite Society always refers to it as town."

"My first lesson learned from you, Your Grace," he said, smiling.

"Have a seat," the duke said. "Caleb, you are free to leave us. Join us at tea, though." Seaton glanced to Seth. "You will stay for tea, won't you?"

"I would be honored to do so."

Caleb Strong excused himself, saying he would see them in two hours' time.

Those two hours passed quickly, the duke and Seth spending time reminiscing about their years at sea on separate shipping lines. Seth was surprised at how honest and open Seaton was, sharing how he had been kidnapped as a young boy and taken to sea. Seth shared how his experience was the exact opposite, and how his uncle had arranged for Seth to be a cabin boy on a Strong vessel.

"My bride is the former Sophie Grant," the duke revealed. "I made certain that she retained ownership of Neptune Shipping. She will continue to run the company."

"I know little to nothing about the *ton*, Your Grace, but I believe that has to be incredibly unique."

Seaton smiled. "My Sophie is most unique herself. Most men would be appalled to hear that I insisted she keep Neptune in her name. Yes, good business would have had our lines merge, especially since we are one another's chief competitors. However, Sophie and I are working on a plan now where our vessels will sail to different parts of the world and bring back different goods to Britain. We would no longer be in direct competition with one another, which should be good for both our companies. It is one of the reasons we will return to town tomorrow. I daresay we'll spend much of our marriage in London since we both have shipping lines to run. Fortunately, my cousin is steward here at Shadowcrest."

"Mr. Strong has offered to tutor me in estate management while my own steward is absent, spending time with his father, who is very ill and near death."

"I can heartily recommended Caleb as a tutor, Hopewell. My cousin has already taught me so much about Shadowcrest in the limited time since we came here for a brief honeymoon. I am a seaman at heart, however, and so I will leave the running of this estate, and the others in my possession, to Caleb and my other stewards. I will keep a light hand in them and focus most of my time on my enterprises in London."

"I know from my solicitor that I have invested in Strong Shipping, along with a few other businesses, but I suppose I will spend a majority of my time at Hopewood. That is why I wish to learn all I can about how to run it."

The men chatted for another hour, swapping tales of their time at sea, before Caleb Strong appeared again.

"We are all having tea in the drawing room," he informed the pair. "The ladies are gathering there now."

The duke smiled. "I hope you won't be overwhelmed by my family, Hopewell. Besides my wife and my stepmother, there are six young ladies in the household. Four of them are my sisters, while two of them are my cousins, Mr. Strong's sisters." Seaton chuckled. "And that doesn't even count my aunt and the girls' governess, making it a total of ten women."

"Then I am happy we had this long talk, Your Grace, for I fear the conversation will be dominated by feminine topics with so many women present."

The duke and his cousin laughed. "You are probably right, Hopewell. Shall we go upstairs?"

They mounted a wide staircase and made their way to the drawing room. As Seaton had said, the room was already packed with ten women. Under normal circumstances, it might have seemed overwhelming to a man new to Polite Society. But his gaze went immediately to Lady Philippa, and Seth saw both the surprise flicker in her eyes and the blush stain her cheeks.

Seth decided this would prove to be a most entertaining teatime.

Chapter Six

As always, Pippa had changed into a gown for teatime. While Mama did not mind her donning breeches to go about the estate, Pippa was mindful that was a privilege, one which she would not wish for her mother to end. Effie and Lyric also would dress in male clothing from time to time, Effie when out riding or hunting, and Lyric while gardening. An unspoken agreement existed between all three of them that they would present themselves as ladies by teatime each day.

Pippa had returned from her impromptu encounter with the new Lord Hopewell a bit shaken. She had never been interested in men. Having grown up in a household full of females, she had witnessed firsthand that women were just as capable and intelligent as their male counterparts. They never had guests while in the country, and in town, Mama and Papa had attended numerous *ton* events during the Season, which none of their daughters did. No gentlemen paid morning calls upon them, so Pippa's experience—even exposure to men—was limited.

The extremely attractive and very manly viscount had caused her heart to flutter wildly and her belly to feel as if were turning upside down. She didn't share any of this with anyone. Instead, she had retreated to the study. It was the last place James would be, since he was besotted with his new wife. No one else would go there. Being in the room had given Pippa time to reflect on the short time she had spent in Hopewell's company.

She had liked him. At least, until he had offended her. Yes, it was unusual that she had struck up a friendship with his uncle, but Hopewell had been a most unusual man.

The new viscount seemed to realize his mistake, though. That was in his favor. From what she could gather, men blundered about, doing whatever they wished, never thinking of the feelings of others. Women, in particular. She wondered if she would see him again. If he would remain in the country as his uncle had or if he would choose to spend most of his time in town.

He was terribly attractive. Pippa knew she had responded to that. He hadn't flirted with her, but then again, they had only spent a brief time together. Besides, why would he? She had been in her usual attire. Gentlemen, even former sea captains, would not think much of a woman traipsing about dressed as a man. And once he met Georgie—if he did—Pippa would never have a chance. Not that she wanted one with him. But it would be nice to have a man pay her a bit of attention.

As she washed and dressed with Millie's help, she decided she worried over nothing. The new viscount would have no desire to speak with her in the future. He would be busy learning what he needed to in order to *be* a viscount. In a way, she felt a bit sorry for him. He looked so at home in the captain's uniform he'd worn. In fact, he had started to introduce himself as the former sea captain he was.

Seth. That was his given name, which he had let slip. She would think of him as Seth. That is, if she thought of him at all. Pippa decided that would be a waste of her time. A man such as Hopewell would have little use for a young lady who had yet to make her come-out. Why, he would go to town for next Season and be fussed over by both married and single women alike, thanks to his good looks. He would most likely return with a wife in order to get his heir. He would probably never even speak to

Pippa again.

"Thank you, Millie," she said to the maid. "That will be all."

Georgie entered the room. "What have you been up to? I haven't seen you all day. You made yourself scarce."

"I went for a long walk. Then I invaded James' study and stayed there for a few hours."

Her twin's face lit up. "Oh, what a marvelous place to read. And we both know James would not be needing it." Georgie smiled softly. "He is so in love with Sophie. I think it marvelous, especially after him being gone all these years. He has found happiness."

"Sophie, too," Pippa pointed out. "I cannot imagine wedding a man so much older than I was. At least he was kind to her and taught her how to run his business. I quite admire Sophie."

"I do, too." Georgie eased a pin from her hair and smoothed her hair before replacing the pin. "Are you ready for tea? I am famished."

The sisters made their way to the drawing room. They arrived to several conversations going on, which wasn't surprising, seeing that eight other women already occupied the drawing room.

She went to her aunt and pulled her aside, saying, "Things went well. I spoke with Mama, James, and Sophie at the same time. We left it at being a delay in my come-out. At least for a year."

Aunt Matty smiled. "I think that a wise move, Pippa, darling. You are a very special young woman. I would not want you to be lost in the chaos of this upcoming Season. Why, to think Dinah and I will be bringing out four of you at the same time is almost unheard of as it is."

She grinned. "You will certainly have your hands full. When pandemonium reigns, just think of the peace and quiet I will be indulging in here at Shadowcrest."

The room grew quiet, and Pippa turned, wondering what caused the sudden silence. She saw James and Caleb had entered the drawing room.

With Viscount Hopewell in tow.

Pippa froze, feeling the color rush to her face. Her gaze met his—and she saw he was amused. That riled her, and she cast her own gaze down, trying to calm her racing heart.

"Everyone, we have a guest for tea today," James said, as everyone rose to their feet. "Our new neighbor, Lord Hopewell." The duke glanced to the viscount. "I will introduce you to everyone, my lord, but I promise there will be no quiz coming afterward."

Lord Hopewell smiled, and Pippa swore she heard a few sighs. Damn him for being so handsome. She had no doubt he would charm every female present, her being the exception.

"I was worried I would have to earn my teacakes by remembering so many names," the viscount said. "It is good to know I will not starve if I forget a name or two."

"You are bristling, dear," Aunt Matty said quietly. "Have you met Hopewell?"

"This morning," she admitted in a whisper. "I'll tell you more later."

By now, James had brought their guest forward and was introducing him to Sophie and Mama. With her and Aunt Matty at the far end of those gathered, Pippa was able to observe the viscount meet all those in the drawing room. His smile seemed sincere and remained in place. He repeated the name of each person presented to him, and she saw he committed it to memory.

Finally, he reached them.

"This is Lady Mathilda Strong, my lord," James said. "My aunt and sister to my father."

Her aunt offered their guest her hand, and Hopewell bowed and kissed it. "A daughter, sister, and aunt to three different dukes. You are quite accomplished, Lady Mathilda."

"Being born into a family and those relationships are not accomplishments, Hopewell," Aunt Matty said. "I do hope I have done more with my life than being fortunate enough to be related to several dukes."

"I stand corrected, Lady Mathilda," the viscount said easily. "Looking about, I see a bevy of young ladies who have benefitted from your wisdom."

"Better," her aunt said. "You will get there in time."

"Let us hope that I do, my lady."

Finally, Hopewell turned his attention to Pippa as James introduced them. He bowed and reached for her hand, which she had been too spellbound to offer. His lips brushed across her fingers, and the most delicious tingles reverberated through her.

"It is good to see you again so soon, Lady Philippa."

She heard the intake of breath from several of her relatives as they overheard his remark. "Likewise, my lord. I did not know you would be calling at Shadowcrest so soon."

"Neither did I," he said, his gaze penetrating her, and she feared he could see far too much about her.

He still held her hand, and Pippa tugged gently on it. For a moment, Hopewell tightened his grasp, letting her know he was aware of what he did. Then he released it, his gaze still pinning hers.

"Might we all sit?" Mama said. "The teacarts have arrived."

She stepped back a few paces, needing to put distance between her and this man. His presence was unsettling. He was far too large for her comfort, and she had no intention of sitting anywhere near him.

"Come and sit here, my lord," Sophie said, indicating a chair for the viscount to take. Her sister-in-law smiled graciously at their guest, and then looked at Pippa a moment. She believed Sophie knew of her discomfort and was grateful the viscount was moving far away from her.

They took seats, and Pippa wound up sitting between Allegra and Effie.

As Mama and Sophie both poured out, with two pots of tea having been brought to the drawing room, Effie spoke up.

"How on earth do you know Pippa, my lord?" her youngest sister asked. "And exactly how are you the new viscount? We heard he was old. You aren't. And you certainly aren't dressed as one."

Leave it to Effie to stir the pot. Her sister missed the frowns Mama and Miss Feathers sent her way.

Lord Hopewell accepted a cup and saucer from Sophie and said, "My uncle was the Lord Hopewell you are familiar with. He passed in his sleep recently. My father assumed the title and only held it for a week before his own death."

"We are sorry for your recent losses, my lord," Mama said sympathetically. "It must have been difficult, losing both of them so closely together."

"Thank you, Your Grace. I regret I had not seen either of them in two years. You see, I was a captain for Strong Shipping. I had only brought *Odyssey* home a few days ago when I learned of both these deaths. I brought Father home to be buried at Crestview. We held the funeral yesterday afternoon."

"I am sorry we did not know of his passing," James said.

"It occurred in town," the viscount shared. "He had not had time to come to Hopewood." He smiled, looking at Effie. "I hope my uniform does not offend you, Lady Euphemia. I did see a tailor in the village today. My valet also recommended that I use my uncle's London tailor, and I will make an appointment with him when I am next there."

"I think you look rather dashing," Effie said brazenly, earning a scowl from Mama and titters from a few others. "But you haven't explained how you know Pippa."

The viscount's gaze now landed on her, causing her cheeks to warm. "We met this morning at the lake. I was walking a bit of the land, and I had thought to call at Shadowcrest to bring at item my uncle wished for Lady Philippa to have."

"What was it, Pippa?" asked Georgie. "Did Lord Hopewell gift you a book? I know he was always giving you ones he wanted you to read."

"No, it was a fishing rod," she said.

"Not Felix?" asked Effie, her eyes lighting with interest.

"You know of Felix?" Lord Hopewell asked.

"Only from Pippa," her sister said. "She is the one who fished with your uncle. I do know how to fish, thanks to Pippa, but Lord Hopewell was a bit withdrawn. I never was invited to join him and Pippa when they fished."

By now, everyone had cups of tea, and Mama asked who wanted cake, cutting pieces as Sophie filled plates with sandwiches and scones and passed them along.

"I am hoping Lady Philippa will show me the best places to fish at the lake," the viscount said. "It may seem odd, but I have never fished. Not a single time. I hope to learn how, though."

Georgie spoke up. "Pippa can teach you."

She sent her twin a murderous look.

Lord Hopewell looked pleased, though. Turning to Pippa, he said, "I would appreciate you tutoring me in the finer points of fishing, my lady. That is, if you are agreeable."

It would be churlish to turn him down in front of everyone. Instead, she smiled. "I would be happy to do so, my lord."

If he followed through and approached her about a fishing expedition, she would suggest Caleb work with him. Her cousin thoroughly enjoyed fishing, and it would be more appropriate for him to be alone with the viscount than her. Even if she had yet to make her come-out, Pippa was aware of certain conventions which must be followed in Polite Society. She would not do anything to risk her reputation because it could then reflect poorly upon her sisters and cousins.

Thankfully, Effie quit pestering Lord Hopewell, and conversation turned to things other than fishing. James and the viscount swapped several stories about their time at sea, while Sophie chimed in about what she looked for in a captain. From the traits her sister-in-law listed, Pippa determined that the viscount must be quite an impressive man beyond his good looks if he had been placed in charge of one of the ships in her family's shipping line.

They told Lord Hopewell a little about the village and the surrounding area and suggested some of the other neighbors he might call upon.

"I was eager to meet His Grace because of his connection with Strong Shipping. Imagine my delight when I learned he, too, had sailed the Seven Seas before he gained his title," Hopewell said.

"We are happy that you called at Shadowcrest today," James answered. "Especially since we will head back to town in the morning."

Pippa hadn't known this, and she sighed. "We have only begun to get to know Sophie," she complained. "And face it, Seaton. You have monopolized her for much of the time you have been here. Why, you barely have come out of your rooms."

Her brother smiled broadly. "That is the way with newlyweds, Pippa. You'll discover that someday."

Her face flamed, thinking of what men and women might do in private together, and it grew more heated when she thought about doing whatever it was with Lord Hopewell. He caught her eye and smiled cheekily, as if he knew exactly where her thoughts strayed. She turned away, biting off more sandwich than she should have, chewing repeatedly to get it down.

Lord Hopewell looked to Sophie and Mama. "I don't wish to overstay my welcome, Your Graces. Thank you for entertaining me at tea, dressed as I am. I promise the next time I come calling, I will be more appropriately garbed."

"I think your uniform is most impressive, my lord," Mirella said.

"I agree," Lyric added.

"Quite dashing," Allegra tossed in, smiling prettily at their guest.

"Come anytime, my lord," Mama said. "It is important to get to know your neighbors. I hope you will think of us as new friends."

"When you are next in town, my lord, you must come and

visit with us," Sophie added. "I would be happy to show you around Neptune Shipping, and I know His Grace would enjoy talking of the sea with you."

"Thank you for your kind offer, Your Grace," Lord Hopewell said. "I believe I will be remaining in Kent for a while, however. My steward is gone off to tend to his ill father, and Mr. Strong, here, is going to tutor me in the finer points of estate management until Hunt's return."

"Shall we go and look at a few ledgers now before you leave for Hopewood, my lord?" Caleb offered. "That way, you can go home and know a bit about what to look for in your own."

"Yes, I would like that, Mr. Strong." The viscount paused and then turned to her. "Might I have a word, Lady Philippa?"

An odd fluttering rushed through her. "Yes, my lord." Pippa supposed it would be about fishing. "I will walk down with you and Cousin Caleb to his office."

Aunt Matty said, "Go ahead with Lord Hopewell, Pippa, dear. I need to ask Caleb a quick question."

There was no question. Of that, Pippa was certain. The question she had was why was her aunt giving her an opportunity to speak with Lord Hopewell alone?

She stood. "This way, my lord."

Pippa crossed the drawing room at a brisk pace, entering the corridor. She didn't bother to wait for the viscount and simply moved along the hallway.

He caught up to her, clasping her elbow. His touch caused a spark. She halted in her tracks, her jaw falling. Aware of that, she clamped her mouth shut.

"Slow down a bit, my lady. I am not in that big a hurry to look at rows of numbers in a dusty ledger."

"You can learn a great deal about an estate if you study numbers, my lord," she said, starting to walk again, irritated when he slipped her hand through the crook of his arm.

"I'm sure I can. I am a blank slate regarding my knowledge of country estates. I know I have much to learn."

"Then you probably won't have much time for fishing," she snapped.

"Oh, I will make time for fishing," he replied, smiling at her, stealing her breath with that simple gesture. "I also will need to do quite a bit of riding. Do you ride, my lady?"

"I do, my lord. Quite well," she bragged. "In fact, I taught all my younger sisters and cousins to ride."

"Then I would be forever in your debt, Lady Philippa, if you would teach *me* to ride. Might we have our first lesson tomorrow morning?"

CHAPTER SEVEN

SETH CLOSED THE ledger he had been studying while he ate breakfast. He had been consumed with a need for knowledge about Hopewood. Thanks to Caleb Strong's tutelage yesterday, he understood the entries Hunt had made. If he hadn't spent time with the Shadowcrest steward, Seth would have had no idea what he was looking at.

He would definitely spend more time in Strong's company. He liked the younger man quite a bit and could see how knowledgeable Strong was. Even though the steward was self-taught, Seth was impressed by the breadth and depth of Strong's knowledge.

He finished his cup of coffee, enjoying the rich taste of the coffee beans. He looked about the room, two footmen and his butler silently staring ahead, ready to anticipate any need he might have. Being a titled gentleman was so very odd. He supposed being the lord of an estate truly was like being captain of a ship, with his servants and staff serving as his crew. It still would take him time to adjust to being a landlubber again after all those years at sea. Time there had been broken down by segments of the voyage. Here at Hopewood, time would be recognized by the seasons. When to plant. When things grew. When to bring in the harvest.

He also knew of some livestock on the property since Hunt had referenced it within the ledgers. Seth had so much to learn. He wasn't afraid of learning or hard work, though, and he would do everything in his power to make Hopewood successful. After all, it had taken him years to learn everything about a sailing vessel. How to navigate a ship. The ways to manage a crew. Handling his estate would be the same. Some parts would come naturally to him. Others would take more time for him to master. And once Hunt returned, he would have someone close by to answer questions and guide him. Until then, Seth would rely on Caleb Strong.

He rose and went to his steward's office, replacing the latest of the ledgers he had combed through. Caleb had suggested looking at the previous year's ledgers first in order to familiarize himself with what was occurring most recently on the estate, then he was to go back a decade and move forward. Caleb said it would help Seth get a solid grasp on what had been done over a decent amount of time, giving him a way to compare season to season. He was to look for trends. How weather and rainfall affected his crops. Noting the price received for crops and how it varied. It seemed there were a hundred different things to analyze.

But Seth was up to the task. After all, this estate was not only his present—but his family's future. Decisions he made would affect his own children and their children for decades to come.

He left the house, telling Robb he was going to the stables. He thought the butler would assume that Seth would find a groom to give him his first riding lesson about the estate.

Instead, he would be taking it with Pippa Strong.

He liked the nickname. She looked like a Pippa should. A bit mischievous. While he had enjoyed meeting all her sisters and cousins, some of them quite beautiful, he liked Pippa's looks. She was pretty without being beautiful. She had a freshness about her, like a morning after a spring rain. Pippa Strong was alive in a way he wasn't used to seeing in women, and Seth had certainly seen his share. Every time his ship had come into port, he had found a different woman to amuse himself with. Most of them had bored him. A few interested him, but they had been forgettable once he sailed off for new adventures.

He doubted he would ever be able to forget Pippa. She had made a deep impression on him. She had a mixture of youthful innocence coupled with curiosity and intelligence.

In other words, she would make for a perfect partner and whatever a viscount's wife was called. That was how little he knew about Polite Society. A duke's wife was a duchess, but beyond that, he didn't know what titled gentlemen called their spouses. An earless? A viscountess?

It didn't matter. Seth had decided he would make the most of the opportunity given to him. That meant being the best viscount he could be and seeing that his estate and investments thrived. It also meant selecting the right woman to aid him in this venture.

And he wanted Pippa Strong as that woman.

It was ironic that he had been such a womanizer in the past, yet after meeting Pippa, he could only see himself with *one* woman. And not just any woman, but Pippa alone. The trouble would be convincing her. To him, Pippa seemed almost like an animal in the wild. Happy and free. He had no idea how to settle down himself, much less with a wife. Perhaps it might be something they might learn together.

Of course, even he knew not to tip his hand too readily. If he did, he could see her taking flight and escaping forever. Seth had no idea how to court a woman, much less the daughter and sister of a duke. Surely, there were protocols to follow, but he had no idea how to go about making Pippa his.

If Seaton were still in Kent, he might have asked him. Their connection as longtime sailors would have made him comfortable in doing so. But the duke and duchess had left this morning for London. Perhaps he could somehow bring up the topic with Caleb Strong. Not right away, but in the near future. He could invite Strong for dinner, and then they could retire to their brandy and cigars, with no servants present. Seth was still getting used to having servants follow him about wherever he went, standing as stone statues during meals. He had no interest in airing his inquiries in their presence. Hopefully, though, Strong would be able to clarify things for him.

Heading toward the stables, anticipation at seeing Pippa again kept his heart rate slightly elevated. He had a spring in his step that was missing before. Seth only hoped she showed up at his stables. He knew he had taken her by surprise when he asked her to give him riding lessons. The good manners ingrained in her had not allowed her to turn down his request. Her cousin had joined them immediately after she had agreed, and upon learning of the scheme, the steward encouraged his cousin to give Seth riding lessons.

Still, Pippa saying she would do so and her actually showing up might be two different things.

As he reached the stables, he caught motion in the distance and focused on the rider coming toward him. It was Pippa—and she seemed at one with her horse, almost as if she were a centaur, that fabled race of creatures who were half human and half horse. He couldn't imagine a woman so slight having such control over a beast so large, but she handled her mount with ease, riding up and stopping just two paces from him.

Her cheeks were flushed with color, making her utterly appealing. Suddenly, the idea of wanting her as a man wants a woman overwhelmed Seth. He had been thinking logically before, believing Pippa would make for a good wife because of her breeding and intelligence.

Now, he was very aware of her as a woman and longed to kiss her.

That would probably earn him a slap, and he chuckled.

"Whatever is so amusing, my lord?" she asked, climbing from the horse's back.

He saw she wore a man's coat and breeches as she had before, when they had met by the lake. He wondered if anything lay between those breeches and her skin.

"I was merely thinking how practical you are to wear breeches as you ride. I see you straddle your horse as a man does when he rides."

"Side saddles and riding habits are what most women stick to," she said. "I prefer having better control of myself and my mount. Men, dressing as they do, have it much easier than women. Yes, when I ride, I do dress in this fashion."

"It suits you," he said, recalling her retreat yesterday and her delicious derriere and legs, snug in their breeches.

"Are you ready to begin?" she asked.

"I know nothing," he admitted straightaway. "I was raised in London. My father was a solicitor's clerk. We rarely even took a hansom cab, so I have never been upon the back of a horse."

"You really are a novice," she marveled. "Nevertheless, you have a better attention span as an adult, although a child often has less fear. Still, I should be able to make a rider out of you after several lessons."

"Oh? It will take several?" He hadn't known that and liked hearing he would need to see her on more than a single occasion for things to take.

"I predict four or five lessons should do it. I will teach you the basics, Lord Hopewell, though I will forgo the lessons I learned in tacking up a horse." She paused. "That means preparing him to be ridden. Ideally, you should groom your horse first, then prepare your tack—your equipment. Being a viscount, your groom will saddle your horse, adjusting its girth and stirrups and readying the reins."

She paused. "It wouldn't hurt, though, for you to learn these things. It would make you more prepared. I will leave that to you, to meet with a groom and learn about those areas. Have you a horse in mind that you wish to learn upon?"

Seth shook his head. "I will be visiting my stables for the first time with you, my lady. Remember, I only came to Hopewood two days ago, when I buried my father. Yesterday was my first full day on the estate."

"Well, riding is definitely the easiest way for you to get around in the country. You'll need to ride your estate often. You simply cannot do so in a carriage. I advise you to get to know your tenants. Not merely their names and faces, but those of their families. Talk with them. See what they need. What they are concerned about. What you might do in order to smooth the way for them. In return, they will be loyal to you."

"All sage advice, Lady Philippa."

She sniffed. "You might as well call me Pippa. Lady Philippa is so formal, and we will be spending several hours together over the next few days, thanks to these riding lessons. Though refrain from doing so around others, my lord. It is important not to seem overly familiar toward a lady when you are with others of your own rank."

"I see," he said, again learning a lesson about the new class he belonged to. "Pippa when we are alone, and Lady Philippa when others are present. I do have a lot to learn about being a viscount, Pippa. Perhaps beyond these riding lessons, you might teach me a thing or two about belonging to the *ton*. And I might also teach you a few things."

Such as how to kiss . . .

She frowned, clueless as to his agenda. "What things, my lord?"

He avoided her question. "Seth," he replied. "If I am to call you Pippa, you must address me as Seth." He grinned at her. "But please refrain from doing so around others," he added, echoing her own words.

She laughed aloud, with gusto. He liked her laugh.

He liked her. Quite a bit.

Seth thought it would be important for them to like one another if they were to wed. They would certainly spend a great deal of time in one another's company if they did so. But he was getting ahead of himself. He warned himself not to push her too hard or too quickly.

Else he might lose her altogether.

"Let us begin," she said, turning serious. Stroking her horse's nose, she said, "This is Starlight. She loves being petted. You try."

He stroked the horse where Pippa had. "She doesn't feel like I thought she would."

Pippa kissed the horse on the nose. "Starlight is gentle, but she can be fierce."

For the next few minutes, she pointed out different parts of the saddle and showed him where the girth was and how it could be adjusted. She also showed him different parts of Starlight and had Seth touch the horse until he seemed comfortable doing so.

"I may choose one mount for you to learn on and ask you to stick to it for a few weeks. Once you are more comfortable in the saddle, you'll want to challenge yourself. For now, we will keep to a horse with a sweet temperament and a tough mouth."

"Why tough?"

She laughed, a sound which was like music to his ears. "Because beginners tug needlessly on a horse's mouth. I will chastise you unmercifully until you exhibit a light hand with your reins." She paused, her eyes twinkling. "Come, Seth. We need to find you a horse now."

After talking with his head groom, Pippa decided on Orion and asked for the horse to be saddled for him, also asking for a lunge line. She explained to Seth how children and many women used a mounting block to climb atop a horse.

"As a grown man—and a very large one, at that—you can simply place your left foot in the stirrup and toss your right one over, landing in the saddle."

She demonstrated for him, and he asked her to do so again, simply enjoying watching her in motion.

And thinking about her mounting him.

Seth shook his head, trying to clear such thoughts. This horse business was new to him. He couldn't afford to let his mind wander. He wanted to prove himself to be a good pupil and not take a spill because he couldn't keep his focus, allowing randy thoughts to distract him.

The groom led Orion outside, where they had waited, and handed Seth the reins.

"Good luck, my lord," he said jauntily.

"Practice is important," Pippa said once the groom was gone. "We will do things because repetition is crucial and will help you become more comfortable atop a horse. All that practice will allow your muscles to remember the motions and habits you have formed even when your brain is tired. Now, I want you to mount Orion, Seth. Please sit gently in the saddle. Your left foot will carry your weight."

He did so a dozen times. At first, he seemed a long way from the ground because the horse was so tall, but after half a dozen times, he began to feel better. She adjusted his stirrups after the second mount, and he instantly recognized the difference. She also told him to center the ball of his foot on the stirrup, not his toe or heel. Again, it made a big difference.

"Getting off takes a little more thought than mounting," she told him. "Obviously, you are at a standstill now, but never attempt to dismount until you bring your horse to a complete stop," she cautioned. "Hold the reins firmly. You don't want to pull on your horse's mouth when you dismount."

After that, Pippa taught him about correct posture in the saddle, having him concentrate on his upper body being straight and tall and how to hold his horse's reins.

She attached the lunge line and said, "I will keep this on Orion the entire time. It is merely a long lead so that I have control of him in case you have a lapse in concentration and lose control. I want you to focus on your posture. Keeping your balance. I will be steering Orion, not you. Let's try walking a bit."

They did so, and Seth rather liked being atop the horse. He did as Pippa asked, thinking about his body and how to hold it as she had instructed. It made it easier without the added complication of steering Orion.

Pippa stopped and said, "You will have four speeds. Walking

is first. If you walked Orion for an hour, you would travel three to four miles, not much faster than if you walked yourself. Trotting is next. Of course, it depends upon a horse's weight and stride, but you can easily make eight—even ten—miles an hour if you trot.

"Next, is cantering. This takes things up a notch. You are pushing your horse slightly, but he is not going as fast as he can."

"How far would cantering take me in an hour?" he asked.

"Again depending upon the horse and the rider's weight, anywhere from ten to seventeen miles."

"Impressive," he said, holding the reins in one hand and scratching Orion between his ears.

"Oh, he has the most blissful look upon his face, Seth. He likes that." Then she became a tutor once more. "Galloping is the final speed. Many horses can only canter at their very best, but a galloping horse can cover quite a bit of ground. Of course, you can't keep them at a gallop for too long a time, but I would say their top speed would be around thirty miles per hour."

He laughed now. "I hope we can save galloping for a later lesson."

"How are you feeling?"

"Much more confident than when I first climbed atop Orion."

Pippa nodded thoughtfully. "Then I will take off the line, and we will walk our horses together. If you feel brave enough, we might trot a bit."

"Would I impress you if I agreed to trot?"

Color flashed in her cheeks. "Are you flirting with me, Seth?"

He waited a beat. "I just might be, Pippa."

"Hmm."

She moved toward him, and his heart slammed against his ribs, thinking she might act upon the flirtation. Then she unbuckled the lunge line and wound it up. His heartbeat slowed.

Pippa climbed atop her horse. "Shall we walk together, Seth? And just maybe we'll trot," she told him.

Was that a wink?

He couldn't tell because the sun came from behind a cloud, shining on her face.

"Lead the way, Pippa," he said.

"Come on, Starlight," she urged, her tone purring.

Seth wished she would speak to him that way. He shook his head, trying to clear it, and then took up his reins.

He decided he would follow Pippa Strong wherever she led him.

And his heart . . .

Chapter Eight

Pippa couldn't believe she had actually winked at Lord Hopewell.

She had no idea why she had done so. While her family teased her of being impulsive, she had never done something so . . .

She was so baffled by her behavior, she couldn't even think of a word to describe it.

Yet Lord Hopewell did seem interested in her. No, Seth. She liked the name. It suited him. And she was also interested in him. Like a woman would be interested in a man. Being around him had her insides doing all kinds of mad flips. She blinked, trying to focus on the task at hand.

Growing stern, Pippa said, "You must always focus when you are atop a horse. Any slight distraction, any wandering of your thoughts, and the horse might take off. Riding is serious business, Seth."

"I understand," he said. "Orion is quite large."

"Yes," she agreed. "A good seventeen hands."

"I can feel the power in him, even if you and the groom said he has a gentle nature. I understand I am a beginner at all of this, Pippa. I promise to concentrate. On the horse. And not you." He paused, his gaze intent. "At least for now."

She grew hot at his words. Her core seemed to seize up, and for a moment, she couldn't breathe.

Do not lose your head, she warned herself.

"To signal your horse to walk, give him a gentle squeeze with your lower legs. Keep your posture tall. Look straight ahead, between his ears and not at the ground."

Seth shifted his legs slightly, and Orion began walking. She fell into place beside him.

"It might be hard, but no more squeezing because it will confuse him," she said. "Your legs should stay long and still, with your weight firmly settled in your heels."

"I understand."

She walked him through steering with his reins and knees, and he quickly picked up on these. It was obvious he was a natural and would take to riding with ease once he had enough practice.

They fell silent, walking their horses side-by-side. She knew he was concentrating, as well he should. Riding was a new activity to him, and Orion was a large beast, though the groom had assured them both of the horse's sweet nature.

Pippa continued to observe Seth and said, "You are growing in confidence."

"I am," he agreed. "I thought it would feel odd, being off the ground, but I quite like it."

"Since you feel comfortable, would you care to try a trot?" she asked, thinking it not too soon to challenge him. A man such as Seth would grow bored quickly. It would be good to keep him on his toes.

He glanced toward her, his clear blue eyes intense. "If you believe I am ready."

"You are," she said, smiling. "Bring Orion to a halt if you would, so we can talk about it."

Seth did as she asked, and she could see he was excited to push himself to the next level.

"Try and remain calm," she told him. "Horses are sensitive

creatures and attuned to their rider's moods. If you are fearful or nervous, they will sense that. If you panic, they might, too."

He stroked Orion's neck. "Good boy," he said, and suddenly Pippa had a vision of him stroking her, causing her to grow hot all over.

"I want you to sit the trot. That means you'll rise slightly out of your saddle with each stride Orion takes. Orion will bounce up and down as he trots. Naturally, you will bounce a little, as well. You will want to go with his flow."

Understanding lit in his eyes. "Ah, it's like being on the water. Walking Orion has been like a mild swaying of a boat. Trotting would be as if the waves become a little rougher or higher."

"Likening it to your experience on the water is clever," Pippa said encouragingly. "Let us run with that idea." She thought a moment. "You will want to stay afloat on your horse when trotting. I want you to sink into your saddle. Your instinct as Orion's speed increases will be to squeeze your knees and legs to hang on. Never do so. Stay relaxed, sunk into the saddle, your legs still loose, with your weight in your heels.

"Then you will post, rising slightly out of your saddle as you watch Orion's movement. Posting keeps you from bouncing while he trots. To use your analogy again, you will be going with the flow. Let's try it."

They both nudged their horses, and Pippa tried to stay next to Seth as they trotted. She saw him struggling to get his rhythm, and she had them slow and then come to a halt.

"You are being bounced from your saddle when Orion pushes off with his back legs, Seth. Think of it as a dance. One-two, One-two. Feel the beat. The rhythm of the trot. You will rise and sit with each of those beats."

He laughed. "I have never learned how to dance with a woman, and here you are asking me to do so with a horse."

She smiled. "I am atrocious at dancing myself. Our dance master constantly tells me to feel the music, but I cannot. I can, however, catch the beat of the trot. Watch me."

Pippa demonstrated for him, riding half a minute away from Seth and then trotting back toward him.

"Could you see and count the beat as I trotted?"

He nodded enthusiastically. "Actually, I could."

"Let's try it again. This time, try using your thighs and knees as your pivot point. Swivel up and forward. Watch Orion's shoulder. When it moves forward, rise. When it moves back, sit. And remember to relax."

They tried again, trotting for half a minute at a time, then walking their horses half a minute before repeating the trot again.

"I feel it," he told her when they slowed to a walk. "That rhythm you mentioned. Before I sensed it, I was tensing up. Now, I understand more how to relax."

"You have learned quite a bit today, Seth, but I think we should go back to the stables. I am going to let you ride ahead of me, so I can study your form."

"All right," he said. "Here goes."

He nudged Orion and started off, his back straight, looking ahead. Pippa watched him ride for a full minute before she spurred Starlight to follow.

She was experiencing feelings, both physically and emotionally, which she never had before. This man stirred things within her that she ached to explore.

But Pippa wasn't certain she should act on this.

Catching up to him, she slowed her horse from canter to trot, and they arrived back at the stables. Quickly, she dismounted and handed her reins to the approaching groom.

"Wait a moment, my lord," she told Seth, reverting to a more formal address since they were no longer alone. "I want you to dismount very slowly because you will feel a bit wobbly. Your knees will be weak."

He smiled, warming her insides. "It is just like disembarking from a ship. As you walk the deck, you learn to move with the rolling of the waves. Every time I descend the gangplank and am on dry land, it feels odd since land is still."

"This will be just like that," she assured him. "Be careful."

He swung his leg from the horse and touched the ground, removing his left foot from the stirrup. Handing his reins to a second groom who had appeared, he said, "Take care of both horses. Lady Philippa is going to stay a while."

"Yes, my lord," both grooms echoed and led the horses to be rubbed down.

"I am?" she asked.

"You are," he said, moving to her. "Oh, I do feel a bit odd."

She slipped her arm through his. "We should walk a bit. It will help."

"Then let's stroll the gardens," he suggested.

They did so, with Seth discussing riding with enthusiasm. He was like a little boy, and she caught his excitement. Then one leg seemed to give out. She steadied him.

"I see a bench," he said. "I'd better sit a moment."

They ventured to the stone bench and took a seat. He was a large man, and he took up a good portion of the bench as they sat, their shoulders pressed together.

"I can already tell that I am going to be sore. Today, not tomorrow."

"You will," she said. "Riding stretches muscles that other physical activities never touch. You will experience soreness in your back. Abdomen. Legs."

Her face flushed. "Groin. My advice is that you soak in a warm bath with Epsom salts tonight to prevent stiffness. You may wish to repeat it again tomorrow morning. I will warn you now—it will be extremely hard for you to get out of bed in the morning after a night of inactivity in bed as you sleep. Even experienced riders can feel soreness, but once you build the muscles needed to ride, you won't be as sore."

His gaze burned into her, and she saw the heat in it. Her body prickled in response, and her breath grew shallow and rapid.

Seth turned so that he faced her. His hand came to her face, cradling it tenderly.

"I am going to kiss you, Pippa," he said softly. "If you will let me."

She licked her lips, eliciting a groan from him, causing her to be aware of a feminine power she had never known she possessed.

"I have never been kissed, Seth," she admitted. "I might not be any good at it."

His other hand rose, her face now framed with his long, strong fingers. "I am very good at kissing," he told her. "You were an excellent teacher for my riding lesson. Let me return the favor and tutor you in kissing."

Pippa shivered. Not from cold.

From desire . . .

She wanted him to kiss her in the worst way, but she was afraid it would destroy the ease between them.

"It has been a long time since I made a new friend, Seth," she said. "I think . . . I think if we kiss . . . it might change things between us."

He smiled knowingly. "Oh, it definitely will change things, Pippa. But I believe for the better. Are you willing to try? One kiss?"

Her heart beat so wildly now that she feared it might burst from her chest. Curiosity won out, though. She knew nothing about kissing. And she *wanted* to kiss him.

"Yes," she said breathlessly. "One kiss."

She thought it would only take a few seconds.

Pippa was very wrong about that.

Seth continued to hold her face as his lips moved to hers. Anticipation flooded her. She felt the heat of his skin as their mouths met. Ever so softly, he brushed his lips against hers, quickening her heart's beat. His lips were firm yet soft, and they seemed meant to be against hers. Her hands moved to his broad shoulders and settled upon them, gripping them as he pressed his mouth against hers. Soft at first, and then more demanding.

He kissed her. Broke the kiss. Kissed her again. Harder. Broke it again. Her heart began fluttering, and her belly exploded with butterfly wings beating rapidly. Seth's thumbs caressed her cheeks and then one hand slipped to her nape, anchoring her. His other hand moved to her back, again holding her steady as his mouth returned to hers.

His tongue teased her mouth open and then slipped inside, bringing shock waves through her. She had no idea kissing involved tongues.

But she liked it. Very much.

Seth's tongue caressed hers, causing her bones to seemingly melt. She clung to him, even as he brought her closer to him. Pippa began to answer his call, her tongue moving against his, now warring with it, both of them seeking to dominate the other, knowing whichever won was a victory for them both.

He tasted divine, a combination of coffee and a sweetness she could not define. He continued to stroke her tongue with his, and then he leisurely explored her mouth.

The warring of tongues was over. Victory was his.

She was his.

And he knew it.

Pippa lost track of time, only knowing that she needed Seth's kiss like she needed the very air she breathed. How she had survived without kissing—without him—amazed her. It was as if they were destined for one another.

Finally, he broke the kiss, both of them panting. He rested his forehead against hers, their breath mingling, their blood calming.

Seth was the one who drew away first. Her hands fell from his shoulders as his released her. They stared at one another, neither speaking. It was as if they feared a single word would break the spell between them.

He brought the back of his hand to her cheek, rubbing it. "Are you glad you tried a kiss, my lady?"

She smiled. "I daresay that was more than one kiss, my lord. But yes, I am glad for the experience."

"Was it what you thought it might be?" he prodded.

"Nothing like I thought," she admitted. "Georgie and I have talked about kissing before. She has even practiced kissing her pillow." Grinning, Pippa added, "But it certainly didn't know how to kiss her back."

His rich laughter was like music to her ears. "You did kiss me back, Pippa. I liked it. Very much."

She looked at him wistfully. "Can we stay friends after having kissed?"

He grew thoughtful. "Do you want us to be friends?"

She hesitated. "I had thought we might be. Kissing . . . well, it might change that. I caught James and Sophie kissing a few times. They never saw me, though. I would come across them and then dart away, not wanting to embarrass them or me."

"They are newlyweds. And in love."

"Yes, it was definitely a love match between them." She paused. "Yet they do seem like friends. More than friends, actually."

"It is because they are lovers, as well as friends," Seth said. "Making love can bring a closeness between two people. Much as kissing can bring a man and woman closer together."

"I liked kissing you, Seth," she admitted. "But I am not certain we should do it again. That is, if we are to remain friends."

His gaze scorched her, and Pippa wet her lips.

"I will not kiss you again," he said. "Unless you ask me to."

Seth pushed to his feet and helped Pippa to hers. "I think it is time you go home to Shadowcrest. Will you come again tomorrow for another riding lesson?"

She swallowed. "Do you want me to?"

He smoothed her hair. "Yes. I want you to very much, Pippa."

"And we won't kiss."

"Not unless you demand we do so," he said, his eyes now twinkling.

"Demand is quite a strong word."

"So is desire," he said, his voice low and rough. "If you desire to, then we will kiss again."

He captured her hand, bringing it to his lips and brushing a kiss along her knuckles. The tender gesture almost did her in, and Pippa had to lock her knees to keep from collapsing against him.

"I will escort you to the stables," he told her, tucking her hand through the crook of his arm.

They walked in silence. She enjoyed being near him and enjoyed his company. He was unlike anyone she had ever known.

But she was afraid to kiss him again. Afraid she might actually fall in love with him.

The only question would be if she could overcome her fear—and see what the future might hold for them.

CHAPTER NINE

PIPPA HAD TO find Georgie.

She rode home to Shadowcrest and handed Starlight off to a groom, not bothering to tell him the horse had already been rubbed down at Hopewood. Let Starlight be spoiled a bit.

Entering the rear of the house, she cut through the kitchens, asking for hot water for a bath be sent up to her. Leaving the kitchens, she went to the music room, hoping she might find her twin there. She had not slept with Georgie last night since her sister shared she had a headache and had taken a tray in her room instead of coming to dinner. Georgie had passed along a message to Pippa through Millie that she wanted Pippa to sleep in a different bedchamber because of her aching head.

Georgie rarely had headaches, and Pippa was concerned, especially since her twin had not even come down to say goodbye to James and Sophie this morning before they departed for town. Since she herself had left for Hopewood soon after their departure and had been gone for so long, she hoped her sister's headache had subsided and Georgie was back to her usual self.

The music room stood empty, as did the drawing room. She decided to have her bath and then look for Georgie again afterward.

Kitty helped Pippa to bathe and dress in a warm gown since

the autumn day had turned increasingly cold.

After Kitty had brushed and pinned up Pippa's hair, she asked, "Do you know where Lady Georgina might be?"

"The last I saw her, she was in the library, my lady."

"Then I will go and see if she is still reading. Thank you, Kitty."

When Pippa arrived in the library, she found Georgie sitting in the window seat, a cushion behind her back, her legs stretched out in front of her. An open book lay in her lap, but her twin was not reading. Instead, she stared out the window, looking morose.

Pippa came and sat at Georgie's feet, asking, "Are you feeling any better? I worried when you did not come down to see James and Sophie off."

"You worried so much about me that you still went off to give Lord Hopewell his riding lesson?"

Georgie's tone told Pippa everything she needed to know. Her twin was feeling neglected and left out.

"You are angry with me," she said.

"I have the right to be angry, Pippa," her twin snapped.

Her sister was usually the calmest of creatures and slow to anger, and never angry at Pippa.

"I apologize," she said quietly. "I should have told you that I met Lord Hopewell when I was on my walk yesterday."

Her twin looked at her with unshed tears glimmering in her eyes. "I thought we told one another everything, Pippa. And yet you never mentioned a word to me about not doing a Season until you went to Mama. That alone blindsided me. I am terrified of making my come-out, much less without you by my side."

She reached for Georgie's hand and squeezed it. "You have nothing to be troubled over," she insisted. "You are the beauty in our family, Georgie. And you are as beautiful inside as you are on the outside. Men will fall at your feet. You will have your pick of them."

"I know that," her sister said, desperation in her voice. "I have never traded upon my looks, but sometimes, they are all that people see, Pippa. I fear my appearance and large dowry will make me a target to chase. I already know men left and right will be offering for me. I was counting on you being by my side. Helping me to determine which gentleman liked me for myself. Now, you will be staying at Shadowcrest while I will be caught up in the swirl of social events in town. While I am close to our other sisters and cousins, they do not know all of me, as you do. I have no idea how to go through this without you, Pippa. And now you are running about the countryside, keeping secrets from me."

"I had no idea of your fears regarding the Season," she said. "Especially since you really didn't voice this to me yesterday. If you wish, I will go to town for the duration of the Season instead of spending part of it here at Shadowcrest. I do not want to attend any events, but suitors will be calling upon you the afternoon after those events. I can be present with you. Get to know these gentlemen and see if any are worthy of you."

"No," Georgie said sadly. "You have negotiated your bit of freedom. I would not take it from you."

She squeezed Georgie's fingers again. "Nonsense. I had already told Mama that I would come to town at some point. I will do so once the Season starts. It will still give me plenty of time by myself since all of you will go up early in order to begin having your gowns made up. That will give me time alone at Shadowcrest. To figure things out about myself."

Pippa bit her lip. "I do need to talk to you about something, though."

"Hopewell?" her twin asked.

She nodded. "I am not quite sure why I did not tell you—or anyone—why we came across one another yesterday. He . . . had an unsettling effect upon me, Georgie. Yes, he gave me Felix, and I am very happy to own the fishing rod now. But there is something about him. Something I cannot quite explain. The way he affects me."

"You are attracted to him," Georgie said simply. "I could see it yesterday. And he is attracted to you as well."

A tear rolled down Georgie's cheek. "I did not have a headache, Pippa. I was simply hurt. Bewildered that you would not have told me about your encounter—and feelings—for Lord Hopewell. And then you came back to the drawing room yesterday and announced you would be giving him riding lessons."

Georgie brushed her tears away. "I will admit I was feeling put out with you. Upset that you did not share with me. I didn't want to sleep with you last night. I was afraid you would no longer confide in me, and so I pushed you away the only way I knew how."

Pippa moved and sat closer to Georgie, embracing her tightly.

"I love you more than anyone who walks this earth, Georgina Strong. We will always be close. I know it in my bones. Yes, I am afraid of what marriage might bring, but the bond between us is unbreakable. You will simply need to wed a man who will recognize our closeness and not try to separate us."

Through watery eyes, Georgie smiled. "So now, we must find a man for me who not only likes me for myself—and not my looks or dowry—but he also must have an estate in close proximity of whatever man you choose as your husband." Georgie paused. "Have you chosen someone, Pippa? Has Hopewell chosen you?"

This time it was Pippa's eyes which misted over. "He kissed me, Georgie."

Her sister sat up eagerly. "He *kissed* you? Oh, my goodness, Pippa. Tell me all about it. Is it wonderful? I actually stumbled across James and Sophie kissing the other day, and they looked as if they were having a marvelous time."

"Well," she said, "it is very different from what you and I thought. And . . . you use your tongue to kiss," she said matter-of-factly.

"No!" Georgie gasped. "Your tongue? What exactly do you do with it?"

"It sounds a bit complicated, but it was very easy to catch on. Apparently, Lord Hopewell has done his fair share of kissing."

"I think it is good for a man to be experienced," Georgie said, her practical nature on display. "Else how would you ever figure out what to do together? I know Mama has said she would tell us about coupling, but I think it is something you can hear about and yet not understand until you actually do the deed. Come on, Pippa. Tell me everything."

"We had our riding lesson. Seth is quite good in the saddle. A natural."

Georgie's brows arched. "Oh, so it is Seth?"

She nodded. "Only during the riding lesson. He is not one who is much for formality, Georgie. You have to remember that he is like James in that respect. They come from a much different life, one completely different from the *ton*. James seethes a bit at being a duke and having everyone constantly addressing him as Your Grace. Seth is much the same. He is struggling, too. I cannot imagine coming home after so long a voyage, only to learn my uncle and father had both passed. He has no one, Georgie. I am glad that Caleb has taken Seth under his wing and will help him in estate matters."

"Back to kissing," Georgie reminded her.

"We finished our riding lesson, and he was already stiffening up. I thought it best if he walked it out a bit, and so we went to stroll through his gardens." She grinned. "But even a large, strapping fellow such as Seth was felled by weakness. The exertion of riding the horse and using muscles in a way he had never used before finally got to him. We came to sit upon a bench—and then it happened. He asked if I would be interested in sharing a kiss. One kiss."

"Of course, you said yes," her twin said, her eyes lighting up. "Because you knew what you learned you would share with me."

"I am trying to do so now." She hesitated. "I really do not know if I can convey everything properly. He anchored me so that I did not wiggle about, which was clever on his part, because you know what a wiggle worm I can be. Then his lips touched mine. Brushing them. Pressing against them. He used his tongue to slowly slide back and forth, urging me to open to him. I simply went along with whatever he was doing because he seemed to be the expert."

Pippa sighed. "Oh, what an expert."

"Pippa!" Georgie squealed.

"His kiss made my insides quiver. It was as if a nest of butterflies had slumbered in my belly all my life and suddenly awoke, fluttering their winds, exploding inside of me. That is the best way I can describe it to you. Our tongues . . . played together. Teased one another. Frankly, I could not tell you where one kiss ended and the next began, only that I wanted to keep kissing him forever."

"Do you love him?" Georgie asked, her eyes large and solemn.

"I . . . do not know. What I do know is that I am eager to kiss him again and learn more about it. Seth told me he would not kiss me again unless I asked him to do so."

Georgie nodded sagely. "Then my respect for Lord Hopewell has shot up immensely. He is giving *you* that power, Pippa. I believe most men would not be gentlemen at all in that situation. They would steal a kiss wherever they wanted and not ask for permission at all. It sounds as if he is truly interested in you. That he likes you."

"I do like him," Pippa said slowly, realizing it. "I . . . might possibly grow to love him. I just don't know," she said, exasperation filling her. "It is most complicated."

Georgie took Pippa's hands, squeezing them. "Oh, wouldn't it be interesting if you wed Lord Hopewell? Even before you made your come-out. My, what a coup that would be. You would have the tongues of the *ton* wagging day and night for a good week or two over that."

"You are putting the cart before the horse, Georgie," Pippa admonished. "I have no idea if I am going to kiss Lord Hopewell again, much less allow myself to fall in love with him."

"So, he's back to Hopewell and not Seth?" her twin teased. "Seriously, Pippa, I think you should allow things to develop naturally. Already, we have seen that Hopewell knows nothing about Polite Society. He knows nothing about being a titled gentleman and running his country estate. He would probably be a disaster at the Season if he attended it as a bachelor. It would make sense, both of you not finding a spouse at the Season, but on your own. Together."

"I had not shared this with you, Georgie, but I wonder if I am even meant for marriage. As I said yesterday, I might be more comfortable playing the doting aunt, going from place to place, spoiling my many nieces and nephews."

"Do *not* push aside Hopewell if he pursues you, Pippa," her twin ordered. "If the viscount is so willing to let you be in charge of something as meaningful as a kiss, I believe he would also consider you a partner in other aspects of life. The same way James treats Sophie. Don't you see, that could be the best possible scenario for us? If you wed Hopewell, he would not be a man who would keep us apart." Georgie paused. "Perhaps I am the one meant to be the doting aunt and spoil your children instead. I could do it all from Shadowcrest. I could live out the rest of my life here, only a few miles from you. Why, we could see each other every day."

"Georgina Strong! I will not let you give up your dream of becoming a wife and mother when it is all you have ever longed for. That—and love. I know you, Georgie, down to your very soul. You have a great capacity to love. You need to give your love and receive love in return. It may take you more than a Season to find a man worthy of you, but I have faith that you will find him.

"As to what happens between the viscount and me?" Pippa shrugged. "It remains to be seen. For now, however, I will take things slowly. Very slowly. There is no need to rush into any kind of commitment, with Hopewell or anyone else."

"My impulsive twin is sounding like the very practical me," Georgie teased. "You are usually the one who rushes off and thinks with her heart and not her head, where I am the opposite."

Her sister grew serious. "I want you to trust your heart, Pippa. You are a lovely woman and would make for an excellent wife and mother. Look at what a wonderful sister you have been all these years. You must trust your heart. If it tells you to move forward with Hopewell, then do so. If you develop feelings for him and they grow, it is meant to be."

Georgie studied her a moment. "And if not?" She smiled mischievously. "Then you will have learned quite a bit about the art of kissing and can practice it on other gentlemen until you find the one meant for you."

They embraced, but Pippa's heart already told her there was no way she would ever wish to kiss another man.

Seth had already spoiled all other men for her.

Chapter Ten

SETH LEFT THE house and headed toward the stables. He was eager for another riding lesson—but even more eager to be with Pippa Strong again. The young woman had captured his attention in a way no woman ever had.

He had never pictured himself being a landlubber, much less settling down with one woman. He enjoyed the company of women far too much to ever have contemplated marriage, and he also had been a seafaring man, expecting to spend the majority of his life upon the waters.

Now, however, with the unforeseen circumstances life had tossed his way, Seth was having to rethink his entire life and future. Pippa was not a conventional beauty, but she grew more appealing to him with each encounter. She also did not seem to adhere to the rules placed upon members of Polite Society. A woman such as Pippa could show Seth the way to function within the *ton* and yet remain true to himself.

He had told himself to take things slowly with her, yet he had kissed her yesterday. Repeatedly. She had agreed to one kiss, but once he had started, he'd found it hard to control his desire for her. Thank goodness, he had stopped at kissing and not taken further liberties with her.

He decided it had been smart to put the onus on Pippa. To

have her make the next move. She seemed to be a woman who knew her own mind, yet her inexperience in matters of the heart would most likely have her being cautious around men and him, in particular. He had told Pippa he would not kiss her again unless she asked him to do so.

Now, he had to make certain she made that request. Hopefully, sooner rather than later.

The stables came into view, and he saw Pippa was already here, standing next to Starlight, holding the horse's reins. She smiled when she caught sight of him and gave a friendly wave. The small gesture caused his heart to sing, and Seth began whistling as he approached her, something he rarely did.

"My, you seem to be whistling a jolly tune," she noted. "I cannot whistle one whit."

She demonstrated, puckering her lips and blowing. No sound came out.

"I am hopeless at it," she said. "Your whistle is rather loud, though. Since I am teaching you about riding, perhaps you could teach me how to whistle. Who knows? It might come in handy someday."

"I only whistle on land," he told her. "It is a superstition sailors hold. A seaman never whistles while aboard a ship upon the water, else it might challenge the wind and cause a storm to appear out of nowhere."

"Really? I did not know sailors were a superstitious lot."

Seth laughed heartily. "We are nothing *but* superstitious," he replied. "Why, I could regale you for an hour with things sailors avoid in order to keep bad luck away, along with what we are partial to."

"I would like to hear all about it, my lord. Perhaps after we have ridden today you can enlighten me."

She looked to the groom who lingered near them and said, "Please ready the viscount's horse." She glanced to Seth. "Would Orion do again?"

He nodded, and she told the groom to saddle the horse.

"Yes, my lady," the groom said, vanishing into the stables.

Pippa turned to him. "You did well yesterday. Do you have an idea where you might like to ride today?"

"I want to see as much of Hopewood as we can." Laughing, he added, "As much as my sore body will allow, that is."

"Did you soak in the bath of Epsom salts which I recommended?"

"You will be glad to hear I did so. Twice. Just as you suggested." He grinned. "And I could still barely get out of bed this morning. For the first time since I became Lord Hopewell, I saw the wisdom in having a valet. I was putty in Tompkins' hands. He dressed me as if I were a helpless babe."

She laughed, and he thought her laughter sounded like sweet music. If they weren't in the open—and if he hadn't told her she had to be the one to ask for their next kiss—he would embrace her now and kiss the life out of her.

Her brows arched. As she looked at him, he glanced away, afraid his eyes would give away his thoughts.

"We can stay out as long as you feel up to it," she told him. "Hopewood is a large estate, and it will take several hours to ride it."

"Then I want to see as much as we possibly can. Just like when I was captain of *Odyssey*, I wanted to know every nook and cranny of my ship. I believe it should be the same regarding Hopewood. I want to learn the estate and know it as well as the back of my hand. I also believe, just as I got to know my crew members, I should know my tenants."

"Have you had a chance to review the ledgers as Caleb suggested?" she asked.

"I buried myself in them yesterday afternoon and all of last night. The lessons your cousin imparted helped me interpret what I saw within them. I look forward to my own steward's return from Haselton, so that I can ask him specific questions. I have already a list of them."

"That is wise to do. Georgie is all about making lists. I am afraid I am a bit more haphazard. My twin is the epitome of a lady of the *ton*."

"And you are not?"

"I do no embroidery. No needlework of any kind. I do not even play the pianoforte. Those things are not only time-consuming but tedious to me. I simply haven't the patience to sit still long enough to learn them, much less practice those feminine arts. I prefer being outdoors. Riding. Fishing. Even hunting. Although Effie says my tender heart keeps me from chasing down the fox or whatever creature is being hunted."

The groom appeared with Seth's saddled horse, and he took up the reins. Lifting his left leg to place his foot in the stirrup caused him to groan, while throwing his right leg over the horse almost did him in.

Pippa laughed loudly, saying, "I know that wasn't easy to accomplish. I commend you for agreeing to get back in the saddle two days in a row. Very few people who take up riding are able to do so in the beginning because of how sore their muscles are. Do you need us to review anything from yesterday's lessons, or have things stayed with you?"

"I recall all you told me. I am sitting tall, staying relaxed, my legs loose, and my weight in my heels."

"We should start off by walking our horses and then build up to a trot."

As they set out, he asked, "Will we canter today?"

"Good heavens, no, Seth," she said, and he noticed she had easily reverted into calling him by his given name now that others were no longer present. "You will need to practice trotting for a good week or two before I would even consider allowing you to canter. Remember, it is all muscle memory. You must become comfortable in the saddle with trotting. You need to approach riding as breathing. It should become so natural, so second nature to you, that you do not even have to think about what you are doing. At least consciously. Cantering is a bit frightening to a novice, and it can cause new riders to panic. Everything you are learning now would be tossed out the window if we embarked upon catering too soon. Besides, you wish to see your estate. Keeping our horses to a trot will allow you to do so. With cantering, the countryside would fly by."

"I will bow to your good judgment then," he told her. "Where should we go? You said you have ridden with my uncle here, so you know Hopewood, where I don't."

"Follow me," she said, nudging Starlight to speed up.

Seth followed suit and went through the steps in his mind, trying to even his breathing and sit tall, even as he moved up and down in the saddle. Pippa had called it sitting the post, and at first, he could not find his rhythm, bouncing too much. Gradually, though, he began rising and falling with Orion's gait. He could see why others found riding a horse so pleasurable.

Still, though, it hurt him to do so today. The muscles in his belly and groin were tight and stiff, as were those in his back and legs. Seth couldn't think of a time when he had been more sore, and that included the heavy physical labor he had done on ships. He knew it would take time for his muscles to loosen up today, and so he ignored the pain.

Pippa slowed Starlight to a walk, and he caught up to them.

"This is the meadow where your grooms let the horses out to give them time in nature. It is not good to always keep a horse locked within a stall. They are creatures of the wind and need to be free to run every now and then."

"You do know quite a bit about horses," he observed.

"I have been riding from the time I was quite young. I have spent more time in the stables and on a horse's back than doing any other activity. The last three years were pure misery for me."

"Why so?" He recalled her saying her uncle forced them to remain in London while her father was ill, but he enjoyed hearing her speak so much, he didn't mind hearing more of her story.

"I believe I mentioned to you my father being ill. We were in town for the Season, which my parents attended every year. It was almost time to return to Kent when Papa had his attack of apoplexy. My uncle thought it best if Papa remained in London, close to his doctor. He did not think it would be wise to move Papa to the country."

A shadow crossed her face. "We were there three solid years. My uncle did not allow us to ride during that time, not even in Rotten Row, so I spent many days walking after lessons with Miss Feathers."

Sympathy filled him, but he didn't think Pippa would want him to voice it. Instead, he asked, "What do you enjoy studying with Miss Feathers?"

Her face lit up. "Oh, I adore languages and geography. I know it's ridiculous, but I would love to go to various places around the world. India. North America. I wish to see the Great Pyramids at Giza. And if this blasted war with Bonaparte ever ends, I want to go and test my French in France. Hear how natives speak the language."

"You speak it fluently?"

"Yes. Also Italian and Spanish. Miss Feathers knows several languages, and I am the Strong daughter who took to them most. Why, I even have learned Latin and Greek."

"I was much the same as a boy," he revealed. "Geography was my chief interest. I could stare at a globe for hours. Comb through an atlas and dream of faraway lands."

She chuckled. "I know every page in the atlas at Shadowcrest. I am determined someday to see places beyond Kent and London."

Seth wanted to be the one who took her to those places. He could see that Pippa had an adventurous spirit, much as he did. It only cemented the fact that he believed they were destined to be together.

"Come along," she said briskly. "There are many more places for us to see at Hopewood."

They rode to the far corners of the estate, Pippa pointing out the fields his tenants toiled in. She had them ride to a group of cottages, and they dismounted, leading their horses by the reins.

Several people came out from these cottages, and Pippa introduced Seth as the new viscount. So many pressed near him, wanting to meet him and shake his hand, their numbers growing.

Before he knew it, they had been invited to stay and take a meal. Though the day was cold, no wind was present, and tables were brought outside and lined up together, along with dishes of food. Seth and Pippa sampled everything from lentil soup to venison stew to cabbage pudding.

He leaned back, patting his belly. "I am not certain if I can mount my horse after such a delicious feast. I do thank you all, however, for this warm greeting to Hopewood. I want you to know that I have much to learn. As the son of a fourth son, I never dreamed I would hold this title. I have been away at sea my entire life, the last several years as captain of a ship called *Odyssey*."

Seth glanced around at the smiling faces. "I look upon you as my ship's crew, and as your lord, I am its captain. I promise to take care of you and see to your needs. In fact, while I am in residence at Hopewood, I would like to designate the first day of the month as a time we can gather and talk of your concerns."

A rousing cheer went up, and he believed he had made a good start at forming a bond with his tenants.

Pippa spoke up. "Thank you again for the wonderful meal. It is good to see all of you again after so long a time away."

"You, too, Lady Philippa," a young man called, causing everyone to laugh.

They excused themselves and returned to their horses. Seth had a bit easier time mounting, some of his stiffness having been worked out through their ride, but he knew it would need another soaking in the Epsom salts after so long a ride today.

"I think we should head back now, Seth," Pippa suggested. "You have been in the saddle for several hours, and while you had a break for this past hour, we don't want you to get saddle sores. You can see the rest of your estate tomorrow."

"Will you take me out again? It is obvious you are familiar

with the land, and my uncle's people know you."

"I did ride with his lordship upon occasion. He did not visit his tenants often, but I encouraged him to do so." She grew thoughtful. "Your uncle was a bit of an odd duck, Seth. I would describe him as a loner. He had everything he could possibly want, but he always seemed tinged by sadness. I hope you are appreciative of all that you now possess as Viscount Hopewell, and that you will form a strong relationship with your tenants."

"That is my intention, Pippa."

They began trotting again, and Seth had to concentrate on his riding, so their conversation ceased.

When they arrived at the stables, two grooms took their horses.

He was reluctant to see her leave and asked, "Would you care to walk with me again in the gardens? I do believe the exercise I took after riding yesterday helped alleviate some of the soreness."

Her gaze met his, and he saw she was conflicted.

"I told you, Pippa, I will not kiss you again if that is what troubles you."

"I know you to be a gentleman, Seth," she said quietly. "Your word is your bond. If you said you would not kiss me, then I believe you." She hesitated. "It's me I do not trust," she admitted. "I am afraid if we are alone in the gardens together, that I might ask more of you than I should."

Her words gave him hope, and he said, "Perhaps after a turn about the gardens—with no sitting—you might come inside for a cup of tea to warm you. It is a rather cold day."

Seth saw she wavered and then said, "All right. A brief walk with no stops, then a cup of tea."

Satisfied that he would retain her company for another hour or so, Seth offered Pippa his arm, and she took it.

Chapter Eleven

When Seth tried to lead Pippa around the house, she protested.

"Cut through the kitchens," she told him. "It is far easier and quicker."

"Is that . . . allowed?"

That musical laugh came again, tugging upon his heart-strings. "You *are* the viscount, my lord," she teased. "You can go anywhere you wish in your house. True, not many titled gentlemen make a habit of appearing in the kitchens. Some probably would have no idea where they are even located. And it will probably startle the scullery maids this first time. But I suggest you make it a habit. You need to see what your servants do. They work long hours to make your life easy and see that your household runs smoothly. Get to know their names, beyond your housekeeper and butler. Compliment them when it is deserved."

"You sound wise beyond your years," he said.

"Mama raised all us girls to have an appreciation for what is done for us. We have the good fortune simply by our birth to be born into a household and way of life that few experience. She wanted us to not only recognize—but value—the contribution our servants make upon our daily lives."

Pippa sighed. "Mama had to learn all that on her own. She married Papa when she was quite young. Why, she was only eight and ten when she had Georgie and me. She was Papa's second wife. James' mother died when he was quite small. I think Papa believed a young wife would give him many sons." She giggled. "Instead, he received four daughters from her."

They reached the kitchens, and as Seth had thought, all work came to a standstill. The silence was deafening.

Trying to put the kitchen staff at ease, he said, "I know you are making marvelous things for me and all my servants to eat. Thank you for your hard work." He looked at the stout, older woman who had to be in command of the place. "Especially you, Cook. I recognize your efforts and have been delighted with the meals you have prepared for me since I have come to Hopewood."

Cook's cheeks burned bright red, but she beamed at him. "Happy to be of service to you, my lord. We are all glad you've come to Hopewood."

"If we could have tea brought to the library, Cook, it would be appreciated. Carry on," he said cheerfully as he escorted Pippa upstairs.

He thought the library would be less formal than the drawing room, and she might wish to explore it with him.

As they headed up the stairs, she said, "See how easy that was? And you've a lifelong devoted servant in Cook now. Why, she melted when you smiled at her." Pippa paused. "Your smile is lethal, you know."

"How so?"

She arched a brow. "Do not fish for compliments, Seth. You are an incredibly attractive man and know it. Your smile sets hearts aflutter."

"Including yours?" he asked, his voice husky.

"Possibly," she said, her tone flirtatious.

He laughed and directed them to the library, where she turned in circles, gazing at the shelves of books.

"Oh, what a marvelous room!" she declared. "You must be in heaven. Lord Hopewell—your uncle—was always giving me books to read, but I have never been in the library before."

He indicated a settee, and they settled themselves on it. "He also sent me books over the years. That was part of our arrangement when he helped me go to sea as a cabin boy. He told me as long as I could read and write, I was in charge of my own education and should pursue learning the rest of my life."

Seth paused, thinking back on how happy he had been every time he received a book from his uncle.

"I read various histories. I went mad for Shakespeare's plays for several years."

"So did I!" she said, laughing. "Although I never saw the point of *Romeo and Juliet*. I mean, who would act so foolishly? I enjoyed the aspects of forbidden love and feuding families, but if you are going to be adventurous enough to take something which would make you to appear as if you had died, you had better have a reliable servant who can be responsible enough to get a message to your loved one so he won't murder himself and be dead when you awaken."

He laughed. "I always thought Romeo had the better end, drinking the poison."

"I agree. While poison is vile and I am certain he suffered, all he had to do was down it quickly and let it do the foul work for him. Poor Juliet had to stab herself! Just think of the fortitude it took to do so. Holding the blade. Slamming it into her and twisting it. The agony of lying there, blood gushing from her as her life slowly and painfully ebbed away."

"We are talking of them as if they are real when they are merely fictional characters."

"True, but a good writer will have you invest yourself in his characters," she said. "I truly felt sorry for them, dying so young and never seeing their love come to fruition. And I cannot imagine the guilt those Capulets and Montagues must have experienced, seeing how their foolish disagreement led to the death of two young people."

"Well, it *was* a tragedy," Seth pointed out. "Frankly, I preferred Shakespeare's histories and comedies."

They talked about the Bard's plays for several minutes until their tea arrived. Without being asked, Pippa poured out for them both, and he saw she did so with an ease that came from years of good breeding, coupled with experience. She might not have the patience to sit with a needle and thread, but she moved with grace.

Even in those tight, tempting breeches.

"Tell me more about those superstitions you mentioned previously," she encouraged, handing him his cup and saucer.

"Bananas," he replied, taking a sip of his tea.

"Bananas? That is ridiculous."

"Not to a sailor," Seth told her. "It was the first superstition I heard about as a boy sailing on my first voyage. Most likely it harkened back to the last century. Bananas were said to bring bad luck goes back to ships which disappeared in the Caribbean. A majority of those vessels happened to be carrying bananas. If a sailor learned that the cargo would transport bananas, he would believe the ship would be lost."

"Fascinating. What else?"

He thought a moment. "I have known sailors to purchase the caul which covered the face of a newborn babe before setting off on a voyage. These are rare, but having one supposedly prevents you from drowning. And once onboard, many sailors never trim their nails or cut their hair. Some won't even shave their beard because all those things are supposed to bring bad luck. And egg shells. They must be broken into the tiniest of pieces once a cook cracks one open." Seth grinned. "It's meant to keep witches from boarding the ship and sailing in the pieces of the shell."

Pippa burst out laughing. "I have never heard anything more ridiculous. Go on. This is fascinating."

"If your hat flies off and is lost overboard, it portends the voyage is to be a long one, though most are scheduled to be months or years in length. Oh, you aren't to stir your tea with a fork or knife, or you will bring bad luck upon yourself and the ship. And you never turn a loaf of bread upside down once it's been sliced. That's also a sign of bad luck. Also, the salt pot mustn't be passed from one sailor to another. It must be placed down, and then the next crew member can pick it up. If not, bad luck will abound."

"Do you believe in any of these superstitions?" she asked.

"Not really, but I would never vocalize that because too many of the men whom I sailed with did believe them. Now, the worst superstition of all said that women were definitely bad luck."

"What?" Pippa cried. "How so?"

"If a woman was onboard, that was definitely a sign of bad luck because she would distract the crew from their duties, which would anger the sea. The sea would manifest its anger in storms, high winds, and crashing waves, showing its displeasure."

"But aren't ships often named after women?"

He laughed. "That is true. And a traditional figurehead of a sailing ship is that of a woman, usually bare-breasted. It is believed by sailors that a topless woman has a calming effect on the seas. That she shames the ocean into being calm."

She shook her head. "That is dreadful. Women no more bring bad luck than a man would."

"Oh, sailors also are prejudiced against anyone with red hair. I know of redheaded seamen who shave their heads before they set foot on a ship, and they continue to shave it throughout the voyage to keep their red hairs from sprouting. Have you ever seen a sailor?" he asked.

"Even though my family owns Strong Shipping Line, I can't say that I have. Other than James, none of us has ever been down to the waterfront, much less to the Strong Shipping Lines offices."

"If you had, you might have seen a sailor wearing gold hooped earrings."

"A man wearing earrings? Oh, do tell."

"The most superstitious of sailors wear gold hoops as a way to bring them good fortune. If a sailor has pierced his ear, it means he has sailed around the world once before or at least crossed the equator. Gold traditionally is thought to have the power to protect and heal its wearer."

"Then before I set sail and see the world someday, I will make certain I am wearing gold hooped earrings."

"When you do step foot on the ship which will take you to faraway places, board it with your right foot first. The left is considered evil, so even sailors keep to the right foot each time they board. I will admit that I do it without even thinking after all these years. It simply becomes a part of you after so many trips to sea. Do you like cats, Pippa?"

"I do. Since I have spent so much time in our stables, there are always mousers there, some sweeter than others. Why?"

"Cats aboard a ship signify good fortune," Seth explained. "They kill the rats, which can eat the food supplies and chew through ropes. Every ship makes certain when it sets out to sea, it has at least a cat or two on board."

She sipped her tea and set down the saucer. "You have been a wealth of knowledge today, Seth. I have really enjoyed hearing about these superstitions, as well as things considered to be good luck."

He fought the urge to kiss her, knowing he had given her the power to make that happen.

But he could still flirt with her.

Laying the groundwork, he said, "Many sailors also bear tattoos. Some tattoo a rooster on one foot and a pig on their other one. It is believed if you do so, it will keep you from drowning because they would steer you to shore."

He could see his words intrigued her. "Do you have any tattoos, Seth?"

"I do," he replied. "I have a nautical star. The North Star."

Her eyes lit with interest. "May I see it? Is it on your foot?"

"It is not on a place I could readily show you," he replied

mysteriously. "Perhaps one day when we know one another better, I might show it to you."

She snorted. "I think we have gotten to know one another fairly well, Seth."

He leaned a bit closer to her, inhaling the vanilla scent which clung to her. "We would have to know one another *much* better, Pippa, for you to see it—and where it is."

She wet her lips, driving him mad. He couldn't stop himself and placed his palm against her cheek. He didn't dare breathe as he gazed into her cornflower blue eyes, the shade he had seen in most of the eyes of the Strongs.

"Kiss me," she whispered.

Had he heard her right—or did he hear what he wished to hear?

Seth did not move.

"Kiss me," she repeated, and he saw the yearning in her eyes.

"Are you certain you wish me to do so, Pippa?"

"I think I might go mad if you don't," she said, her honesty refreshing.

"All right."

He wanted much more than a kiss from her, but instinct still told him he shouldn't move too fast or take things too far. All this was so new to her. He didn't want to make her uncomfortable or drive her away for good. In fact, he thought it might be wise to kiss her only a little.

And make her want more . . .

He took her hands, his thumbs caressing them, bringing them up and brushing his lips against her knuckles. Her sigh told him it had been a good move on his part.

Still holding her hands in his, Seth leaned toward her, his mouth touching hers. He gave her light kisses and then kissed her cheek, savoring her scent. He moved his lips to her temple, brushing it softly.

Releasing her hands, he captured her face in his hands, holding her steady as his lips returned to hers. He kissed her softly, and an aching tenderness for this woman filled him. Of all the women he had kissed—and coupled with—Pippa Strong alone moved him like no other had.

It surprised him when he felt her tongue slide along his bottom lip. Pleased that she had been the one to act boldly, he opened for her. Hesitantly, she pushed her tongue inside his mouth, gently exploring him. It took everything he had not to push her back to the settee and climb atop her. He held himself in check, his tongue brushing against hers, now mating with it.

Their kisses grew more heated, and he knew passion stirred within her. He tilted her head slightly, allowing him to deepen the kiss as he now took control. He took from her. She took from him. His arms went around her now, crushing her to his chest. He could feel her breasts' swell and longed to suck on them. That would be taking things too far, though.

Once more, he gentled the kiss, finally easing from her. He liked that she looked slightly dazed and at the same time wore an expression he likened to a cat who had been into the cream.

Satisfied.

Her chest heaving, Pippa said, "You kiss extremely well, Seth."

"You do, too, Pippa."

Her cheeks, already flushed with color, turned even redder. "Please, no."

"What?"

"You do not have to flatter me, Seth. I realize I am a novice at kissing, and you have far more experience than I."

Cradling her face in his hands, he said, "You *do* kiss well, Pippa. Better than any woman I have ever kissed."

She looked both pleased and doubtful. "Truly?"

"I think it all has to do with the fact I like you," he said frankly. "I like you—and I like kissing you. Have I kissed other women? I will admit I have. But none of them have ever made me feel as you do, Pippa. I am attracted to you."

"You are?" The doubt left her eyes, and she looked quite pleased with herself.

"Yes, I am. But as before, I will not kiss you unless you want me to do so." He paused. "Or if you wish us to do more."

"More?" she questioned. "I will admit I don't understand what you are saying."

Oh, she was an innocent.

"I would never couple with you. That is something you will do with your future husband. But . . . there are ways of pleasuring you which would not be that."

She frowned. "I know coupling can result in a babe. I do not want a babe, Seth," she said firmly.

He pictured her with his babe inside her, her rounded belly swollen.

"I understand. But if you want to do more kissing—do more *than* kissing—I am happy to accommodate you."

She grew thoughtful. "I must think on this. While I find your kisses to be delightful, I am not certain about trying something beyond them."

"I promise I will not ask you to do so, Pippa. I am only happy to teach you anything you wish to learn regarding what occurs between a man and a woman."

She stood abruptly, and he followed suit.

"I must go home. Now."

Seth saw panic rising within her. He brought his arms about her, hugging her to him.

"Calm down," he said.

She wriggled a moment and then stilled. He did not move, simply kept his arms around her, like someone who had captured a bird in his hands.

"You are overwhelmed," he told her. "Feeling things you have never felt before. There is no reason to be upset. No need to panic. Take a few calming breaths."

She did as he asked, and he felt her relax. He released her.

"Better?" he asked.

"Yes," she said, her voice shaking.

"Let me walk you to the stables."

Seth did not touch her. They walked side-by-side without speaking. A groom appeared, and he asked him to retrieve Starlight.

While they waited, he said, "I think we should take a break, Pippa. No riding lesson tomorrow."

"No?" she asked, clearly disappointed, which thrilled him.

"I will give my body a day to rest. I have other things on the estate to keep me busy. We can try again the day after tomorrow."

"I see. You . . . you aren't angry with me, Seth?"

"Not at all, Pippa."

"And you liked kissing me?"

He smiled. "More than I can say."

"All right. I will come again the day after tomorrow. But if you change your mind and wish to ride before then, just send a note to Shadowcrest. And don't go out without me. You are still too inexperienced to be riding alone."

The groom appeared with her horse, and Pippa swung into the saddle.

"Thank you for coming today," he said. "I enjoyed getting to see a large part of Hopewood and meeting my tenants."

"I enjoyed showing it to you. And being with you."

She turned Starlight and took off, galloping away, woman and beast moving as one. As he watched her ride away, the stark truth hit Seth.

He had fallen in love with Pippa Strong.

Chapter Twelve

SETH AWOKE AFTER a restless night. As a ship's captain, he had always had to take decisive action, particularly when the weather changed so quickly. A storm in the form of Pippa Strong had entered his life without warning, and he needed to deal with it.

Yes, he acknowledged to himself he had feelings for Pippa, because of the proximity they had shared, but mostly for the friendship they had built. That had led to the desire he felt for her.

Since he didn't know how to handle the way he felt about her, he decided the wisest thing would be to put some distance between them. It would give him time to clear his head and look at his situation more objectively. It would also give Pippa the chance to see if she had a fondness for him and missed him during his absence.

He rang for Tompkins and raised himself for the day, telling the valet they would be leaving for town as soon as breakfast concluded.

"My lord, you are to see the Crestview tailor. He did send word that you could come this morning."

Seth had forgotten about his appointment, but he hoped the man would at least have something ready which he might wear to London.

"Then we will stop in the village first and claim anything that is ready to go. While we are in London, I will be seeing another tailor to take care of the bulk of my needs."

The valet's eyes lit. "That is a good thing, my lord."

He chuckled. "Tired of seeing me dressed in my captain's uniform, Tompkins?"

"You wear it quite well, my lord," the servant said diplomatically. "However, you have a new rank in life and need to be dressed appropriately for your station."

Seth went down to breakfast, where he informed Robb of his decision to head to town.

"I should be there no longer than a week. Perhaps by then, Mr. Hunt will have returned. For now, I will dine and leave. Please see that my coachman has the carriage readied."

"Which of your staff do you wish to take with you, my lord?" the butler asked. "Since Lord Hopewell rarely went to town, he had no servants remain in London. Various ones were chosen to accompany him each time."

Peabody had told Seth about that unusual arrangement, saying if Seth wished to end it, it would be wise. The solicitor assured him that he had ample funds to hire staff to remain in London and care for the townhouse.

"Everyone but Tompkins will remain at Hopewood," he told Robb. "I will be hiring servants who will be in charge of my London home. When I travel to town in the future, you will be able to send a message to my butler there, and he will have the house readied for my visit."

Robb's relief was visible. "A most wise plan, my lord." He hesitated. "If you need me to do so, I can accompany you and help in the hiring of the staff."

While he thought his country butler efficient, Robb was still his uncle's man. Seth wanted to begin to put his own mark on the viscountcy, and a good start would be with hiring his own servants.

"The Duchess of Seaton has promised to aid me in this endeavor," he said crisply. "But thank you for your offer, Robb."

After eating, Seth went to his study to compose a message to Pippa. He decided to make it brief.

Lady Philippa –

I have been called away to London for several days, perhaps as long as a week. I am sorry to have to delay our riding lessons. Perhaps by the time I return, my soreness will have worked itself out, and we can pick up where we left off.

Sincerely,
Hopewell

He read through the few lines and decided the note was adequate, wondering if she might read into his line about picking up where they'd left off. He made certain he had not addressed her in a familiar fashion, not knowing if anyone would read and screen the contents of the note before it reached her. It was better to be on the safe side.

Going to the foyer, Robb told him the carriage was waiting for him. He handed over the note, asking that it be delivered to Lady Philippa at Shadowcrest, so that she would know not to come to Hopewood for his riding lesson tomorrow morning. In return, the butler awarded Seth with the keys to his townhouse before he made his way outside. As before, Tompkins sat next to the driver.

"We are stopping in the village so I might see my tailor, then we are off to London. You know where the horses are to be exchanged, I assume."

"Yes, my lord," the coachman replied.

They made it to the village within minutes, and Tompkins accompanied Seth inside, where the tailor greeted them.

"Lord Hopewell, thank you for coming so promptly."

"I find I must journey to London and thought I would stop before I left to see if anything you had already made up would be suitable for me to wear while I am there."

"I believe so, my lord. Shall we have you try on a few things?"

The tailor had made up three coats, along with waistcoats and breeches. Everything fit him to perfection, with no adjustments needed. Seth gazed into the long mirror and couldn't help but admire the figure he cut, wondering what Pippa would think of him in his gentleman's clothes.

"I don't believe any adjustments need to occur, my lord," the tailor said.

"I agree," Tompkins chimed in. "I have brought a trunk for his lordship's wardrobe. I'll fetch it now so that we might pack up his things for him."

While the valet retrieved the trunk from the carriage, the tailor said, "I know you will see a tailor in town, my lord. The quality of fabrics in London will be more luxurious than what I had to offer you, but please know I am always here and ready to be of service to you if you need anything while you are in Kent."

"Thank you for the quick work. I am pleased with what you have created for me and happy to wear this from your store into town. It is time I retire my captain's uniform."

Tompkins returned and packed what the tailor had sewn, along with the uniform Seth had discarded. Soon, they were on the road again. They changed horses once, and then arrived at his townhouse an hour and a half later. Peabody had driven him by it before they went to the country, and he was curious what it looked like inside.

He told Tompkins, "I will be coming to town regularly and will take my seat in the House of Lords and also attend the Season. I think it wise to have a staff in town, and I will be hiring several servants while I am here. For now, I am off to see my solicitor and the Duke of Seaton. We will have to rough it for a few days, with it being just the three of us. We can eat from the street vendors until a cook is hired."

"The horses need a rest, my lord," the coachman pointed out.

"That isn't a problem. I will simply take a hansom cab on my errands."

He decided before even seeing Peabody that he would go to the wharf area and see if the duke or duchess were at their places of business.

Walking along his street, he found and hailed a hansom cab, giving the driver instructions to take him to the London docks.

Seth disembarked and paid his driver, walking closer to the water, seeing two different ships in dock. He thought he might be sadder than he was to see them, knowing he would never go out on one again as its captain, but he was eager to face the new challenges confronting him.

Especially Pippa Strong.

He was familiar with where the Strong Shipping Lines was located, having reported to them after returning from sea voyages. The warehouse sat opposite of the offices he had gone to. He thought he might find Seaton at Neptune Shipping, however, and decided to make his way there first.

Stopping a passerby, he inquired where Neptune was located, obtaining directions to his destination. He soon found himself at its doors. The warehouse was on the ground floor, while the shipping offices were above it. He made his way up the stairs, giving his name to the secretary and asked to see Her Grace if she were available to Lord Hopewell.

"Her Grace is with His Grace in the conference room, my lord. Let me see if they night speak with you."

Less than a minute later, Seaton himself appeared, offering his hand.

"It is a surprise to see you here, Hopewell. I thought Mr. Samuel was wrong, but here you are."

"I had some unfinished business in town and thought to call upon you and Her Grace."

"You've come at a fine time. Please, accompany me to the conference room."

He entered and greeted the duchess, meeting Mr. Barnes, who helped run Neptune Shipping with her, and Mr. Compton, who was in charge of Strong Shipping.

Across the conference table, a large map was unfolded. He saw it was of the world and marked with various trade routes.

The duchess smiled. "Instead of both our shipping lines duplicating the same routes, we are dividing and finalizing which routes each of our companies will now take. It will be easier to concentrate our ships on fewer routes and not be so scattered as before."

She launched into an explanation of which company would be taking which trade routes, and Seth was astounded at the depth and breadth of her knowledge.

When she had finished, the duke said, "I may know all that goes on while at sea, but Her Grace has the head for business in our family." He smiled at his wife. "It is what makes us such a good match. We are an excellent balance of one another and complement the other."

They spoke a little more about business and then returned to Her Grace's office, which was smaller than Seth would have expected.

"Why have you come to town?" she asked.

"For one thing, I need to see a tailor." He indicated what he now wore. "While I have a few decent coats to my name now, my solicitor urged me to visit a London tailor as soon as possible."

"Then you must come and be fitted by mine," Seaton insisted. "He did a remarkable job outfitting me from head to toe. You will have to look the part you now play, Hopewell. Why don't I take you to see him now if you are free to do so?"

"That is a marvelous idea," the duchess agreed. "And if you are free, my lord, you should join us for dinner this evening."

"Thank you for your kind invitation, Your Grace. I will take you up on it since I have no servants in town to cook a meal for me."

"Oh, dear. No servants?" she fretted.

"My uncle was a bit of a recluse and rarely left the country. When he did, he merely brought a handful of servants with him from Hopewood. One thing I wish to do while I am here is to hire a staff to manage my London townhouse."

The duchess grabbed a pencil and scribbled something on a piece of parchment. Handing it to him, she said, "This is the employment agency I have used in the past. I have been most pleased with them."

"Why, thank you. I had no idea where to begin."

"I will accompany Hopewell to my tailor, my love," Seaton said, bending and kissing his wife on the lips.

The gesture surprised Seth because even he knew open affection amongst the upper classes was rarely—if ever—seen in public.

The duchess smiled warmly at her husband. "I will see you later."

"I will be back to escort you home," he promised. Turning and slapping Seth on the back, he asked, "Shall we go?"

His Grace took them to his carriage, simply the grandest vehicle Seth had ever laid eyes on.

"I know little of horseflesh, but the team drawing your coach are magnificent in appearance."

"They are, aren't they?" the duke said, pride evident in his voice. "I rode briefly as a boy, before I went to sea. Pippa has promised to refresh my skills. She says it is the only way to get about the country."

They entered the carriage and he said, "Yes, Lady Philippa has already given me two riding lessons so far. Let me warn you, Seaton, you will be sorer than you have been in your entire life after that first time back on horseback. I almost thought I wouldn't be able to get back on my horse yesterday, but your sister is an excellent teacher."

"That is good to hear."

"Unlike you, I had never been atop a horse. We seamen had little need to learn how to ride."

As they drove to the tailor's shop, Seaton explained all the items Seth would need to purchase.

"I had help with this, and I am happy to offer guidance to you. The tailor we will visit will handle your coats, waistcoats, and breeches. His brother has a shop next door, and he is a shirtmaker. You will be astounded at the number of shirts required of you. Why, I believe I own over three dozen."

"What?" Seth asked, floored by the number.

The duke shrugged. "You keep some of them in town. Some in the country. Surprisingly, a titled gentleman changes clothes quite a bit. It makes it easier for servants to launder and care for your clothing if you have numerous pieces. I also can recommend a bootmaker to you, a brother-in-law to these two brothers I have mentioned. He has made me three pairs of boots, and they are the most comfortable I have ever worn. The expense for all of this is great, but it is expected of you."

Seaton chuckled. "I have to consider not only my own reputation but that of my sisters and cousins. I must look and act as the duke I am. Many of them are coming of age and will be making their come-outs during the upcoming Season this spring. The exceptions will be Pippa and Effie."

Seth frowned. "I know Lady Euphemia is too young to make her come-out, but why would Lady Philippa not do so when her own twin will?"

Seaton shrugged. "She apparently doesn't want to. She told me she is not ready for marriage. Pippa wants to have a bit of freedom. Frankly, I think it has been hardest on Georgina. The twins are quite close, and Georgie will certainly miss not having Pippa attend balls with her."

Hearing that Pippa wasn't ready for marriage deflated Seth. He would keep to himself his intentions toward her.

For now.

Thinking that, he realized he was ready to make a commitment to Pippa. He would certainly need to walk on eggshells now since he'd learned she wasn't ready for marriage.

They entered the tailor's shop, and the duke was greeted effusively.

"This is my good friend, Viscount Hopewell. I would ask that you do for him what you did for me. He is a fellow sea captain who has come into his title, and he must look his best for Polite Society."

Seaton grinned at Seth. "I am sure you will attend this upcoming Season and possibly be looking for a bride."

Seth was fussed over, measured from head to toe, and asked to look at many fabric samples.

"I will leave that to you and my valet," he told the tailor. "I will send Tompkins to you first thing tomorrow. The two of you can make these decisions for me. I trust his taste—and yours."

Seaton accompanied him next door to the shirtmaker and then to the bootmaker and a hatmaker. At each place, His Grace emphasized the need for speed and quality, saying his friend would be returning to the country soon. Every establishment promised to have numerous items ready, while they would send other finished things to the countryside once they were completed. All noted that since they were between Seasons, it would be easier to accomplish this.

"It is late, so you might as well accompany me back to Neptune to claim Sophie. Then we can proceed home for dinner."

Seth waited in the carriage while the duke went inside, returning minutes later with the duchess. They went to the ducal townhouse, and Seth was astounded at the sheer size of the place.

"It is a lot to take in," His Grace said. "I was dumbfounded to think I would be living here."

They entered the townhouse and went up to the drawing room. The duchess excused herself, saying she would join them in a few minutes.

When she returned, a footman appeared with a tray of drinks, and Seth accepted one.

"We can sit for a few minutes," Her Grace said. "Powell will let us know when it is time to go into dinner."

After they seated themselves, the duchess asked, "What have you been up to since we last saw you, Hopewell?"

"I have spent a good deal of time reviewing my estate's ledgers. Thanks to Mr. Strong, I had a good idea what to look for as I did so. I also have been taking riding lessons from Lady Philippa."

"Oh, I haven't ridden in years," Her Grace said. "And my husband hasn't for many years. I will need to work with Pippa to refresh my own skills. Have you enjoyed these lessons, my lord?"

"I have taken to riding," he shared. "It has allowed me to go out on the estate with Lady Philippa and see it better. She says riding is the best way to get around in the country, and after seeing how easy it is to cut across and go where no roads do, I completely agree."

At that moment, Seth changed his mind about talking to the couple in regard to Pippa. While they were in the drawing room with no servants present, he asked, "May I speak frankly to the both of you?"

His Grace nodded. "I hope you understand that you are amongst friends. Especially with us being neighbors, I hope that we can build upon our acquaintance so that we will become good friends."

"But you want more, don't you, Lord Hopewell?" the duchess asked. "You have come here to ask us about Pippa, haven't you?"

"Have I been that obvious?" he asked, and she nodded, losing the fight to suppress a smile.

"Perhaps I noticed because I felt such an affinity with James—His Grace—when we were brought together recently. Our feelings for one another were quite powerful. I thought I saw something between the two of you and wondered if you might pursue it."

"You are correct, Your Grace. While I had never thought to wed since I anticipated spending my entire life at sea, I have had to rethink things. Holding a title, I know I must pass it along someday, which means providing an heir for that title."

He swallowed, nerves filling him. "And that means claiming a wife. I don't believe because of my background that most ladies—

and their fathers—would find me suitable, despite my title. I do believe a marriage should be a partnership, though, and I am quite taken with Lady Philippa. I find her quite unique."

The duchess nodded in agreement. "It is true that Pippa is not a typical lady of the *ton*. How does she feel about you, my lord? Or have you yet to make your feelings known to her?"

"She knows that I am interested in her, but not to the extent of asking for her hand in marriage," he replied.

"That decision will be left to my sister," Seaton said. "I understand, thanks to Sophie, that most women in Polite Society are held hostages to the wishes of their fathers or guardians. I would never force Pippa—or any of my sisters—to wed."

The duke took his wife's hand, gazing upon her tenderly, and Seth could feel the power of their love.

"My own wife had no say in her first marriage. While it turned out Sophie wed a good man who taught her many things, he would not have been her choice. She was able to make her own choice this time." He kissed her fingers. "I would not deny Pippa and keep her from following her heart."

The duke turned to look at Seth. "I like you, Hopewell. We both do. But it will be up to Pippa as to whether or not she wishes to wed in the first place, and she will be free to make her own choice of husbands if she does."

"I understand, Your Grace. I feel the same. I want Pippa to choose me because I am the man she sees herself with. I can assure you I would never place her in a box. She would be free to be who she is." He grinned. "Breeches and all."

"Whether my sister agrees to wed you or not, I hope we can enjoy being neighbors and friends. Because of that, I ask that you call me James."

"And I am Sophie," the duchess quickly added.

"I am Seth." He smiled. "The man who hopefully will become family someday."

CHAPTER THIRTEEN

PIPPA ATE BREAKFAST with her family, wondering what she was going to do today. She had never thought about that when she was in the country. She had simply gone wherever the spirit moved her.

Lord Hopewell had changed all that.

She was frustrated with herself because she could not stop thinking about the irresistible viscount. It had been a week since she had last seen him, and he dominated her waking thoughts. She still had no idea of when he might return from town and wasn't sure that she wanted to give him riding lessons anymore.

A footman entered the breakfast room and whispered something to Forrester. The butler smoothly moved to Mama.

"News has arrived from the tenants, my lady. Mrs. Foster has given birth to a healthy boy."

"Then I finished the blanket I knitted for the babe just in time," Georgie declared. "I should take it to her today." Her twin looked to her. "Would you like to go with me, Pippa?"

"Of course," she said, thinking she had nothing better to do than mope about, hoping to receive word from Hopewood of the viscount's return.

"I want to go, too," Mirella said. "We can take food from Cook to the family. May I be excused, Mama? I will go and tell

Cook what we need."

"Yes, my darling," Mama said.

Half an hour later, they were ready to head to the Fosters' cottage. They decided to take a horse and cart since it would be too difficult to carry on horseback all that Cook had provided for them. Pippa had a groom saddle a horse to a cart and after two footmen had loaded the contents into its bed, the three sisters set out.

When they arrived, they were warmly greeted by Mr. Foster, who beamed with pride, being a first-time father.

"You should see how perfect he is, my ladies," the father said. "And you have brought an abundance of things for us. You are very kind to think of us."

"We are happy to do so, Mr. Foster," Georgie said. "May we come inside and see your wife and the babe?"

"Come with me," the farmer said, lifting the large pot of stew Cook had provided. "I'll come back for the rest."

They entered the cottage and found the new mother nursing her babe. She was thrilled by their visit and shared that her labor had been long but without complications. Pippa still didn't quite understand all that it took to become with child, much less how the child came out. Maybe it was time to press Mama to explain such matters to her.

After burping her newborn, Mrs. Foster asked, "Would any of you like to hold him? We have yet to name him."

It didn't surprise her when Georgie spoke up. "I would."

The new mother handed over her babe, and Georgie held the sleeping infant gingerly, gazing down at him with a soft smile.

They talked a bit about things happening in the neighborhood, and then Georgie looked to Pippa.

"Would you like to hold him?"

She wasn't sure if she wanted to or not, but agreed to do so, mostly to please her sister.

"Yes, give him to me," she said, accepting the babe from her twin's arms and nestling him in her own.

Pippa gazed down at the child and felt a deep yearning within her, something unknown to her before now. Her twin had never made a secret of how much she wanted children, but Pippa had not even given the issue a thought. Looking down at this beautiful babe, though, she found herself changing her mind.

Having a child would be the right thing to do—with the right man.

Her thoughts drifted to Lord Hopewell and the kisses they had exchanged. Of course, he would want an heir.

But would he want to make a babe with her?

She found herself conflicted. She needed to see Hopewell. His absence had only caused her to think of him constantly, and she didn't know if she missed him or the idea of him. Even then, who was to say if he might think of her as marriage material. Of all her sisters and cousins, Pippa seemed the least maternal. Yet the pull on her heart caused by the babe in her arms was causing her to rethink things.

Could she be who she had always been and still fit into Polite Society? Could she be as good a mother as Mama?

She was getting ahead of herself. While Lord Hopewell had kissed her, he had mentioned nothing of courting her, much less marrying her. She needed to thrust these thoughts from her mind, and turned to Mirella.

"Would you like to hold him now?"

Her younger sister's face softened. "Yes. Please."

Pippa rose and placed the infant in Mirella's arms, thinking how natural both she and Georgie appeared when holding the newborn. A restlessness filled her, and she did not know how to fill it.

After a few more minutes, she gave Georgie a look, and her twin said, "We should be leaving now. We know you must get your rest, Mrs. Foster, and we do not wish to overstay."

"Thank you so much for the food you brought, and especially the blanket you knitted, my lady," the woman said. "Every time I wrap my child in it, I will be wrapping him in love."

They said their farewells and returned to the cart. Pippa was quiet as she took up the reins and drove, Georgie and Mirella chattering the entire way home.

When they reached the stables, a groom met them. Effie emerged, leading her horse.

"I was just going for a ride," her sister said. "Would anyone care to join me?"

"I would," Pippa said immediately, needing to be on horseback, galloping, banishing her thoughts.

Her other two sisters demurred, heading back to the house, saying they wished to practice their music.

Pippa and Effie took off from the stables, galloping for several minutes before slowing their horses. Then Effie began peppering her with questions.

"When will Lord Hopewell be returning? How are your riding lessons going with him? Is he taking to being atop a horse? I cannot imagine having lived my entire life at sea and then being stuck on land. Pippa, why aren't you answering me?"

Effie studied her a moment and said, "Oh, Pippa! I do believe you have feelings for the viscount."

"Hush!" she commanded. "You are talking far too much. It is tiresome."

"I did not mean to offend you," her sister apologized. "Please. Do not be angry with me. I know I speak sometimes before I think. Mama says it is something I must work on in order to improve myself."

She dismounted and began leading Starlight by the reins. Effie did the same, falling into step beside her, and they walked silently for several minutes.

Then Pippa spoke. "I do have feelings for the viscount, Effie. They are confusing me, and it did not help with him leaving to go to town."

"He's quite handsome," Effie said dreamily. "And he seems very nice. You could do worse, Pippa. Do you think you might wed him?"

"It is far too soon to predict what might happen between us, Effie. We have only been in one another's company a few times."

"But it has been for several hours each time, Pippa," her sister pointed out. "Why, girls become engaged to a gentleman after only a few dances during the Season. I have talked to friends who say their sisters have danced with a man a handful of times, and he has called at their house a few afternoons, only to find themselves betrothed. I would wager you have had more conversation with the viscount than those girls have had with the men they will marry."

"There has been no talk of marriage," Pippa said firmly. "I would appreciate if you do not mention this to anyone else, Effie."

Sympathy filled her sister's eyes. "Have you at least spoken to Georgie about this? I know you tell one another everything."

"We have talked briefly about Hopewell. I really do not wish to pursue this topic anymore, Effie," Pippa declared, placing her foot in the stirrup and mounting Starlight once again.

Effie did the same, and they continued their ride, coming across Caleb. Pippa slowed her horse and asked, "What have you been out and about for?"

Her cousin said, "I am coming from Hopewood. The viscount sent a message, asking that I meet with him and his steward."

Pippa hid being upset. "When did Lord Hopewell return from town?" she asked casually.

"He got back yesterday," Caleb said cheerfully. "Mr. Hunt had arrived the day before. Poor Hunt lost his father and had gone to bury him."

While she could sympathize with the steward, she was irritated that Seth was back and had yet to inform her. Why, they could have had a riding lesson this morning if she had only known he had returned to Kent.

"What did you meet about?" Effie asked.

Caleb launch into an explanation, which Pippa ignored. Her

anger grew. She wasn't even sure if she wanted to see Seth again.

Much less kiss him.

"I will ride back to Shadowcrest with you if you are headed that way," Caleb told them.

"Fine," she said brusquely, nudging Starlight and taking off.

"Racing, are we?" Caleb called, thundering after her.

The two of them followed back to the stables, Pippa arriving seconds before her cousin did. She slipped from her horse and tossed the reins to a waiting groom.

"I know Starlight is fast," Caleb said as he dismounted, "but you get the most out of her. You seem to be as one with a horse, Pippa," he complimented. "It is too bad you are not a jockey and race horses for your living."

Effie rode up, dismounting from her horse. "We should go inside and change, Pippa. It will be teatime soon."

They parted company with Caleb, and she went to her bedchamber, washing and then changing into a gown with Kitty's help.

"Did you see your note, Lady Philippa?" the maid asked.

"Note?" Her heart began to race. "From who?"

The maid went to the dressing table and picked up a folded page. "Here it is, my lady. It came after you left to go see Mrs. Foster and her babe. One also came for Mr. Strong."

Now she knew it was from Seth.

"Thank you, Kitty," she said, dismissing the maid.

Once the servant had left the room, she broke the seal and unfolded the page.

Dear Lady Philippa –

I have returned from town, having completed my business. I am not certain you will recognize me because of the new clothes I now wear. I actually look more like a viscount and nothing as the sea captain I once was.

I spent several hours with my steward Mr. Hunt yesterday, and I am asking your cousin to come visit with us today to help clarify a few matters for me.

I hope you have been well during my absence and that you might wish to continue our riding lessons tomorrow morning. If this is convenient for you, I will meet you at my stables at eight o'clock. If you are otherwise engaged, please send me a message as to when you and I might ride again.

Sincerely,
Hopewell

Joy filled Pippa as she read his words, but she was irritated at herself for being so excited simply from a note sent by the viscount. Part of her wanted to make him wait, telling him it would be inconvenient for her to continue their lessons for several days, punishing him for having left her to go to town. Yet that would be petty and spiteful on her part. After all, he was a viscount and new to his title. He must have a dozen things to take care of. Riding lessons with a duke's younger sister would not be a priority.

She decided she would show up tomorrow morning. She needed to see him. Be with him. Find out if her feelings for him were changing—and if he even had any feelings for her.

The next morning, Pippa dressed in her riding clothes, making her way to breakfast. Only Aunt Matty was present when she arrived.

"You are an early bird," her aunt commented. "What do you have planned today?"

Pippa accepted a cup of tea from a footman. "I am to give Lord Hopewell another riding lesson this morning, Aunt," she said matter-of-factly.

"Oh, that is right. Caleb mentioned that the viscount had returned from town. Your cousin seems to think quite well of Lord Hopewell."

She thought her aunt baited her and neutrally said, "Yes, Caleb did speak about his lordship a bit at tea yesterday. And dinner."

"It would be good if they became friends," Aunt Matty said. "Caleb works so hard here at Shadowcrest. He needs to socialize more."

She ate her breakfast, joined by Allegra, Mirella, and Mama. Pippa excused herself and went to the stables, asking for Starlight to be readied for her. She rode to Hopewood, tamping down her growing excitement. It would not do for Seth to see how much she had missed him. Like a gambler, she would hold her cards close, giving away nothing of her true feelings. Truthfully, she didn't even know what those feelings were.

When she saw Seth standing in front of the stables, holding Orion's reins as he waited for her, she marveled at how he was now dressed. While he had cut a fine figure in his captain's uniform, his new wardrobe marked him as the titled gentleman he was. The elegant clothes only added to his masculinity, making him more appealing than ever. Her heart began to soar as she came close, and he gifted her with a smile.

"Good morning, my lady," he greeted. "Thank you for meeting up with me this morning. I have missed being on horseback—and with you," he added, the last words so soft, she almost didn't catch them.

"Good morning, my lord. Did you work out your stiffness?"

He laughed. "I did, but I also told Tompkins to make certain we had a good supply of Epsom salts on hand. I believe I will be in need of them once again after today's ride."

"Mount Orion if you would, my lord."

He did so, and Pippa quickly reviewed with him the lessons she had imparted before he left Kent.

She concluded with, "Are you comfortable setting out now?"

"Very much so. I was one of the lucky ones, in that when I went to sea, I gained my sea legs quickly. I never experienced any nausea from the motion of the waves, as many men suffer. Taking to riding has been much the same. I feel it is something I am born to do."

"We have seen much of your estate, my lord, and I know you

spoke of estate matters at length yesterday with my cousin and your steward. I have something different in mind for today's ride. Shall we ride to Crestview and see the village?"

He smiled again, causing her toes to curl. "I think that sounds like a fine adventure, Lady Philippa. Lead the way."

CHAPTER FOURTEEN

SETH DIDN'T REALLY care where they rode, only that he was with Pippa. He had missed her more than he had imagined possible, and he had forced himself to deliberately stay away a week. In that time, his heart had spoken loud and clear.

Pippa Strong was the one.

He still did not want to rush things with her, especially hearing that she didn't want to go to the Season. Had she made that known before he came into her life? Or was she simply opposed to the idea of ever marrying? He would have to learn those answers.

In the meantime, he would merely bask in her company, getting to know her better, and allowing her to know about him, as well.

As they picked up the pace and began trotting their horses along, she asked, "Have you been to the village yet?"

"I went and had a few clothes made up for me." Panic filled him even as he spoke, and he said, "Pippa, I cannot talk while I'm riding just yet."

"You are right. Concentrate on sitting the post. We'll be to Crestview in no time."

They did arrive in the village within a quarter hour, and they slowed their horses to a walk.

"Let's go up and down the entire length first," she suggested. "I want you to see what Crestview has to offer."

As they moved along the main thoroughfare, Pippa pointed out various shops to him, telling Seth a little about the people who owned and ran them.

"How do you know so much about these villagers?" he asked.

She shrugged. "I have always been interested in everything around me—and that includes people. I have been coming here for a very long time, and almost every shopkeeper is the same as when I was a little girl."

He caught a whiff in the air and inhaled deeply. "Where is that coming from?"

She laughed. "Oh, that is from Mrs. Bailey's shop. She runs a bakery, and her bread is divine. In fact, it is so good, one of our footmen comes to the village daily and buys loaves and loaves from her because it is so good. It also helps to keep our kitchens running more smoothly, with not having to bake bread each day. She even has a few tables and chairs within the bakery, so customers may stay and have a cup of tea and a bite to eat."

His stomach grumbled loudly, causing her to laugh even more.

"I think that is an excellent idea. Are you hungry?"

An odd look crossed her face. "I did not think to bring any coin with me, Seth, since I did not know we would be stopping and eating."

"Allow me to pay for it in exchange for the riding lesson you are giving me today."

She beamed at him, and the warmth of her smile enveloped him. He wanted more of those smiles from her. He wanted more from her.

All of her . . .

"We can leave our horses here," she told him as they arrived in front of the bakery, dismounting and looping her reins about a post.

Seth imitated her action and followed her inside, where incredible smells permeated the air.

"Good morning, Mrs. Bailey," Pippa said brightly. "I would like to introduce you to Lord Hopewell. He is the new viscount, the nephew of the former one."

The woman, with iron gray hair and merry eyes, bobbed a quick curtsey to him. "Good morning, my lord. It is wonderful to meet you."

"I feel the same, Mrs. Bailey. My nose led me here, and Lady Philippa assures me everything you bake is marvelous."

The older woman blushed. "Why, thank you, my lord." Looking to Pippa, she said, "I just took some sticky buns from the oven, my lady. Are they still your favorite?"

"They are indeed, Mrs. Bailey. Might I have one with a cup of tea?"

"Of course." The baker turned to him. "And for you, my lord?"

"I will have the same as Lady Philippa."

"Have a seat, and I will bring things to you when the tea has steeped."

They had their choice of three small tables, two chairs at each, and he pulled one out, seating Pippa and then himself.

"You are in for a treat," she revealed. "Mrs. Bailey's sticky buns are known throughout the area. I have not had one in years and have missed them so."

"Since it is a favorite place of yours, I am surprised you have not visited since your return to Shadowcrest."

"I am saving my coins," she confided. "Next month is Christmas, and I try to purchase a small gift for all my relatives. Miss Feathers, too, because she is like family. In fact, I have been needing to come to the village to do my Christmas shopping. Might we do so while we are here?"

"I am at your disposal for as long as you need me."

Mrs. Bailey arrived bearing a tray, setting down cups of tea and two plates containing the largest sticky buns Seth had ever seen. She also handed them each a rolled up napkin, saying a fork and knife lay inside.

"But I won't tell anyone if you lick your fingers, my lord," she teased, leaving them to their treat.

As Pippa cut into her bun, she asked, "What did you do in town, Seth? You were there what, a week?"

She had asked the question far too casually. His gut told him she had missed him, which raised his spirits considerably.

"One of the most important things I did was to hire servants to staff my London townhouse. My uncle rarely left his country estate. When he did venture into town, he would merely bring a few servants with him from Hopewood. I take my responsibilities seriously and will be happy to take my seat in the House of Lords."

"Parliament is in session during the Season," she told him. "Will you be attending those social events while you are in town?"

"It's possible," he said cryptically, wanting to gauge her reaction, hoping he could get her to reveal her true feelings about the *ton* and its Season.

"Are you going to be in town for the Season?" he asked. "Since I know literally no one but your family, it would be nice to see a friendly face."

Her brows knit together. "I was supposed to have made my come-out this coming spring, but I told Mama recently I was not ready to do so just yet, and she has allowed me to postpone it. You will know others, though. Georgina and Mirella will make their come-outs, along with my cousins Allegra and Lyric. Effie, naturally, is too young to do so, but she will go to town with the rest of the family."

"And what of you, Pippa? Where will you be come spring, if not in London?"

"I had thought to stay at Shadowcrest the entire time, but most likely now, I will go to town in April when the events begin. Since Mama and Aunt Matty are bringing out four family members, they will leave as early as February, so that seamstresses can begin working on the come-out wardrobes. Mama will also need new clothes, as will my aunt. Neither of them went to any *ton* events while Papa was ill those three years. In fact, Aunt Matty was sent down to Shadowcrest because she challenged my uncle about how he was managing Papa's household. She will definitely be ready to see her friends, as will Mama."

She took a sip of tea and then said, "Georgie is worried about deciding upon a husband. She wishes for me to be there to help her make up her mind."

"How will you do so if you don't attend the events?"

"Oh, she can tell me about her various gentlemen she meets. Just the tone of her voice—as well as what she reveals about them—will let me know which suitors she is most interested in. Men who wish to be the suitor of a lady will call the next day, and they also send flowers to show their interest. I told Georgie I would be happy to greet visitors with her in our drawing room. That way, I can get to know these men and see which ones might make a good husband for her."

"What is it like being a twin?" he asked. "I assume you are closer to Lady Georgina than your other sisters?"

Pippa nodded. "We usually know what the other is thinking. We oftentimes finish one another's sentences." She frowned. "That is one thing we are most concerned about: Georgie wedding a man who doesn't understand our closeness. We are both worried he will also live far away from Shadowcrest."

Tears glimmered in her eyes. "We have never been separated. We are each other's best friend and depend upon one another. It will take a very special man to understand that bond between us. It is why Georgie is so concerned and wants me there."

She paused and took a bite of her sticky bun, chewing thoughtfully.

"Don't you have the same concerns, Pippa? You, too, will wed someday, whether you find a husband during this Season or one beyond it."

She shrugged. "I have never really thought about a husband

or children, Seth. It is everything to Georgie, however. I wish for her to be happy and settled first. I even told her that I could always be like Aunt Matty and never wed. She helped raise all us girls. It was a lot for Mama, having four of us and then taking on my two cousins, for the most part."

"Why did she need to do so?"

Pippa's mouth hardened. "Uncle Adolphus is a typical man who sees no value in women. He got two sons off his wife, and then Allegra and Lyric came along. They, too, are twins, and were even born the same day as Georgie and me. Unfortunately, their mother died giving birth to them. Since my uncle had no use for the twins, they have spent a majority of their lives with us. I look upon them more as sisters than cousins, and Mama is the only mother they have ever known."

"I think you would make for a good mother, Pippa," Seth said quietly. "And a good wife."

Color flooded her cheeks, and she picked up her teacup as a distraction. Putting it down, she said, "Well, Seth, you will need to be looking for a wife yourself. Now that you have a title, you will need to provide an heir. Unless you have some brother I do not know about."

"No," he said, sadness washing over him. "I, too, lost my own mother when she gave birth to me. Father loved her a great deal and did not ever remarry. After her death, it was just the two of us for all those years."

"I suppose your family became your fellow sailors since you spent a majority of your time at sea," she mused.

"You are right about that, at least until I became captain of my own vessel. A captain needs to command with authority. He must make certain his crew respects that authority and that they are well disciplined. Because of that, he really can't have any friends aboard his ship. It would not do to show favoritism of one man over another."

She grew thoughtful. "It sounds an awful lot like a gentleman who holds a title. You have a tremendous amount of responsibility as a viscount, just as you did when you obtained your own ship. You cannot truly be friends with your staff because they would not respect you otherwise. We will need to get you some friends in the neighborhood, Seth."

Pippa began talking about others of genteel birth in the area, telling him he would need to call upon each of them, especially now that he looked so fine.

"You like my new clothes?"

"It is very obvious that you have been to London and been fitted by a tailor there."

"I also have shopping to do here," he told her. "I have noticed a few of my servants' uniforms are a bit frayed. Somehow, I don't believe my uncle paid attention to mundane matters such as that. I would like to stop at the tailor's and see if he would be willing to make up new uniforms for everyone."

"My, Seth, that is very generous of you. The expense will be great, though."

"You asked about what I did while I was in London. Beyond hiring staff for my townhouse, I spent time with Peabody, my solicitor. I am quite wealthy, Pippa. So much for one man to possess. I would not begrudge my servants a few uniforms. I can well afford it."

She dabbed her lips with a napkin, drawing his attention to them, and he thought how much he wanted to kiss her again.

"Then we should go see the tailor next," she determined.

He went to pay Mrs. Bailey, but she refused his coin. "It was good to meet you, my lord, and a delight to see Lady Philippa again. She doesn't come in often, but she is one of the kindest, gentlest souls I know."

"Thank you, Mrs. Bailey. I guarantee I will be a frequent visitor to your bakery. In fact, would you prepare some loaves of bread for me to take back to Hopewood? Lady Philippa and I will visit a few other merchants in Crestview, and then we can return for them."

Seth gave Mrs. Bailey money, and she accepted it, promising

she would have the bread for him by the time they returned.

They left their horses and walked a few shops down, calling at the tailor's establishment.

"Lord Hopewell, it is so good to see you again," the tailor greeted. "I see that you are wearing even newer clothes. They must come from London."

"They do, but I was just as proud to wear what you made up for me as what I am wearing today. I do have a project to ask you about, however."

Seth explained how he would like all his servants to be fitted for new uniforms, from his butler down to the lowliest scullery maid and groom.

"Which do you think would be better, two or three uniforms for each employee?"

"I would say two for your lower servants and three for the upper ones, my lord."

"But don't those lower servants work physically harder?" he asked.

"They usually do, my lord."

"Then I believe we should do three uniforms for each of my staff members. How should we go about this?"

They decided it would be easier for the tailor to come to Hopewood, versus having all Seth's servants dribble in one by one to the village. They agreed upon tomorrow, and the tailor said he would be at Hopewood by eight o'clock. Seth would have to meet with Robb in order to create a schedule to get everyone in to be measured.

"Thank you for taking this project on," he said.

The tailor's eyes lit up. "No, my lord, I must thank you. I have never taken on such a grand project, and this will be the bulk of my income for the entire year to come."

"Then I will see you tomorrow morning at Hopewood," Seth said.

"You are a very good man, Seth," Pippa said after they left the tailor's shop. "I cannot think of another gentleman who would be so generous to his servants."

"I realize it takes many of them to keep my household running smoothly. The least I can do is provide new uniforms for them. I will do so on a regular basis from now on. Perhaps that could be my Christmas gift to the staff."

"Well, it will be much appreciated."

"Where are we off to now?" he asked.

"A place you most likely have never been," Pippa said, mischief lighting her eyes. "A dressmaker's," she announced.

He laughed heartily. "I have not visited one. See what a new world you are opening up to me, Pippa?" he asked teasingly.

They entered the shop, which he saw contained many bolts of materials, along with a few hats on display.

"Mrs. Ames," Pippa said, greeting the proprietor. "May I introduce you to the new Lord Hopewell?"

The woman looked old enough to be his grandmother. She curtseyed to him. "I am happy to meet you, my lord. I never even laid eyes on the previous viscount."

"I hope to be out and about more than my uncle was," he said. "But Lady Philippa is not here simply to introduce us. She has gifts to purchase."

The dressmaker smiled, looking at Pippa as if she were a fellow conspirator. "Oh, my lady, what are we going to do for this Christmas?"

"I am thinking gloves for my sisters and cousins. Miss Feathers, too. That would be six pairs in all. Aunt Matty is always cold, and I believe a shawl would be appropriate for her."

"And for Her Grace?"

"Mama is still in mourning, but she won't be forever. You know she loves a pretty bonnet."

"I think those are wise choices, my lady. I have some bonnets on display if you wish to peruse them. If one of them will do, then I will tuck it away until Christmastime. If not, I can make up whatever you desire."

"Let me go look."

Pippa moved away, and Seth looked at the dressmaker. "It seems you have known Lady Philippa for many years."

"Yes, my lord, I have sewn many a dress for her and her relatives. She does love to buy a Christmas present for all in her family. She saves what little money she is given all year long in order to so do."

That thought distressed Seth, Pippa going without something in order to buy gifts for her family members.

"Why don't we let Lady Philippa save her coins this year?" he suggested. "I would be happy to cover the cost of anything she chooses."

Mrs. Ames' eyes widened, and he realized he had blundered badly.

"You see," he said smoothly, as if confiding in the woman, "Lady Philippa has been giving me riding lessons, and I have been trying to find a way to repay her. She refuses to accept payment, but I am still in her debt. If you will allow me to pay for these gifts, I will then tell her they are in exchange for the lessons she has given me. Would you please help me repay the kindness Lady Philippa has shown to me, Mrs. Ames?"

His words seemed to mollify the older woman. "I suppose so, my lord."

Pippa rejoined them, carrying two bonnets. "I couldn't decide between these, and then I realized I have another gift to buy this year, Mrs. Ames. My brother recently wed. I must get my sister-in-law, the new duchess, a gift, as well. I think a new bonnet would make Sophie very happy. Would you please set both of these aside for me? I can pay you the next time I come to the village."

Mrs. Ames smiled benignly, avoiding the question of payment. "Shall we look at gloves, my lady? I can also set those aside for you."

As the two women moved to the far side of the shop, Seth mulled over what he might choose as a Christmas gift for Pippa. That was a little over a month away.

Either he would be buying it for a friend—or for his betrothed.

Chapter Fifteen

Pippa had gotten her mother involved in helping introduce Seth to the neighborhood. Although they were a house in mourning and she didn't feel a dinner party appropriate, Mama said it would be perfectly fine to invite a few people to tea in order to introduce the viscount to others instead of him calling out of the blue upon strangers. She had done so twice, and Seth had met a local baron and his wife, as well as another viscount who was a widower, and the viscount's sister, who had moved in with him to help care for his children.

Today, Lord and Lady Binford were coming to tea at Shadowcrest. The couple had wed at the end of the previous Season and had recently returned to Kent after an extended honeymoon in northern England, where the bride had extended family, and Scotland, where Lord Binford's mother had come from. In her reply, Lady Binford had asked if they might bring along her brother, Viscount Plemons, who was visiting the couple. Mama had been agreeable to the suggestion, always enjoying meeting new people.

Pippa had ridden with Seth earlier in the day, as they did most mornings these past three weeks. She had grown to enjoy these rides together. Seth was different from anyone she had ever known. He would sing her songs from his days on the seas and even told her a few ghost stories, which had caused her to look over her shoulder even in the light of day. He had come to tea several times, and her family all thought highly of him.

And still he had yet to kiss her.

She knew it was because she hadn't asked him to do so. Bloody fool that he was, he was holding out for her to do that very thing. Pippa wanted to ask him. In fact, she was desperate to ask him. Yet something held her back. She worried that even though he had seemed to enjoy their previous kisses, he would grow tired of her and her inexperience.

Or maybe she was merely afraid to ask him because if they did begin kissing, she didn't think she could stop doing so. She knew kissing led to other things, unknown things, but she was smart enough to know those things could result in babies. She couldn't have a baby when she wasn't even wed. Why, it would ruin the come-outs of her sisters and cousins, and Effie's eventual come-out, as well.

Because of that, Pippa had made a choice not to ask Seth to kiss her again. She did not want to be the person responsible for the downfall of all the women in her family, including Mama. She hadn't thought about it until recently, but Mama was only in her mid-thirties. She might wish to wed again someday herself. So, Pippa would keep her lips to herself. Seth was too much a gentleman to kiss her without her approval.

Sometimes, she wished he wasn't quite such a nice gentleman, though.

It hurt because despite no kissing, her feelings seemed to grow stronger for him each day. She did look upon Seth as a friend and thought friendship would be a good basis for marriage. Most women weren't friends with their husbands, but Pippa thought it was an excellent idea. Polite Society's unwritten rules called for a man to do the talking. It was men who were the ones who offered marriage to women. Men who made the decisions. Pippa preferred keeping Seth as her friend rather than voicing her feelings for him. She was afraid if she asked for more kisses and told Seth how she felt about him, it would be the end of everything between them.

She rang for a maid to help her change her gown since she didn't like the color of the one she currently wore. Millie helped her into a gown of pale blue, which she thought went well with her Strong eyes. Once again, she was grateful Mama hadn't made them dress in mourning colors once they had returned to Shadowcrest. While Mama said she would remain in mourning until the next Season began, she said it wouldn't be necessary for all her daughters or their cousins to do so, saying they were in the country and would see little of society while there. Beyond having a few people over for tea and attending church services every Sunday, the Strongs kept to themselves for the most part. With the neighborhood knowing of the loss of the Duke of Seaton, they had not received the usual invitations while in the country.

Mama didn't mention the fact that none of them had been close to Papa. She did say that Papa had been ill for so long, it was as though they had all mourned him for the past three years he was incapacitated. She said youth should not be wasted, and she wasn't going to have her girls pretend to pine for a man who had had so little to do with them.

Pippa thought that quite practical—and generous—of Mama.

She went to the drawing room and found Georgie and Caleb already there. Mama had said it would be too overwhelming for guests trying to make Lord Hopewell's acquaintance if everyone came to tea, so the rest of the family were having their tea in the library. Mama said it would still be a large group, with the four Strongs, Lord Hopewell, the Binfords, and Lord Plemons, and that there would be plenty of good conversation to be had. Aunt Matty would preside over tea with everyone else.

"I cannot wait to meet the new Lady Binford," Georgie said. "I will admit I used to swoon whenever I saw Lord Binford at church. He has always been so nice-looking."

Mama joined them, accompanied by Seth. He greeted everyone.

"How was your ride this morning?" Caleb asked.

Seth described where he and Pippa had ridden, saying they were cantering now. "It is a step up in my riding lessons. I finally could talk and ride as Lady Philippa and I trotted our horses, so she believed I could move to the next level."

"Are you enjoying riding, my lord?" Georgie asked the viscount.

"Very much so, my lady," Seth replied. "And I could not ask for better company."

Pippa sensed her cheeks heating and turned away, walking to the window. "Oh, I see the Binfords have arrived."

Soon, Forrester appeared, announcing the couple and Lord Plemons. Introductions were made and two teacarts rolled in. She found herself seated next to Lord Plemons, who looked to be a few years older than Pippa and quite tall.

"I know Lady Binford must be glad you have been able to come and visit her," Pippa told him.

Lord Plemons smiled. "We were close in age and fellow conspirators growing up," he said easily. "If trouble were to be found, one or both of us were a part of it."

"I cannot picture you being mischievous, my lord," Mama said. "Both you and Lady Binford both appear quite angelic to me."

The viscount laughed. "That is what made us so successful in our wicked endeavors, Your Grace. With our hair being silvery-blond and faces which resembled cherubs, no one wanted to think ill of us." He grinned. "We certainly used that perception to our advantage."

"Why am I only hearing of this now?" Lord Binford complained good-naturedly. "I thought I married a paragon of virtue."

Lady Binford said, "You did, my dearest. I reformed a long time ago from the misdeeds my brother dragged me into. He is still the one who stirs up trouble wherever he goes."

"Betrayed," Lord Plemons said, pretending to stab himself in the heart. "By my own kin. You have thrown me to the wolves, Sister. And here I was trying to impress Lady Philippa."

Though she knew he was teasing, Pippa felt pleased. The attention Lord Plemons gave her might spur Seth into action.

Mama finished pouring out and passing along saucers and teacups to everyone. She now invited, "Please, make plates for yourselves. Cook has outdone herself today."

Pippa handed Lord Plemons a plate and kept one for herself. "You must try the raisin scones," she recommended. "And I know it sounds odd, but after you have smeared them with butter, add a bit of marmalade."

He smiled at her. "I will only do so because you suggested it to me to, my lady. Might I get a sandwich for you? It looks as if it is roast beef."

"Yes, please."

She passed her plate to him, and he placed a sandwich on it. As she accepted it again, she happened to see Seth looking at her intently, so much that she grew hot all over. She averted her eyes and concentrated on her plate.

The talk was lively with so many present. She had thought of everyone in the neighborhood, Seth would take most to Lord Binford. They were the closest in age, and Pippa had always heard the earl was friendly and kind. Lord Binford asked several questions about Seth's sailing days and how he came to be a captain at such a young age. She was interested in those answers herself, but she found herself paying more attention to Lord Plemons, who seemed to want to talk just to her.

"I finished at Oxford last summer," the viscount told her. "My sister and I grew up on our country estate in Oxfordshire, not ten miles from the university. I always knew I was destined to attend it."

"Where are you now, my lord, since you completed your studies?"

"I am still at our country estate. My father is in poor health, so I am seeing to the running of the estate. Our steward recently passed away, and I have stepped in to replace him for now."

"How long will you be visiting in Kent?"

He gazed at her intently. "I had thought to leave in a week or so. Perhaps now I have a reason to extend my visit, however."

Pippa had enjoyed talking with Lord Plemons and was only sorry that the viscount had not had more time to visit with Seth.

"It would be good of you to stay longer," she encouraged. "That way, you might be able to spend a little time with Lord Hopewell."

He chuckled. "You mean the man who has glared at me throughout this entire teatime?"

She stole a look in Seth's direction, but he was talking with Lord Binford. Glancing back to her companion, she said, "I believe you are mistaken, my lord."

Plemons looked to Seth and back. "Do you have an understanding with Hopewell, my lady?"

Her cheeks burned with the question. "No, not at all, my lord. In fact, I have yet to make my come-out."

"I did not mean to be so blunt. I usually display more tact than that, my lady. It is just that Hopewell has looked at the two of us fairly often."

"He probably is regretting not getting to visit with you more, my lord," she said. "After all, this tea was so you could get to know him better. Perhaps I should change seats so that that you can—"

"Don't," he said softly. "I am rather enjoying our conversation. Perhaps we might extend it. Do you ride, Lady Philippa?"

"I do," she said cautiously. "Do you?"

"I live to ride. Would you care to do so with me? You could show me more of the neighborhood."

"I could. When would you like to do so?"

"Tomorrow morning?" he suggested.

"I usually ride with Lord Hopewell each morning. I am teaching him to do so since he grew up at sea."

"Then we should all ride together."

She glanced over at Seth again and saw something in his eyes, a coldness she had never seen before, as he contemplated Lord Plemons.

"We could make a day of it," the viscount suggested. He looked to Seth. "Lord Hopewell, I hear you are riding each morning with Lady Philippa."

"Yes," he said curtly.

"I suggested coming along," Plemons said easily. "We could take a picnic with us. I will wager Lady Philippa knows of a scenic spot we might stop."

Pippa looked at Georgie pleadingly, and her twin spoke up. "May I come along? I love to picnic."

"In this weather?" Caleb asked. "It's early December, Georgie. I know we're not the north of England, where it is already frigid, but it is downright chilly to be picnicking."

Georgie smiled sweetly. "But it would be a wonderful way to show Lord Plemons the neighborhood. It would also give Lord Hopewell a chance to challenge himself in the saddle, after all his lessons with Pippa, if we made a day of it. Come along, Caleb. It will be fun. I will even have Cook pack things you like."

"All right," her cousin agreed. "What time shall we leave—and from where?"

She relaxed, knowing others would be coming along, and decided to squash the idea of a picnic.

"Caleb is right. While I have never minded riding in the cold, stopping to eat might prove difficult, especially if it is windy, as it has been the last two days. We could, however, stop at an inn for luncheon. I am sure they could accommodate our party."

Lord Plemons favored Pippa with a smile. "I like the idea of that even better. Good company by a roaring fire and a meal on top of that. Good thinking, my lady."

She fought—and lost—the blush which tinged her cheeks. "Then let us meet at Lord Hopewell's stables. I will see if anyone else wishes to join us. Shall we say nine o'clock?"

Everyone seemed in agreement, and Pippa felt the tension

release within her. Tea ended soon after, with the Binfords and Lord Plemons leaving together. Knowing their guests had left, the other Strongs began showing up in the drawing room, though Seth had remained behind, drawing Caleb into conversation. She assumed it had something to do about estate business since the two men were forever talking about it.

"We are thinking of taking a long ride tomorrow," Pippa said. "Georgie and Caleb are coming, along with Lord Hopewell and Lord Plemons. We would stop at an inn for a repast."

Mirella sniffed. "I am not much for riding when the weather turns cold."

"I agree," Lyric said. "Besides, Allegra and I are supposed to go to see the vicar's wife about sewing some new altar cloths."

"I will go with you," Effie said, eager as always to get in the saddle. "It sounds like fun to me."

"Say that when you come home with a red nose which is running like a fountain," Allegra said. "You will be calling for hot water bottles for your bed."

"It isn't that cold," Effie said. "Besides, you know I enjoy riding."

"I think it will be a nice outing for those who do go," Mama said.

Pippa decided to join Caleb and Seth. As she thought, they were talking about livestock, but Caleb wrapped up their conversation as she approached.

"I should be leaving," Seth said. He looked to her. "Might you walk out with me, Lady Philippa? I believe you were going to give me the book you mentioned. The one in your library."

She had promised no book to him and figured he wanted to speak to her in private. "Oh, that book. Yes, come along, my lord. I can retrieve it for you."

They left the drawing room and headed toward the library. It surprised her that Seth remained silent.

Until they reached the library.

Once he closed the doors behind them, he latched onto her

elbows, spinning her around, backing her into the door they had just entered.

"What is going on, Pippa?" he asked, his voice low and rough.

His tone irked her. "I have no idea what you are referring to, Seth." She wriggled, but he held fast.

"With Plemons," he said. "He monopolized you the entire time at tea."

"We did speak to one another quite a bit," she agreed. "I found him to be interesting. I have told you I enjoy meeting new people."

His face moved closer to hers, causing her breath to hitch.

"More interesting than I am?"

Pippa swallowed. "You are very interesting, Seth. You have led an extraordinary life of adventure, what with being at sea."

"And the viscount?"

"He enjoys being in the country. He finished his studies at Oxford recently and is managing his father's estate. I gather his father is in poor health, and Lord Plemons has become the estate's steward."

Seth lowered his head, his lips inches from hers. "I didn't like how he looked at you, Pippa. Not one whit."

"How did he . . . look at me?" she squeaked, her body humming, being so close to his, his hands scalding her elbows.

"Like he wanted to gobble you up."

She almost laughed aloud.

Seth was *jealous*.

"You mean the way you are looking at me now, Seth?"

His body's proximity had made certain she wasn't going anywhere. He now placed his hands on her shoulders.

"Are you ever going to ask me to kiss you again, Pippa? It has been a long time since we kissed. Several weeks, in fact."

She swallowed, her gaze locked on his. "Do you want to kiss me, Seth? If you do, you should. I wouldn't protest."

The last word had barely escaped her lips when his mouth came crashing down on hers.

Chapter Sixteen

Pippa had no time to think. She only responded to Seth's insistent kiss. He was not following his usual pattern, beginning gently and then deepening the kiss.

No, this kiss was heated from the start. It was as if he were an invading army, trying to conquer a lesser one, his tongue seeking domination over hers. For a moment, she allowed herself to give in to the kiss. To soak up the thrill of it. To become lost in the headiness. To surrender to the heat and desire. It had been far too long since he had kissed her, and she reveled in the physicality of the kiss and the emotions it brought bubbling to the surface.

She liked this side of him. She liked the fire within him because it was lighting one within her. Who knew a man's kisses could make one's blood sing?

Tamping down the temptation she faced, she forced herself to think reasonably. Stopping Seth now, before things went further, had to occur.

Because he was kissing her for the wrong reason.

For the first time, she turned her head, breaking a kiss between them. She raised a hand, placing it between them, and said, "Stop."

Seth had been leaning in to steal another kiss, but he lifted his head and studied her, respecting her wish to bring a halt to what they were doing.

"What is wrong, Pippa?" he asked, concern in his voice, which was low and rough.

She was taken aback for a moment, seeing the heat in his eyes, heat that almost singed her.

"You tell me. Why are you kissing me right now, Seth?" she said bluntly.

He gave her that sunny smile which must have melted the hearts of dozens of women over the years.

"You know why I am kissing you, Pippa. It is because I enjoy doing so. I thought you, too, enjoyed our kisses."

"I do. You are not being honest with me, however, Seth."

He frowned deeply. "I have been nothing *but* honest with you, Pippa. Why would I lie to you now? I would think you would understand what I meant by my kiss."

She nodded, his words confirming what she thought. "I do know what you mean by your kiss, Seth. In the past, you have kissed me because you wanted to. Because you liked to. And I believe because you liked that I liked doing so with you." She hesitated a moment. "But you are kissing me now as if you are trying to brand me. As if you wish to make me forget about my conversation with Lord Plemons."

He cursed under his breath. "Pippa, do not go there," he warned.

"I have every right to go there, wherever *there* is," she snapped. "You are kissing me now as if to prove a point. Well, I do not like being used in such a manner. While I am flattered and it makes me feel good that you have missed our kisses, I will not continue to do so under these circumstances. You do not own me, Seth. You cannot tell me what to do. if I want to sit at tea and speak with Lord Plemons—or any other man—then I will do so freely. Is that understood?"

She saw a grudging respect for her in his eyes which hadn't been there before. "You have a fire within you, Pippa. I don't know of many men who would stand up to me and call me out, much less a woman."

He leaned in to kiss her again, and this time, Pippa threw up her palm, pushing it against his hard, muscular chest. She deliberately ignored the thoughts that came to her. How she would like to investigate those hard muscles beneath her fingers, with no barrier of clothing between them.

"We are done here, Lord Hopewell," she said formally. "Let me go and find a book to give you."

She stepped away from him and went to the bookshelves to the left of them, pulling out a book on husbandry.

"Try reading this. Perhaps it will cool your ardor and bore you enough so that you calm down. And I want you to be perfectly behaved when we go riding as a group tomorrow. No angry looks tossed Lord Plemons' way. No cutting remarks, either. You will enjoy the ride. It will be a challenge for you, for we will be in the saddle far longer than you and I have been up to this point. Am I clear?"

Seth didn't speak for a long moment, and she thought she had perhaps pushed him too hard.

Finally, he said, "I hear and understand your expectations, my lady. I will be on my most gentlemanly behavior. You will find no fault with me."

"I am delighted to hear that, my lord."

Pippa opened the library door and sailed through it, expecting Seth would follow her. When they reached the landing of the stairs, she said, "I believe you know your way out, my lord. I will see you tomorrow morning."

He stood gazing at her a long moment, and she almost relented, taking back everything she had said to him. She had desperately missed his kiss. She wanted his kiss. But she would not be used in some fashion, simply because he had been jealous she had spoken to another man. He was not a suitor to her, much less someone she would be betrothed to anytime soon. She knew that she did interest him, but in the long run, Seth would need to find a wife who would be much more suited to be his viscountess than Pippa Strong. Her heart told her he was merely amusing himself with her while he was in the country, and when he went to town for the Season, he would find himself a bride.

The thought saddened her because she had come to enjoy his company a great deal. She admitted to herself that every day was a new and better one when she saw him. It would be important to prepare herself, however, for when that day came when he no longer needed her. He had already begun cantering a week ago. He was a natural in the saddle and could probably gallop on his own with ease. The time for their lessons to come to an end had arrived. After tomorrow's outing with the group, Pippa would tell Seth—no, Lord Hopewell—that she had no more to teach him. The sooner she put some distance between them, the better it would be for her heart.

Because what it told Pippa now was that she had fallen in love with Seth Atwell.

SETH WENT TO the stables and had a groom saddle Orion for him. He took the offered reins and waited by the horse for the others who should be arriving soon.

As he stroked Orion, he decided Pippa had been right. He had been immensely jealous of the time Lord Plemons had spent monopolizing her during tea yesterday. When Seth had gotten her alone in the library, he had wanted to brand her as his. He had thought to kiss her until they were both breathless and then finally tell her of his feelings for her. Instead, she had shut down his actions and called him out, not afraid to do so.

It made him love her all the more.

Pippa Strong was just as her name proclaimed – a strong woman who knew her own mind. A woman who would make for a wonderful wife. While she was unconventional in both dress and her outspokenness, those things only endeared her more to him. While Seth wanted to make her his, now that he knew he was in love with her and wanted to build a life together, he was afraid to speak up after yesterday's spat between them. If he offered for her now, Pippa might think he was trying to prevent her from being friendly with Lord Plemons or any other man she might meet. Yes, he had been jealous of Plemons, but he didn't want her to think that was the only reason he was bringing up marriage. He walked a fine line now and would monitor her mood carefully, hoping not to push her away from him—and into Plemons' willing arms.

He saw movement and watched as Lord Plemons rode toward him. Seth would admit the viscount had good looks and had been quite charming at tea yesterday. In other circumstances, he might even have befriended the man. For now, he would do as Pippa had asked and simply be courteous.

But there would be a limit to just how civil he could be.

Plemons reached him and gracefully dismounted. "Good morning, Hopewell," he said cheerfully. "A pleasant day to ride."

"Yes, quite so. While cold, the sun is out. We should be able to see a great deal today."

"Lady Philippa said you are a novice in the saddle."

Seth gritted his teeth and then forced his jaw to relax. "I am learning, but I have always been a fast learner. And Lady Philippa is a marvelous instructor."

The viscount nodded. "She seems to be a quite capable young lady." He paused. "Ah, it looks as if she is coming now."

He glanced to where he saw four riders approaching, recognizing Pippa right away. Accompanying her were two of her sisters and Caleb. Seth had grown quite fond of Caleb Strong, and the two men were becoming fast friends.

"Is she wearing . . . trousers?" Lord Plemons asked, clearly taken aback.

Smiling, he turned to the viscount. "Why, yes. Lady Philippa always does so when she rides. Is there a problem with that, my lord?"

"Er . . . no."

Seth saw that Pippa's manner of dress did bother Plemons.

And he was very happy about that.

The party of four reached them, and Caleb called out, "Good morning, my lords. An excellent day to ride."

"I agree," Lady Georgina said. "Lord Plemons, this is our youngest sister, Lady Euphemia."

The viscount had recovered from his shock and smiled charmingly, even though Lady Effie also wore trousers. "It is nice to make your acquaintance, my lady."

"Thank you for inviting me along," Lady Effie said. "I think we will be able to show both of you much of the neighborhood, including some of the ruins left from Roman times."

"Do you know much of Kent, Lord Plemons?" Pippa asked as Seth mounted Orion and Plemons also climbed into the saddle.

"Not really," the viscount admitted. "I haven't an interest in history, my lady. The past is the past. I am all about looking to the future."

Pippa sniffed. "The people of Kent have a motto—*Invicta*—which means unconquered. They claimed it after William of Normandy invaded Britain. The Conqueror was unable to bring Kent to its knees, unlike other areas. Kent negotiated very favorable terms with William, and it became a county palatine the year after the invasion."

"I have no idea what that is," a perplexed Plemons told Pippa.

She smiled smugly. "It means Kent enjoyed a special autonomy, apart from most of the rest of Britain and the new William the First's kingdom. William's half-brother became its nominal ruler. We people of Kent are most stubborn, my lord."

"I can see that," Plemons replied. "Especially in your unique dress, Lady Philippa. And yours, too, Lady Euphemia."

"Enough talk," Caleb said. "Let's see some of Kent."

Caleb told them where they would ride first, and everyone turned their horses to the north, beginning to canter. Seth was glad he had grown comfortable in the saddle. Orion responded well to his commands.

They stopped at various places to see scenery. Sometimes Pippa or Lady Georgina would share a bit of history regarding the sites. They also went through a few villages without stopping.

Around one that afternoon, Lady Euphemia announced they should stop for something to eat.

"It will also allow the horses to get a bit of a rest," she added. "There is a town less than a mile ahead. It should have an inn or two with decent food."

The group rode to the town, where they stopped at the first inn they came across. Caleb said he would see if someone could care for their horses, and Seth volunteered to go inside and arrange a place for them to dine.

The innkeeper he spoke to had a large upper room and was delighted to serve their party. Seth told he innkeeper they were hungry and asked for him to arrange a hearty meal, saying he would trust the man's judgment as to what might be served.

Returning outside, he saw the others dismounting, with a few young lads collecting the horses.

"The horses will be watered and fed," Caleb said. "I hope we will be, too."

"We have a room upstairs, and a meal is being sent up to us," he assured his friend. "Shall we?"

They entered the inn, and the innkeeper's wife met them. "Right this way," she said, leading them upstairs and opening the door to a room which actually overlooked the tavern below, with walls on the other three sides.

"I hope this will do, my lord," she said to Seth.

"Yes, thank you," he said.

Going to the table, he pulled out a chair. Lady Georgina was closest to him, and she took the seat. He hadn't spoken to Pippa the entire morning, even when they stopped and explored various places, but he had hoped he could sit near her while they dined. She wound up taking the seat directly across from him, Lord Plemons quickly seating himself on her left. At least Seth could look at her and engage her in conversation.

If he could think of anything to say to her in front of everyone.

The innkeeper's wife appeared again with a serving wench, both bearing trays with cider and ale.

"I can bring wine, too, if you wish," the woman said.

"This will do nicely," Lady Georgina said. "Thank you."

As they talked of what they had seen on their ride, their luncheon was brought up. They started with a white soup, followed by a cabbage pudding. Next was beef with roasted potatoes and carrots and a crusty bread with warmed butter. They finished the meal with a rum cake.

"This was heavenly," Lady Effie said. "I am so full, I could easily nap for two hours."

"I do not think sleeping atop your horse is a good idea," he teased, liking Pippa's little sister very much, as well as her other relatives.

"I could do so effortlessly, my lord, and my mount would take me home," she bragged. "You, on the other hand, Lord Hopewell, are still new in the saddle. Orion might steer you to the English coast instead of home."

Everyone laughed, and Pippa said, "I think Lord Hopewell has grown quite comfortable in the saddle, Effie. In fact, I do not think I have anything left to teach him."

He smiled at her for standing up for him but realized she was ending their riding lessons. The excuse he had to see her on a daily basis would now come to an end.

Protesting, he said, "We have not even learned to gallop, my lady. I would be more comfortable if we continued as we have for another week or so."

"We will see," she said, her tone sounding like a parent telling a child no without using the actual word.

Disappointment filled him. Seth would have to become creative to invent ways to see her in the future. He also worried Lord Plemons would do the same, despite his initial reaction to what

Pippa wore today. The viscount had paid quite a bit of attention to her, the same as yesterday, and she had chatted happily with him.

"I think we need to get back in the saddle and head for home," Caleb suggested. "That will end your sluggishness, Effie. Come along, and we'll reclaim our horses."

"I am going to ask the innkeeper's wife about the cabbage pudding," Lady Georgina declared. "It was delicious. I want to get the recipe for Cook. I believe it had nutmeg in it, and I want to be certain."

"I will settle our bill," Seth volunteered.

"I will be downstairs in a moment," Lord Plemons said. "I am going to have a few last bites of this delicious beef."

"I will stay with you, my lord," Pippa volunteered. "We will be down shortly."

Everyone left them, Caleb and Lady Effie heading outside and Lady Georgina to the kitchens. He hated leaving Pippa with Plemons but didn't want to cause a fuss.

He found the innkeeper, saying, "Thank you for your hospitality. Our meal was delightful." Seth gave the man several notes to cover the meal.

He then waited until Lady Georgina appeared, curbing his desire to rush up the stairs and bring Pippa down.

"I was right. Nutmeg and fennel seed," she told him. She glanced up the stairs. "Have they not come down yet?"

"No. I shall fetch them," he said as Caleb entered and said, "Our horses are ready."

Seth strode across the room and up the stairs, going a short distance down the hallway and opening the door. He opened his mouth to inform them it was time to go and stood there, shocked.

Lord Plemons held Pippa in an embrace—and was kissing her.

Chapter Seventeen

Pippa watched as Lord Plemons took a bite of the beef from his plate and said, "Our food was quite good. I usually find at an inn you can get a tasty meal."

The viscount smiled at her lazily. "It was rather tasty, and the company was excellent."

"I have always enjoyed the company of my family a great deal," she told him. "I know some siblings do not get along well, but that has never been the case with me and mine."

"Besides Lady Georgina and Lady Euphemia, do you have other sisters? Or brothers?"

"I have one other sister. Mirella. She is a year younger than Georgie and I, but I also have two cousins who are my age. They were brought up in our household for the most part."

"Why so?" the viscount asked.

"My aunt died giving birth to Lyric and Allegra, and my uncle Adolphus is not known for tolerating females. He basically handed the twins over to Mama, and she raised them, alongside us."

"Six girls in a household? That is quite a lot," Plemons observed.

"It never seemed strange to me because that was simply the way things were. I am happy, though, to be back at Shadowcrest because I am getting to know my cousin Caleb better. He serves as Shadowcrest's steward and has done so for the past three years. He is Allegra and Lyric's brother."

"You also seem quite friendly with Lord Hopewell," the viscount said, and she thought she caught disdain in his tone, which bothered her. Up until now, she had thought Lord Plemons to be pleasant.

"Actually, I was quite good friends with his uncle, who previously held the title. Hopewell is our closest neighbor, and the deceased viscount took me under his wing. He shared books with me, and we discussed them at length. We also went riding and even fished together. I miss him a great deal, but I am forging a new friendship with his nephew."

"It seems Lord Hopewell wants more than friendship from you, my lady."

"He is friendly with my entire family," she said, feeling the heat rise in her cheeks. "We are introducing the viscount to the neighborhood. It is why we asked Lord and Lady Binford to tea yesterday. Mama thought with Hopewell and your brother-in-law so close in age, they might become friendly with one another."

He laughed. "Hopewell may become friends with Binford, but I doubt that offer of friendship will extend to me—because of my interest in you."

"Why *are* you interested in me, my lord?" Pippa asked boldly, wanting to put a stop to unwanted attention. "Georgie is much prettier than I am. I would have thought you would have sought her company over mine."

"Your sister is quite the beauty, but you have a spirit about you that is quite appealing, Lady Philippa."

Plemons sat down his fork and stood, capturing her wrists and bringing Pippa to her feet.

"I am a viscount now, my lady, but my father is ill, as I mentioned to you before. I believe within the next few months, I will become an earl. Though I am young, I know the importance of seeking a wife."

He gazed at her intently, and she felt her blush extending to her roots.

"What are you saying, my lord?"

"I am making my case to you, Lady Philippa. Although you have yet to make your come-out, I find you to be everything I would wish for in my future countess. Do you have any attachment to Hopewell? Or anyone else?"

"Nothing formal," she said faintly, the blood rushing in her ears.

Pippa found Lord Plemons interesting, and she was curious about how she would feel about him if they kissed. She gazed up at him, seeing that he wanted to try a kiss.

Encouraging him, she said, "I think it would be appropriate if we shared a kiss, my lord, to see if we suit one another."

He smiled at her, like a cat who had been caught in the cream. "My, you are a bold one, aren't you?"

Plemons released his hold on her wrists and wrapped his arms about her. Lowering his head, his lips touched hers.

She felt nothing.

She allowed him to kiss her, but she did not kiss him back, something she had learned how to do with Seth. Instead, she let him continue to see if anything changed between them.

The viscount eased open her mouth, his tongue sweeping inside. Again, she felt dead inside. None of the rush of feelings which occurred when Seth did the same happened now.

Her heart had told her that she loved Seth, and this failed kiss spoke volumes, giving her all the proof she needed.

Pippa turned her head, breaking the kiss, one hand nudging Plemons' chest. His arms fell away, and he took a step back from her.

"You are a very nice man, my lord, but you are not the man for me," she stated bluntly.

His eyes glimmered with understanding. "You did not feel anything when we kissed, did you, my lady?"

"No, my lord, I most certainly did not."

"But you have been kissed before, haven't you?" he pressed.

"Yes, I have. I will not deny it. Only by one man, but the experience was vastly different from this one."

He nodded sagely. "Then I think it wise for you to pursue that particular relationship, Lady Philippa. In the meantime, I hope we might become friends."

She smiled, relief filling her that he had taken the news so well. "I would be more than happy to be your friend, Lord Plemons."

"We'd best go downstairs. We have kept the others waiting long enough," he told her.

They left the upper room and the inn itself, emerging through its doors to find the rest of their party already mounted up. Pippa went to Starlight and swung into the saddle. She glanced at Seth, but he stared straight ahead.

"Where to next?" Effie asked.

"As I said, we should begin to head toward home," Caleb said. "If we find anything interesting along the way, we can always stop again."

They reached Hopewood two hours later, and Seth and Lord Plemons both thanked them for today's outing.

"Hopefully, I can return the favor and have all of you over to my sister's soon," Lord Plemons said, waving jauntily and riding off.

Pippa tried to catch Seth's eye, but he still refused to look in her direction. She wanted to talk with him further, and asked, "Do you think you will be up for a riding lesson tomorrow, my lord, or will you need an extra day to rest after today's long ride?"

His gaze finally met hers, and she saw it to be colder than winter. "I thought you meant for my riding lessons to be at an end, my lady."

Desperate to spend time with him, she said, "We still have to conquer galloping, Lord Hopewell. You mentioned that yourself."

"Then perhaps we can do so later in the week. Or next." He

looked at the group. "Thank you again for a lovely outing today. I saw so much and improved upon my riding skills."

Caleb said, "I have time tomorrow if you wish for us to go out to look at your livestock together."

Seth nodded in agreement. "That will do in place of my riding lesson with Lady Philippa and will prove to be much more productive."

His words stung her, but Pippa kept her face neutral. The men arranged a time to meet up, and they bid the viscount goodbye. Once they arrived at Shadowcrest, she wanted to be by herself. They had already missed teatime, and she had a couple of hours before dinner would be served.

Retreating to the library, she went to her favorite window seat and gazed out the window, wondering what had really happened today between her and Seth.

She heard the library door open and saw Georgie coming across the room. Pippa scooted over so that her twin could sit beside her.

Georgie put an arm about Pippa's shoulders. "You seem very downcast. Do you wish to talk about it?"

"Lord Plemons kissed me," she blurted out. "And it was terrible."

"Did you encourage him to do so?" her twin prodded.

"He wanted to kiss me, and I let him know I would have no objection if he did." She faced her sister. "Georgie, kissing a pillow is more exciting than kissing Lord Plemons. I felt nothing at all—and I told him so."

"Oh, dear," Georgie fretted. "That must have been difficult for him to hear. How did he take it?"

"Rather well," she shared. "I simply wanted to compare his kiss to that of Lord Hopewell."

"And Hopewell's kiss pleases you, doesn't it?"

She sighed. "Oh, Georgie. I cannot describe the joy in my soul when Seth kisses me. It is if I have ascended to the heavens, and all is right with my world. But he was so distant today. He never addressed me directly. Not a word was spoken between us until we were departing from Hopewood."

Tears welled in her eyes. "Should I tell him of my feelings? Would that be simply too much, a woman sharing how she feels about a man before he has told her if he has feelings for her?"

"I believe Lord Hopewell is a very good man, Pippa. I also think he likes you quite a bit. He might possibly even love you."

"I think I love him, Georgie," she confided to her twin.

"Can you see yourself spending the rest of your life with him? If so, you must make him aware of that. If he returns your feelings, then you will have risked nothing and gained everything. If he does not feel the same way, however, at least you will know for certain."

The thought of Seth rejecting her caused her to draw in a quick breath.

"Yes," her twin continued, "you might face some heartbreak, but I think it wiser to speak up than remain silent forever and never know. You have to remember, Pippa, Hopewell is quite new to the world he finds himself in. Even a man with his intelligence and life experience would flounder a bit, being so unfamiliar with Polite Society. He may long to tell you of his feelings for you, but he may not believe he is good enough for you, despite the title he now holds."

She hugged her twin tightly.

"Thank you, Georgie. When do you think I should tell him?"

"You need privacy for something so important. I would say ask him to tea or dinner, but it would be too difficult to get a moment alone together to have such an important discussion. I believe you must confess your feelings for him on one of your rides, when no one can interrupt you."

"And what if he no longer wises to do so? You heard how dismissive he was earlier when I mentioned continuing his lessons."

Her sister thought a moment. "Then do not give him a choice. Write a note and send it to him. In it, act as if nothing has changed between you. Simply tell him that you will show up for your usual riding lesson the day after tomorrow. Caleb can deliver the note for you when he sees Hopewell tomorrow, and the viscount will know to expect you the next morning."

"I hope he feels the same as I do," Pippa said. "If he doesn't, I do not know if I will be able to go on."

"If Hopewell does not return your feelings, you can do one of two things. You can stay home and brood at Shadowcrest—or you can change your mind and make your come-out with the rest of us. The swirl of social activities would do you good and keep your mind off him, and you would meet countless men. One who just might be the one meant for you if Hopewell is not."

"You are right," she told her twin. "I will speak to Seth during our next ride together. If I bare my soul and he rejects me, then I will tell Mama I have changed my mind and wish to make my come-up after all, alongside the rest of you."

Georgie stood and pulled Pippa to her feet. "I requested a bath for both of us. Effie, too. Shall we go upstairs now? Our hot water should be delivered soon. We can bathe and dress for dinner."

They did so, bathing and changing, and then Pippa wrote the note to Seth, informing him she would arrive for their next riding lesson the day after he saw Caleb. She even let Georgie read it over and received her twin's approval.

"It is polite and succinct," Georgie commented. "Exactly as it should be."

They went downstairs and regaled the rest of the family regarding their adventures during dinner. Effie had been so pleased to be included on the outing, and Pippa noticed for the first time how grown up the youngest Strong now appeared. She would be ten and six on the first of March, less than three months away, and already showing signs of the beauty she would become.

When the meal ended, both Pippa and Georgie excused themselves, claiming they were exhausted after such a long day in the saddle. They called for a maid and changed into their night rails, climbing into bed together, lying side-by-side and holding hands until they fell asleep.

CHAPTER EIGHTEEN

SETH MULLED OVER his options as he sat at breakfast. He could go down to the stables and meet Pippa—or send a footman with a message, telling her he was busy with estate business and they would need to put off their lesson for another time.

Knowing Pippa, she would march up to the door and talk her way into the house, banging on his study's door until he granted her entrance.

He didn't need for that kind of drama to play out in front of his servants, so he would keep to their plans. Actually, her plans. Seth hadn't wanted to see her.

Not since he had witnessed the kiss between her and Lord Plemons.

Just thinking about it brought a rush of emotions to the surface. Rage. Jealousy. Disappointment. Bitterness. Obviously, he was more invested in her than she in him, else she never would have allowed Plemons to kiss her.

And what if she preferred Plemons' kiss to his?

The thought made him panic.

Here he was, a former ship's captain, a man who had faced down everything from pirates to crippling weather. Yet the thought of losing Pippa Strong to another man had him acting as a callow youth instead of the experienced, mature man that he was.

"I'll face her," he muttered under his breath, thinking he wouldn't let any woman dictate how he should feel. Hiding would not be an option.

He would meet Pippa head on.

Finishing his meal, he left the breakfast room, retreating to his study for a few minutes of quiet time. He vacillated on whether or not to tell Pippa of his feelings for her. If she did not return them, it would be humiliating. But better to know that now and move on, than sit and pine for her. After all, everyone kept mentioning the Season to him, where there would be a bevy of young ladies being introduced into Polite Society. If Pippa Strong did not want him, surely one of these debutantes would. After all, he was a wealthy, titled gentleman with all his teeth and hair. He would be considered quite the catch.

In his heart, though, Seth knew no one would ever hold a candle to Pippa.

Steeling himself for whatever lay ahead, he left the house and headed to the stables. A groom caught sight of him and asked if he wished for Orion to be saddled.

"Yes, please do so. I am riding with Lady Philippa this morning," he informed the servant.

Waiting in front of the stables, he shivered. The air was chilled today. It had rained heavily throughout the night, and dampness hung in the air.

He saw Pippa appear on the horizon, galloping on Starlight, the two seemingly one. Seth couldn't help but admire the skill she showed as a rider. Her years in the saddle showed just how experienced she was.

She arrived, her cheeks flushed from the cold, a hat pulled low on her forehead, wearing a man's greatcoat. It only made her appear even more feminine.

"It is very cold this morning, Lord Hopewell. You might wish to dress more warmly."

"My greatcoat still awaits finishing," he told her. "I had word only yesterday from my London tailor. He wishes for me to come to town for another fitting. The coat is among the items he holds."

She frowned, blowing out a breath, which he could see. "I am disappointed, but I think it best if we do not ride today. I would not want to be responsible for you catching a chill."

Seth snorted. "In this weather? I have faced down far worse, my lady. I've been drenched by waves as high as these stables, water so frigid that it almost shocks the heart into stopping. I am wearing an adequate coat. Besides, a great deal of energy is exerted when riding. I will warm up soon."

He turned, seeing the groom leading Orion to him. "I would only be worried about your health, my lady."

She waved her hand dismissively. "I have my coat and hat. I will be fine, my lord, but I thank you for your concern."

Seth slipped his foot into the stirrups and tossed his leg over, taking up his reins. "Shall we?"

"Wait a moment," she urged. "I know you are eager to gallop. I will admit galloping is great fun, but just like other speeds, we need to discuss it."

"All right," he agreed, nodding to the groom and dismissing him.

"First of all, you never begin at a gallop. It is important to build up your speed gradually. If you rush things, you could lose control of Orion. You must start with a trot, move to a canter, and only then break into a gallop."

"That makes sense," he admitted. "A babe learns to crawl, then walk, before it ever runs."

"Once we are cantering, you will want to lean forward and raise your body slightly from the saddle. As before, you will use the pressure from your legs to signal Orion to move faster. Watch how you hold the reins. Do not pull on them. Keep your reins between your thumb and forefinger with each hand, with a short length of them lying across Orion's neck. I rest my hands on Starlight's neck when I gallop. It gives me more control."

She demonstrated and watched as he mimicked her action.

"Good. More than anything, you do not wish to go too fast. Even experienced riders must think in order to keep control of their horses when they gallop. There is a difference between giving a horse his head and letting him run freely, versus an all-out gallop which you cannot manage."

"I understand. I will not succumb to temptation and ride too fast," he told her.

"We'll practice starting a gallop, galloping, and then slowing the gallop several times," Pippa continued. "When you wish to slow your horse, sit in the saddle and pull on the reins. The rest is simply gauging your horse's rhythm and moving in and out of the saddle as you have done with trotting and cantering. It will take a lot of practice to gallop, however. Do not rush the process. Do not be disappointed if you suffer a setback today. You are feeling out Orion as much as he is you. You will come to a happy medium."

She cleared her throat. "One more thing. Sometimes, you may wish to stop—but your horse chooses not to. My best advice is to keep sitting straight in the saddle and steer Orion in smaller and smaller circles. He will need to go slower and slower to keep his balance, and that will allow you to force him to come to a stop. You can also shorten the reins. That will also help slow him."

Pippa stroked Starlight's neck fondly. "More than anything, think of galloping as a partnership between you and your horse. You'll work up to higher speeds gradually. Feeling comfortable at various intervals and then increasing your speed will take weeks of work between you and Orion."

"Enough talk," he said impatiently. "Let's ride."

Seth took off, trotting away from Pippa. She soon caught up to him, and they continued to the meadow, where he had first learned to trot and canter. He urged Orion on and began cantering, getting a feel for the horse beneath him.

Then he nudged Orion further, and the horse broke out into

a gallop. Seth felt his heart in his throat, and for a moment, panic rippled through him. He quickly shut it down, not wanting to fall off his horse in front of Pippa. The many rides they had already been on helped his muscle memory, and Seth adjusted to Orion's gait, moving up and down.

Suddenly, he caught the magic. The breeze in his face. The thrill of the speed. The strength of the beast beneath him.

"Slow down, Seth," Pippa called from behind him, and he obeyed her, asking Orion to do the same. The horse slowed his pace to a canter, and Seth kept to that for half a minute before telling Orion to trot. Another half minute passed, and Pippa appeared at his side.

"Very good," she praised. "You had good form. You also sat tall in the saddle when you asked Orion to lessen his speed. We will try it a few more times, and then I want you to come to a complete halt from your gallop."

They practiced for the next half-hour, and he grew in confidence. Still, each time he galloped, he understood how fragile his control over the horse was. It would take many more hours in the saddle before he truly became comfortable with galloping.

"You have caught on quickly. I think we might go ahead and practice coming to a quick, full halt now," she told him. "I will watch you. Listen for my call."

Seth turned Orion and started the horse off, bringing him to a full gallop, racing across the meadow. He steered the horse in a wide turn and brought Orion back in the other direction.

When he reached the midpoint, he heard Pippa call out to stop. He did as she asked, excited when his horse did exactly as asked.

As she rode toward him, Seth cried, "We did it!"

She rewarded him with a smile. "You most certainly did. You are a true partner with Orion. You should be very pleased with the progress you have made, Seth."

"I want to try again," he said, enthusiasm bubbling through him.

"All right," she said, laughing. "Have at it."

Seth asked Orion to gallop and stop twice more. The third time, he allowed the horse to slow gradually, before walking it up to where Pippa sat waiting.

"I know Orion must be thirsty after all this," he said. "Shall we walk our horses to the stream nearby?"

"That is a good idea," she agreed, bringing Starlight around and walking the horse next to him.

They reached the stream and both dismounted, leading their horses to the water. Orion bent low and greedily guzzled, while Starlight was more prim and proper, lapping water gently.

Exhilaration still filled him. "That was incredible."

"I knew you would like it," she said. "As much as we have practiced other gaits, you will need twice as much practice at galloping. You never want to be overconfident. At all times, remember how powerful your horse is. Galloping is dangerous if you do not practice restraint."

"I understand, Pippa," he said, using her name for the first time.

Then he felt the mist in the air, which quickly turned to raindrops. "I think it is about to pour," he told her. "We should seek shelter."

"There is that abandoned cottage not far from here," she said, swinging onto her horse's back. "Follow me."

Seth mounted Orion and stayed close to Starlight as they ventured toward the unoccupied cottage. It was on his list of things to do, seeing its roof shored up and the holes in the walls repaired. While it would let some rain in, they should be fairly protected.

They reached it and steered their horses into the shed next to the cottage, tying them up and hurrying into the structure just as the bottom fell out. He closed and latched the door, looking up.

"Leaks are there and there," he pointed out. "We should be safe if we stick to this side."

Dragging the two abandoned chairs from the center of the

room, Seth brought both to the corner. Pippa sat in one, shivering.

"It did not look like rain earlier. We had already gotten so much last night," she mentioned.

"I thought we had gotten too much and that you would send a note, canceling our lesson," he said.

Her gaze met his. "No, I wanted to keep to our lessons, Seth."

He liked the way his name formed on her lips. She had avoided using it until now.

"Are you angry with me?" he asked, laughing when she asked the exact question at the same time.

"Why would you think me angry at you?" he asked.

"Because you never really spoke to me yesterday," she said. "You avoided me."

"Well, you said I didn't need any more riding lessons. I was put out with you for that. And for . . ." His voice trailed off.

"For what?" she pressed.

He might as well say it. "For kissing Lord Plemons."

Her face flamed instantly. "You *saw* that? Oh, I am mortified. I only let him kiss me a moment. I cannot believe you saw that brief encounter."

Anguish washed over him. "It hurt, Pippa. To see you in another man's arms. To know you were enjoying it."

She burst out laughing. "It was awful, Seth. Truly terrible. I told Georgie kissing a pillow was more exciting than locking lips with Lord Plemons. I felt absolutely nothing."

Hope swelled within him. "So, you are saying you did not enjoy the viscount's kiss."

She placed her gloved hand on his knee, the touch sending a shock through him. "I find I only enjoy one viscount's kiss." She wet her lips. "Yours, Seth. Only yours."

He jerked her to him, their lips colliding. It was as if he were drowning, and she the life line that would save him. Seth kissed her with everything he had, wanting to convey to her the love he felt for her.

For her part, Pippa kissed him back, and he could tell she gave it her all. He believed her when she said she did not care for Plemons' kiss.

Seth believed in them. Together.

He broke the kiss, pulling her from her chair into his lap, kissing her again until they were both breathless, the storm raging not only outside but within them.

"I love you, Pippa," he murmured against her mouth.

She jerked away. "What did you say?"

He looked at her sheepishly. "I love you."

Pippa beamed at him. "Say it again, Seth. Please."

"I love you," he said loudly. "I love you," he repeated.

Tears filled her eyes. "Oh, Seth, I love you, too. I have for what seems like forever."

Kissing her again, he reveled in her taste. Her scent. This woman made him come alive in a way he never had been before.

Breaking the kiss, Pippa said, "I love you. I let Lord Plemons kiss me to see if I was wrong about my feelings for you. And I wasn't, Seth. Plemons is a nice man, but his kiss did nothing for me. Or to me. When you kiss me, I soar."

He yanked off his gloves, wanting to feel her skin. Brushing his fingers against her cheeks, he said, "I once told you I could give you pleasure without creating a babe." He hesitated. "Might I do so now, Pippa?"

"Yes," she said breathlessly, grabbing his face and pulling him toward her for a long, slow kiss.

She finally broke it. "Does it involve kissing?"

"It can," he said mysteriously. "This would be easier if you wore a gown, though."

She frowned. "Why?'

"Then I could dance my fingers under it and touch your womanly core more easily."

Her face burned. "What?" she gasped.

"Do you trust me?" he asked, need for her growing within him.

"Yes," she said, her face full of innocence, yet her eyes betraying her desire for him.

"Then I'm going to need you to lower your breeches."

Shock filled her face. "But . . . I have nothing on underneath them, Seth."

"I know," he said, grinning wickedly at her.

Frowning, Pippa asked, "Are you certain what we do won't make a babe?"

"Absolutely. You can feel pleasure in many ways. This will be one of them."

Pushing off him, she stood. "All right. But close your eyes."

Seth wanted to see her—all of her—but he knew what an innocent she was. "If that's what you wish."

He did as she asked and then sensed her moving about, clothing rustling. "Do I have to remove my breeches entirely?" she asked, her voice small.

"No, love. You can leave them on. Just push them down to your ankles."

Pippa chuckled. "I might as well take them off if they'll only cover my feet. Hmm. But I have my boots to deal with. I am pushing them down, Seth. But they and my boots are staying on."

She sat in his lap again, wriggling her bare bottom against his thighs and groin. He felt the heat rise within him. But this was about Pippa. Helping her explore her femininity. Her sexuality.

Seth wrapped an arm about her waist to anchor her and then placed his hand on her calf. Slowly, he began exploring it, moving his hand to her knee. Past her knee and to her thigh, his fingers dancing along her skin.

"That feels good," she admitted. "Your hands are rough, still that of a sailor's, but I like your touch, all the same."

"Good," he whispered, his mouth closing over hers, kissing her as his fingers moved along her bare skin. Pippa smelled like vanilla. He would always associate the scent with her.

His hand slipped between her thighs, and her breath hitched.

"I won't hurt you," he said. "I only want to help you unlock the power within you."

"I trust you implicitly," she said, her gaze connected to his.

He caressed the seam of her sex, and she nearly flew off him.

"What are you doing?"

He grinned. "Hoping to make you very, very happy. Relax. In fact, close your eyes. Experience it through touch alone."

She bit her lip, driving him up a wall. "All right," she said quietly, closing her eyes.

He kissed her again deeply, allowing his fingers to stroke her. Then he pushed one inside her, hearing her gasp. He broke the kiss but saw she kept her eyes closed.

"Good girl," he said softly, kissing her lightly and then stopping, wanting to watch as she claimed her ecstasy.

Seth's fingers worked their magic, stroking her deeply, moving in and out of her, a second finger joining the first. Pippa began to pant, her breathing short and shallow. He found her sweet nub and encircled it, pressing against it, causing her to whimper. Soon, she was writhing in his lap, moaning softly, then loudly.

"What are you doing to me?" she asked, her breaths short and swift now.

"Bringing you to orgasm," he said. "Hoping you will find pleasure beyond words."

A few more caresses pushed Pippa over the edge. She clutched him, moving, whimpering, his fingers feeling her spasms. She called out his name, over and over, tears streaming down her face. Finally, she stilled, her eyes opening.

"That was . . . I have no words for it, Seth," she said, wonder in her eyes and voice.

"Let's see if you do this time."

Her eyes widened. "You are going to do it again?"

"Yes, but in a different way."

"Different how?"

"Oh, you'll see."

Seth had Pippa sit in the chair this time, first taking off his coat and draping it over the seat so no splinter would lodge in her delicious derriere. He parted her thighs and got down to business, using tongue and teeth to bring her to the heights of ecstasy. Her cries became music to his ears, as she fisted her hands in his hair, holding him to her as he pushed her to new heights.

Pippa shuddered violently, crying aloud, and then sagging in the chair. He helped her to stand, placing her hands on his shoulders, bringing her breeches back up, smoothing them, his hands cupping her derriere, his mouth finding hers again in a searing, passionate kiss.

When he finally broke it, he held her face tenderly, saying, "You are now all mine, Pippa Strong. My best friend. My lover. You will be my partner and wife. Mother to our children."

His words obviously caught her off-guard as she gazed at him, dazed.

"Are you . . . *offering* for me, Seth?"

"I want you in my bed, Pippa. As my wife. So yes, I am proposing that we wed. What say you, love? Are you willing to become an Atwell and my viscountess?"

Her sunny smile would light the darkest of nights. "I am more than ready, Seth." She smiled shyly. "Especially if you can do again what you just did to me—and if you can teach me how to bring you pleasure, too."

Seth kissed her hard, staking his claim to this woman.

And to their future happiness.

CHAPTER NINETEEN

PIPPA SAT ON Seth's lap, his arms nestled about her as they waited for the storm to subside. She couldn't believe her feelings for this incredible man were returned and that they would build a life together as husband and wife. She was glad she would not have to go through a London Season—even more than one—in search of a husband. Instead, she had found true love on her own with Seth and could not wait to start their lives together.

"When would you like to wed?" he asked. "I have no idea how to go about it since I never thought I would do so."

Realizing he had spent most of his life at sea and would not be aware of British marital customs, she told him, "We have a few options. One, we can call the banns. That means for three consecutive Sundays at our local church in Crestview, there will be a call to see if anyone objects to our union."

He frowned. "Why would anyone object?"

"I cannot truly answer that. It is merely the way things are done. Once the three Sundays have passed and the banns have been called, we can be wed in the church between eight and noon by the vicar."

Seth cradled her face with his palm, his thumb caressing her cheek. "Is there any way we could avoid waiting three weeks, Pippa? I am very eager to consummate our love."

She couldn't help but laugh. "You are a very sensual man, Seth."

He smiled shamelessly. "And it's one of the reasons you love me, I'm certain."

"It is," she agreed happily. "But I love you not merely for your handsome looks. You are a kind man, Seth. An intelligent and interesting one. Your travels have made you so."

"I know that you, too, have longed to travel. Although I had thought to take my seat in the House of Lords for the upcoming Parliamentary session, I now find that I have other priorities. Mainly, you." He kissed her nose. "I want to take an extended honeymoon, Pippa. I want to show you places I have been. Share them with you."

He kissed her softly, and Pippa was filled with need for him.

She broke the kiss, saying, "There are three other ways we could wed more quickly. We could elope to Scotland. Just across the border from England is a town called Gretna Green, and couples travel there to wed." She smiled wryly. "Usually ones whose families do not approve of their match, which is why they are eloping in the first place."

He snorted. "Scotland is too far away. What else might we do?"

"We could wed by special license. I must warn you that they are expensive, however."

Seth laughed. "I do not foresee that to be a problem, love. You are marrying quite a wealthy man. Where would I purchase this special license?"

"At a place in London called Doctors' Commons," she told him. "From what I gather, the license allows a couple to wed at any time and place of their choosing while it is valid."

"I like the sound of that. What is the final choice open to us?"

"There is something called a bishop's license. It involves a short wait. I believe it is a week, and then you can marry."

"Do you have a preference, Pippa? I want to please you. While I would like to rush into marriage so I can have you all to myself, I don't want to skimp on any of your expectations regarding the ceremony itself. I suppose it would involve new clothes for both of us, at the very least. I know it takes time to make up a gown for a woman."

"I am not like Georgie. She has dreamed of her wedding day for years now. But I *would* like to look nice for you, Seth. I think I would like to wear a new gown, perhaps one sewn by Mama's modiste in town."

"How long does it take to make up a dress?" he asked.

"If a dressmaker focuses solely on a single project—and at this time of year, it would be easy for her to do so—three days should suffice."

"Well, if I am to buy this special license, and that is what I plan to do, that means a trip to London. I would be happy to escort you and your mother to town in order for you to see this modiste." He paused. "I suppose I should speak to Her Grace and ask for your hand."

"I think it would be a good idea," Pippa said. She thought a moment. "And since James is my brother and the head of the Strong family, you should also ask permission from him, as well. You are a titled lord now, Seth. That means marriage settlements will have to be drawn up between us by solicitors."

"What are those?" he asked, clearly clueless about the process. "I have never heard of these."

"It is really only for those in Polite Society, although there is a growing merchant class within England, and I believe daughters of those businessmen are beginning to ask for marriage contracts to be drawn up, as well. Basically, the matter of my dowry is settled, along with planning for our future children and their futures."

She blushed, thinking of those children—and how they might be made—still unaware of the exact process but eager to explore it with Seth.

"Usually, a bride brings a certain amount of monies into a marriage, called a dowry. Sometimes, the groom will absorb the entire dowry. Other times, parts of it are earmarked for future daughters and their dowries, or funds can be designated for future sons, beyond the heir apparent. It also provides for what is to happen to the bride herself after her husband's death and what monies will be settled on her as a widow."

"I know our oldest son will receive my title and the bulk of my wealth and properties. It would be wise to provide for other sons if they come along," he agreed.

"It is tradition amongst the *ton* for second sons to go into the military, while third sons usually enter the church. Sons beyond that have to make their own way in the world if they are not taken care of in the marriage settlements."

"Much as my own father did," Seth shared. "Father was a clerk at Mr. Peabody's office for the majority of his life. Ironically, Peabody is my own solicitor now."

"We should strike up our plan then, Seth," Pippa said. "I think you should speak to Mama first. I know she will give her approval to you. If you would like, I can speak with her first about it. Then if I am to have a gown made up for our wedding, we can journey to town for that. There, you may talk with James and ask his permission."

Seth grinned shamelessly at her. "Actually, your brother already knows of my interest in you."

"What?" Shock filled her. "When have you spoken to James about us?"

"When I went to town a few weeks ago." He lifted one of her hands and pressed a kiss upon her knuckles. "I knew even then, Pippa, that I wanted to make you my wife. I called upon Their Graces, and your brother made it clear that he would not stop me from pursuing my case with you."

She marveled that Seth had felt so strongly about her that he would already have spoken to James.

"He was of a mind that although he is head of the Strong family, it would be your choice. Her Grace agreed with that."

It did not surprise her that Sophie would have been in her

corner regarding this issue.

"Still, I think you should speak with Mama as soon as possible and make a formal offer for my hand. Then if we wish, we can travel to town to share our happy news with James and Sophie."

"Do you have a particular place in mind where you would like to hold the ceremony? You mentioned something about the village church."

"Actually, there is a small chapel on Shadowcrest lands. It is used for marriages, baptisms, and funerals. I would like to wed in it, Seth, if you have no objections."

"Christmas is in two weeks' time," he said. "Would you like to wed before or after it?"

"Before if everything goes as planned. We could do so a couple of days before Christmas Day. I am certain James and Sophie will come to Shadowcrest to celebrate the holiday with us. I most definitely want them present at the ceremony."

He looked up at the leaking roof and said, "I don't see any more rain dribbling in. I think it is safe for us to venture from this dilapidated cottage."

They returned to the shed where they had stabled their horses and mounted, riding back to the Hopewood stables.

When they arrived, Seth dismounted and said, "I will go inside and make myself presentable before heading to Shadowcrest and calling upon your mother. I will come in two hours' time."

He took her hand and squeezed her fingers.

"Then I will make certain Mama knows to expect a call from you," Pippa said.

She turned Starlight and headed for home, making certain she kept her head out of the clouds and focused on the ride, especially with the ground so slippery.

Cutting through the kitchens, she called for a couple of jugs of hot water to be sent up. She didn't have time for an entire bath but wanted to freshen up after their ride and being caught in the rain.

Finding Forrester, she asked," Where is my mother?"

"Her Grace is in her sitting room, Lady Philippa."

"Thank you, Forrester."

Pippa headed to the sitting room, knocking twice before entering. Mama was sitting with Georgie, and they both were busy with their needlework.

"You are certainly looking bedraggled," Mama said. "I suppose you got caught in that dreadful downpour as you rode with Lord Hopewell."

She crossed the room but didn't want to sit since her coat and breeches were still damp.

"Yes, Mama. We wound up taking shelter in an empty cottage for the worst of the storm." She swallowed, looking to her twin.

Georgie immediately picked up on Pippa's feelings and asked, "Do you have something to share with Mama and me?"

She nodded, seeing Mama set aside her needlework, asking, "What is it, dearest?"

"Lord Hopewell is going to call in the next couple of hours, Mama. He wants to ask you for my hand in marriage."

Georgie squealed, leaping from her chair and rushing to Pippa, embracing her.

"I am so happy for you, Pippa," her twin said, her eyes glimmering with tears.

Mama also rose and came toward her, enveloping Pippa in her arms.

"This is what you want, Pippa?" her mother asked.

"Very much so, Mama. I love him with all my heart."

Mama smiled, smoothing Pippa's hair. "I am very happy to hear this news. Lord Hopewell is a very fine man, and I have seen his interest grow in you. Selfishly, I am glad he offered for you because it means you will not be far from Shadowcrest, living at Hopewood. He does make you happy, doesn't he?"

"Happier than I could have dreamed possible, Mama," she answered truthfully. "I could never see myself with anyone but

Lord Hopewell."

"Then he will receive a warm welcome into the Strong family," her mother promised. "We should ask James for his permission, though, just to make things official."

She chuckled. "I believe James will not have any problem with the marriage, Mama. Seth actually spoke to him and Sophie when he was in town a few weeks ago."

"I see," Mama said. "Did you know of this?"

"No. He never said a word to me about it, but he wanted to make certain that James had no objections."

"Then my permission granted today will merely be a formality," Mama said. She cradled Pippa's face. "I am so very happy for you, dearest. It is not often a woman makes a love match. I can see the difference in you already. You are glowing."

Pippa felt a blush heat her cheeks, thinking of what she and Seth had done in the abandoned cottage today, wondering if her own parents had done something like that themselves. Something told her they had not. What had passed between her and Seth had simply been pure pleasure for Pippa. She could not see her father and his coldness ever wanting to please Mama. Papa had merely wanted to get sons off his second wife.

It made her look at Mama with new eyes. She had recently thought of how young her mother truly was. That she might also wed again someday. Pippa fervently hoped that Mama would find a man who would make her as happy as Seth had made Pippa herself.

"Seth—Lord Hopewell, that is—will be asking not only for my hand in marriage, but he also wants a wedding as soon as possible."

Mama nodded knowingly. "He wishes to purchase a special license. Is that correct?"

"Yes," she said. "We do not want to wait three weeks for the banns to be read. I thought we could marry in the Shadowcrest chapel a few days before Christmas, once James and Sophie have returned to the country to celebrate the holidays with us. I had also hoped we could see your London modiste and have her create a wedding gown for me."

"She will have to do more than that for you, my darling," Mama declared. "You are getting married, Pippa! You will need an entire new wardrobe. We will start with your wedding gown and then have Madame Dumas and her staff begin sewing the rest of your wardrobe."

Mama paused, thinking a moment. "I believe I will have her start on my wardrobe for the Season and Georgina's, as well. That will keep her busy until we return to town in early February. At that time, Madame can measure the others and begin on those wardrobes for the Season, as well."

Her mother embraced Pippa again. "I am so happy for you, Pippa dear. You will have what I never had myself. A loving husband."

"Perhaps you might have that one day yourself, Mama," Pippa encouraged. "After all, you are young enough to wed again."

Mama cocked her head. "Who knows what this next Season might bring? I am hoping it will be husbands for Georgina, Mirella, Lyric, and Allegra. Perhaps I should think of marrying again, though."

"So, I am to go with you to town?" Georgie asked, excitement dancing in her eyes.

"Yes, Madame Dumas can take your measurements and begin on your come-out wardrobe, Georgina. I know your sister will be happy to have your company while we are in town."

Mama went to her desk and sat. "I am going to write a note to let Madame Dumas know we are coming. I will also write to James and Sophie and let them know we will arrive tomorrow. Go freshen up, Pippa. Lord Hopewell will most likely want to see you after he has spoken with me."

"Yes, Mama," she said, linking fingers with Georgie and departing the sitting room.

As they mounted the stairs, Georgie said, "You are so fortunate to have found love, Pippa. Oh, I hope I will be so lucky and do the same."

"You are far prettier than I am, Georgie. I have already told you that you will be the most popular debutante of this coming Season. A diamond of the first water."

They went to their shared bedchamber, where the hot water was being delivered. Georgie herself helped Pippa to bathe and dress.

"We should go to the library," her twin said, after she finished brushing Pippa's hair and twisting it into an elegant knot. "You will want to be nearby when Mama sends for you."

They found Forrester and told him where they would be, and Pippa informed the butler that Lord Hopewell would be calling soon to see the duchess.

Understanding lit the servant's eyes, and he smiled. "Very good, my lady."

Pippa and Georgie went to the library, where they opened the atlas and began pouring over it.

She said, "I have always dreamed of traveling. Seth wants to take me places around the world, Georgie. He has talked about an extended honeymoon, with us traveling to lands he has visited."

"That sounds exciting," her twin said, but Pippa saw Georgie's smile was small.

She recalled that her twin had wanted her to come to town to help her make the decision regarding a husband during the upcoming Season. Perhaps Pippa should ask Seth if they might delay their travels.

At least until this Season came to an end.

CHAPTER TWENTY

THEY ENTERED LONDON in two carriages, the first being Seth's vehicle, which carried Pippa, Lady Georgina, and their mother, along with him. The second carriage was one from Shadowcrest, and it bore two maids and their group's luggage. He had directed his coachman to head to the Duke of Seaton's townhouse first, where the ladies would be dropped off, while Seth wanted to go about obtaining the special license.

"It seems so odd to be here at this time of year," Lady Georgina said.

"We were here for three years at this time," Pippa reminded her sister. "I hated not spending Christmas at Shadowcrest."

He knew his bride-to-be preferred the country over the city, and he was glad they would be able to spend their first Christmas with her family as man and wife. Seth was eager, however, to take Pippa on a long voyage, where they would visit places he had been from his youth through the time he had captained his own ship. They had yet to discuss their ports of call, but Seth figured they would be gone a good year—and possibly two. He worried a bit about Pippa being separated from her family that long, especially her twin.

"The traffic is as heavy as ever," Her Grace commented. "Sometimes, I wonder why I even bother coming to town."

Pippa had told Seth that she would be fitted not only for her wedding gown but also an entire new wardrobe. She was of age now, and her mother deemed it proper for her to wear more mature clothing, which would suit her age and her new rank in Polite Society as Viscountess Hopewell. The duchess and Lady Georgina were also going to be measured in order for the modiste to begin making up their wardrobes for the upcoming Season. He had listened as they had discussed the Season in the carriage rider from Kent to London, and he nearly fell off the bench when he heard the duchess explain that at least fifty to sixty ball gowns were to be created for each Strong female making her come-out, not to mention a bevy of other gowns for things such as garden parties and routs, whatever those were.

He glanced next to him at Pippa, wondering if she would mind giving up the Season. Not only this one—but future ones. Somehow, he did not think he was cut out for the social swirl. Then again, he knew they would be in town during future years so that he might be seated in Parliament and have a say in the bills presented in the House of Lords. As long as they were in London, he believed Pippa would wish to go to the various social affairs, especially if her family members would also be present at them. Seth supposed he would grin and bear it to make her happy.

"This is a rather personal question," Her Grace said, looking to Seth. "Do you know how to dance, my lord?"

He laughed. "Only a sailor's jig, Your Grace. Nothing fit for a *ton* ballroom."

"James does not know how to dance either," the duchess revealed. "I think I will hire a dance master to teach both of you together. I am certain the duke will pull you into the card room, and you will hide there during most balls, but it would be appropriate for you to dance a few numbers with your new wife and her siblings."

Wanting to fit in, he replied, "I am at your disposal, Your Grace. Whatever His Grace suffers through, I will be his willing companion in the torture."

The three ladies laughed, and Pippa nudged him in the ribs with her elbow. "You do not have to be an expert at dancing, Seth. I am atrocious at it myself. Our dance master has told me that I have absolutely no rhythm."

"That cannot be, Pippa," he protested. "I have seen you ride, and you have counted out the sequence for me. I would think riding and dancing would have much in common."

She shrugged. "I cannot dance. Georgie cannot sing. But I do ride well, and she plays the pianoforte beautifully. We aren't totally hopeless."

"I hope no suitors will ask me to sing when they come calling," Lady Georgina fretted. "Else they would go running from our townhouse, covering their ears."

"Surely, you can't be that bad, my lady," Seth said gallantly.

The twins looked at one another and burst into laughter.

"Let him hear for himself, Pippa," Lady Georgina encouraged. "Then your betrothed will discover what we mean."

Pippa broke into song, and Seth thought she had a lovely voice, low and melodic. He would teach her some songs from his sailing days, enjoying hearing the words coming from her lips.

Then Lady Georgina took up the song, and Pippa's voice faded away. He couldn't help but wince at the screeches that came from the beauty's mouth.

She quit singing and began laughing. "You should see the look upon your face, my lord. We told you that I could not sing a note."

"Not everyone can do everything well, my lady," Seth said diplomatically.

"Oh, I wish you would call me Georgie, or at least Georgina. After all, you are going to be family and like a brother to me."

"I will only do so if you call me Seth."

She smiled at him. "Seth, it will be."

"It can be so within the confines of this carriage or when we are all together in private," the duchess reminded her daughter.

"Even if Lord Hopewell is to be your brother-in-law and you become good friends, you must address him properly around others, Georgina."

Her Grace looked to Seth. "I agree with my daughter, and I wish for you to call me Dinah when we are with family."

"I am honored to do so, Dinah. I have already been granted leave to call James and Sophie by their given names. Your kind gesture makes me feel truly accepted into the Strong family."

The horses began to slow, and he glanced out the window, seeing they stopped in front of the Seatons' grand townhouse. Again, he was awed by its sheer size.

Several servants poured from the door, and James stepped outside to greet them. The duke himself handed down the three women, and then Seth exited the carriage.

James offered his hand, and the two men shook.

"It is good to see you again, Seth. What are your plans for the day?"

"I had thought to see about purchasing our special license for the wedding ceremony."

"That can wait until tomorrow. You are going to be here several days. I would like to take everyone to the wharf so that you might see our two enterprises in person."

The duke looked to the dowager duchess. "Why don't you ladies go inside and freshen up? Sophie was unable to greet you in person because she had an important contract to sign this morning. She sends her regrets and hopes that you will come down to see the offices now."

"Then I will send my carriage and valet to my townhouse and let my coachman handle rubbing down the horses. I would be happy to visit both Strong and Neptune Shipping."

Seth dismissed his driver, his valet claiming Seth's trunk from the second carriage, which would remain at the Seaton's.

He went inside with the others, and the ladies made their way upstairs, while he and James headed to the ducal study.

"So, it's Pippa for you, after all," the duke said.

"Yes. I knew when we last spoke that I wanted her as my wife, but there is an independent streak running in her Strong veins. I knew I couldn't rush her. That if she discovered she returned my feelings, she would do so in her own time."

James steepled his fingers. "Still, you persuaded her to do so in only a few weeks. I suppose our solicitors will need to sit down and hammer out the marriage settlements while you are in town."

"Pippa was telling me about these. I most certainly want to take care of her and any offspring we might have. I will send word to Peabody and tell him to start drawing them up. In fact, I may go see him in person in order to clarify any questions he might have regarding my wishes."

"I had forgotten Arthur Peabody was your solicitor. He is the Strong solicitor, as well. It should make things quite easy. We will go see him together and make quick work of things."

They chatted a bit about their country estates and the help Caleb Strong had given Seth in helping him understand his responsibilities.

"I had my first meeting with my tenants at the beginning of this month," Seth shared. "It is something I wish to do every month I am present at Hopewood. In my absence, I will expect Hunt, my steward to continue the practice, so that their needs may be made known and addressed. I want them to lack for nothing."

He paused. "Pippa and I may be gone for quite a while, however. She has yearned to travel for many years, and there are places I wish to introduce her to."

"Will you leave directly after the wedding ceremony?" James asked.

"We wish to wed two days before Christmas, so we will stay and celebrate the holiday with family. Come the new year, though, I am going to see that we board a ship and sail for a more tropical climate."

"I do not want her in danger, Seth," James admonished. "You

have to remember that we are at war with France."

"We will sail far from Europe, and Bonaparte's influence," he shared. "I would like to take Pippa to the Sandwich Islands. The Far East. India. Places I am familiar with after so many years at sea."

"Although I have not been back with my family for long, I want you to think carefully about this trip, Seth. Pippa and Georgie are tremendously close. It might prove difficult for them to be apart for so long a time."

James' words confirmed his fears. "I will discuss this with Pippa and acquiesce to her wishes."

"Good," the duke pronounced. "I know if my sister is wedding you, she must love you a great deal. It is important to always communicate with your spouse. Sophie has taught me that lesson. If you are willing to compromise regarding your trip, perhaps making it shorter rather than longer, you would have a happy wife."

A knock sounded at the door, and the butler entered.

"The ladies are waiting, Your Grace."

Both men rose and followed the butler to the foyer.

"I cannot wait to see Strong Shipping," Dinah said. "Even though it was owned by my husband, he did not believe women should cloud their head with matters of business, and so I was never allowed to visit the premises. Sophie is the new example in our family for what women can be and what they can accomplish."

James laughed. "My duchess is teaching me more about business each day. Come, our carriage is waiting."

They went to the ducal carriage and traveled to London's wharf area. The vehicle deposited them beside the river, and James pointed out a ship at the docks, cargo being unloaded from it.

"This is a vessel from the Neptune Shipping Line. Sophie and I have decided it is more practical for our two lines not to be in head-to-head competition with one another. We have drawn up plans and are now implementing them. We will no longer call at the same ports, nor will our ships bring back the same merchandise."

"It is so large," Georgie said, awe-struck. "How many men does a ship this size carry as a crew?"

Seth and James took turns answering the questions from the women for a few minutes, and then the duke said they needed to go to the Neptune Shipping offices and collect Sophie.

"They are only a short ways from here," he told them as they set out amidst the bustle along the docks.

They reached Neptune Shipping, and James explained how it was all within one facility, with the warehouse on the ground floor and the offices above it.

Their group went upstairs and was taken to a large office, where Sophie and Mr. Barnes were deep in conversation.

The duchess sprang to her feet, crying out, "I am so glad you have arrived!"

Embraces were exchanged between the women, and then Sophie came to him. Seth, too, was warmly embraced.

"I am delighted you are going to be part of the family, Seth," Sophie told him. "Pippa could not have made a better choice for a husband. But come, let us go to the conference room. I want you all to see what James and I have been up to, with Mr. Barnes' and Mr. Compton's help."

They entered and once again, Seth saw the large map dominating the table. Sophie explained in simple terms to the three women the routes Neptune ships would now be sailing and where Strong Shipping Lines would send their vessels.

"We did not want to merge our two companies," Sophie explained. "While our oldest son will inherit Strong Shipping, the rest of our children will hold shares and be able to run Neptune Shipping."

"Even the girls?" asked Pippa.

Sophie laughed. "Especially the girls."

"Why don't we go see our family's facilities now?" James

suggested.

Once more, they went through the warehouse and walked a quarter-mile until they reached Strong Shipping Lines. James led them first to the warehouse, walking them through it, explaining how cargo was categorized and assigned various places within it.

They crossed the street and went to the offices, where he introduced them to Mr. Compton, who now headed and managed the line for the Strong family.

"I am working closely with Mr. Barnes at Neptune Shipping," Compton told them. "Dividing the trade routes was simply a brilliant idea on Her Grace's part. It will allow our fleets to cover different places throughout the world and bring back varying goods. I believe profits will rise exponentially."

"Thank you for showing us around, Mr. Compton," Dinah said. "I hope we will no longer be strangers but visit the family business on a regular basis."

"You are welcome to come anytime, Your Grace," the manager said.

"I am famished," James proclaimed. "All of you must be, as well, after your journey up from Kent. Why don't we head home for tea? Cook is expecting us."

They returned to the duke's carriage and journeyed back to Mayfair, where they went up to the drawing room. Two teacarts were immediately rolled into the room, and Dinah presided over tea.

As they talked and ate, Seth felt a sense of belonging, something he had never felt before. Yes, he had loved his father, but it had been only the two of them. Even on the various ships he had sailed on throughout the years, while he thought of the crew as his family, it wasn't true kin.

These Strongs, however, had taken him in as one of their own. While he hoped he and Pippa had many children, he would remember they were half-Strongs and half-Atwells. He wanted their children to remain true to their Strong roots and planned for them to be close to their cousins. After all, Pippa considered

Caleb and his two sisters as simply more siblings. He liked being part of such a large clan.

He observed how in tune Pippa and Georgie were and decided he would need to get Georgie alone and speak to her frankly about his plans for a long honeymoon. It would be important to receive Georgie's approval—and blessing—before Seth could ever sweep Pippa away from England and her family.

Seth would bide his time while they were in town and find a moment when he could discuss this with Pippa's twin without interference.

CHAPTER TWENTY-ONE

PIPPA WAS DISAPPOINTED when she did not get to spend any time alone with Seth after dinner. Instead, they had all gone to the drawing room. They did have fun, though. Seth and James kept them entertained with story after story of their time at sea, sometimes talking about some of the same wonderful, strange lands they had visited during their years on the water.

She had encouraged her betrothed to tell one of his ghost stories, having them blow out all but a single candle to set the mood. Seth had built the tension slowly, telling of a sailor who had been in love with a woman and how she had sacrificed herself to free him from a debt.

"The woman gave her life for the man she loved, so he would be free of the strangling debt," Seth said in a mournful tone. "But he regretted her action, though not his love for her and hers for him, and he swore an oath to one day reunite with her."

Seth paused, his gaze meeting Pippa's, and she nodded encouragingly, wanting to hear how the tale was resolved.

"One night, she came to him as a ghost while he stood watch with two other crew members in the dead of night. She rose from the waves, beckoning him to follow her into the depths, a smile playing about her full lips. Without thought—and having missed her terribly—her lover jumped overboard, plunging into the ocean."

Georgie gasped, and Pippa linked her fingers with her sister.

"Two sailors had also seen her ghost," Seth continued. "They were witnesses to their friend's leap into the ocean. Both rushed to the spot where he had jumped, peering into the black waters, calling his name in vain. The man never answered them, and they finally backed away, knowing he was gone, reluctant to tell the captain and crew what they had seen.

"Then another wave rose, higher than the deck, and the sailors watched in awe as they saw the lovers together at the peak of the wave, their arms wound about one another, lips locked together in a kiss for all time. The wave froze, the sea growing calm for a brief interlude, before the wave crashed again. Once more, the seamen peered over the side of the ship, seeking their friend and his lover, but they had been swallowed up by the seas, never to be seen again."

The room was silent a moment, and then Sophie said, "Oh, that has given me chills, Seth."

"At least they were together for eternity," Dinah said. "It might be a ghostly tale, but it was very romantic."

James took the lone candle and went about the room, relighting others, until the drawing room was cast in a warm glow once more.

"What are the plans for tomorrow, Dinah?" asked the duke.

"We have an appointment with Madame Dumas," the duchess said. "It is imperative that Pippa's wedding gown be started. I will also have Madame's assistants measure Georgina and me so that our Season wardrobes can be started, as well. Sophie, you should come with us. I know you and James will want to attend at least a few events this upcoming Season. I am certain Madame would be pleased to be given the opportunity to dress another duchess."

Sophie looked to her husband. "What do you think?"

He slipped his hand around hers. "I think I have wed the most beautiful woman in the world and wish to show her off to all of

Polite Society. While I cannot see us going to balls every night of the week, it would be nice to attend some of the events so that the *ton* can know the Duke and Duchess of Seaton are forces to be reckoned with. Go ahead, love, and have this wardrobe created for you."

James looked to Seth. "The two of us shall head straight to Doctors' Commons after we breakfast in order to obtain the needed special license. After that, we will meet with Peabody and see about drawing up the marriage settlements."

Pippa knew Seth would treat her fairly, and with James there to also look after her interests and those of her future children, she didn't think the marriage contracts would take long to write.

Seth left after that, promising to return to the Seaton household tomorrow morning.

"Will you come for breakfast?" she asked him.

"If you wish me to do so." His eyes glowed with love.

"I do," she said pertly.

He took her hand and kissed her fingers. "Then I will take my leave and see you in the morning. Good night to you all."

After Seth left, she and Georgie went upstairs. Oddly enough, they had been placed in two different bedchambers instead of the single one they had always shared. Mama had told them it had been at her direction, but Pippa was having none of it. After getting into her night rail and dismissing her maid, she went down the corridor to the room Georgie was staying in.

Much to her surprise, the door opened before she even knocked. Georgie, also in sleep attire, held a candle in her hand.

"Oh! I was just coming to you," her twin said. "I cannot imagine sleeping alone."

"I thought the same," she said. "Which room shall we use?"

"You are already here, so you might as well come in."

Pippa followed her twin inside, blowing out her candle and resting it next to the bed.

"We don't have that many more times to be together," she told Georgie. "Soon, I will be in Seth's bed. While I am eager to become his wife, I will miss all the long talks we have had over the years after we have blown out the candle."

She climbed into bed, Georgie doing the same, resting their lit candles on the bedstand and then extinguishing them. They threaded their fingers together.

"I wonder what marriage will be like," Georgie wondered. "I do know Seth loves you a great deal. He looks at you all the time, smiling like a puppy at its master."

Laughing, Pippa said, "He would not want to be thought of as a pup. But I do think he will be devoted to me. Mama told me tonight that she and I were going to have the talk. She said she has things to tell me about the marriage bed."

"You will tell me everything, won't you?" her twin pleaded.

"I will tell you what Mama says, then I will tell you if it is true or not after Seth and I couple. I think what we do together will be far different than from what Mama and Papa did."

Georgie shuddered. "I cannot even think of them kissing, much less doing whatever it takes to make a babe. Poor Mama. She was only seven and ten when she wed Papa. He was so much older than she was."

"I doubt Papa loved her," she said. "He merely wanted more sons from her, especially after James disappeared." She hesitated. "Georgie, do you think Mama might wed again?"

"Hmm. I had not even considered it until you brought it up to her previously, but she very well could. She is so beautiful and while she seems old to us, she could still wed and even have another babe or two. Wouldn't that be something, having more brothers or sisters?"

"They would be a half-brother or half-sister," Pippa said. "No, James is our half-brother since he had a different mother from us, but he has insisted we are simply his sisters. We should do the same if Mama does remarry and has children."

"She is having a new wardrobe made up for the Season," Georgie pointed out. "She may very well be considering finding a new husband. Oh, wouldn't it be something if Mama married again?"

"I hope this time she might wed for love," she said wistfully. "I already love Seth so much my teeth hurt. All I can think about is kissing him. Mama deserves happiness."

They fell silent, and soon she heard Georgie's even breaths. She had wanted to talk to her twin about the honeymoon Seth wanted to take, but they could save that for tomorrow.

By the time Pippa and Georgie dressed and went downstairs, Seth was already present at their breakfast table. Her heart fluttered at seeing her handsome fiancé.

He stood and came to greet her with a kiss to her cheek. He was freshly shaved, and she caught the scent of his shaving soap.

"Good morning," he rumbled, slipping her hand through his arm and leading her to a seat at the table. "Are you excited about seeing the modiste today?"

"I am, but I am glad that Mama will be there to help me select the design for my wedding gown. And the others."

Seth returned to his seat next to her as a footman poured tea for her and Georgie. Pippa dropped in a lump of sugar and a dash of cream, stirring until the sugar dissolved.

"Where is Sophie?" asked Georgie.

"She is already at her desk at Neptune Shipping," James told them.

"But I thought she was going to Madame Dumas' shop with us today," she said.

"She will meet you there," her brother assured her. "Your appointment is not until ten o'clock, and Sophie will have already tackled half a day's work by then."

"I wonder what it would be like, going to a job every day," mused Pippa.

"You will have job enough running both our households,"

Seth said. "I know nothing of that, so that will be your strictly your domain."

She smiled at her mother. "Mama has fully prepared us for that."

That reminded her of the chat she and her mother needed to have regarding marriage. It had been put off long enough, and Pippa planned for it to happen today.

They ate their meal leisurely, and then Seth and James left for Doctors' Commons. She couldn't help but be excited that when they returned, Seth would have their marriage license. It was all becoming quite real.

Mama stood. "We have an hour before we leave. I am going to catch up on my correspondence."

She looked at her twin and nodded. Georgie winked at her.

"Mama, I have a matter to discuss with you. Georgie, too. Is this a good time to do so?"

Her sister's eyes widened. "Oh, I think just Pippa wishes to speak with you, Mama."

"No," she insisted. "This way, nothing will be misunderstood."

Mama looked perplexed but said, "Come along, girls."

They retreated to the cozy room Mama used as her retreat while in town. Pippa closed the door behind them, and the twin sat across from their mother.

"Mama, I am about to be married, and Georgie will most likely find herself betrothed by Season's end," she began. "Because of that, we need to get . . . certain information from you."

"Ah," her mother said, nodding her head as she looked at her oldest children. "You wish to speak of marriage. And intimacy."

Georgie squeaked. Pippa said, "Yes, Mama. Whatever you can tell us will be helpful."

"First of all, I must emphasize to you that my experience with your father was vastly different from what I wish for the two of you." A wistful smile appeared upon her mother's face, one which they had never seen.

"What is it, Mama?" she asked.

"You love your viscount, Pippa, and he loves you. That is the major difference between the marriage you will have and the one I experienced. There was no love between Seaton and me."

Her mother proceeded to tell them about the mechanics of lovemaking. Pippa thought it sounded so cold, unlike what had taken place in the cottage that day with Seth, or with any of the kisses the two of them had shared.

"I think that sounds dreadful, Mama," Georgie said once Mama finished. "I do not think I would like to do that at all with any man, even one I loved."

Mama took Georgie's hand. "In all honesty, I did not like it much myself. But it is different when you have romantic feelings for your spouse, Georgina." She paused. "I once loved a boy."

"What?" both twins cried in unison.

"It was before I wed your father. We had grown up together and had been friends for years. Then our feelings changed toward one another. We shared several kisses, and they were magical. I wanted more than anything to marry him. The way I felt when he kissed me made me want to soar through the skies."

"That is how I feel whenever Seth and I kiss," admitted Pippa. "Why didn't you marry this boy, Mama?"

Tears glistened in her mother's eyes. "I was brought up to do whatever my parents asked of me. They wanted me to wed the Duke of Seaton, even though he was so much older than I was. I was a dutiful daughter and did as I was expected to do."

"What of the boy you loved, Mama?" asked Georgie.

"He went to university. Then he took his place in Polite Society. He married a girl who admittedly favored me. They have three children now. I used to see him occasionally during the Season. We never speak. I only hope that he is happy with the wife he chose and the family they have created."

"That is very sad, Mama," Pippa said. "It was unfair of you to be forced to wed a man you did not love."

"Most girls making their come-out have little choice, Pippa dearest. They wed the man they are told to wed. Most families want their daughters to marry a man of wealth. One with a great title. My husband had both, and that is what my parents wished me to have."

"What was it like kissing Papa?" Georgie boldly asked.

"I do not know. We never did so. Kissing is for romantics, Georgina. For those who are attracted to one another. For those who are in love. I was under no illusions such as that. I knew Seaton married me because of my youth and looks. He wanted sons off me." Mama giggled. "Instead, I gave him four wonderful daughters."

"Do you plan to ever wed again, Mama?" she asked. "Georgie and I think you should."

Mama thought a long moment. "I cannot say if I will or I won't. I will tell you this. I am comfortable with the life I have now. I have the four of you, and Allegra and Lyric are happy additions. Caleb, now, too. If I did choose to do so, it would only be for love."

Pippa took Mama's hand. "Then I hope you do find love, Mama. I am so happy with Seth. I wish you could also find happiness of your own." She turned to her twin. "You, too, Georgie. You deserve a man who will treat you as kindly as Seth does me." She smiled. "And one whose kisses you cannot live without."

"Enough of this talk," Mama said, pulling away and dabbing her eyes with her handkerchief. "We mustn't be late for our appointment with Madame Dumas."

They left for the modiste's shop, traveling in the ducal carriage James had left for them. Madame Dumas was a woman of no-nonsense. Her assistants measured the three of them, and then Sophie joined them, also having her measurements taken. Once that was completed, they sat with the modiste, talking of Pippa's wedding and the gown to be made up for it. Madame quickly drew a design that was both beautiful and pleasing.

"That is perfect," Pippa said. "Seth will love seeing me in this."

"What else?" Madame asked. "Her Grace said that you need an entire wardrobe, Lady Philippa."

They spent an hour, the dressmaker drawing designs and altering them based upon Mama's suggestions. Then Madame Dumas began designing gowns for both Georgie and Mama.

"We will start on Lady Philippa's wedding gown at once," the modiste said. "Come back in two days' time for a fitting. We can make any necessary adjustments, but I will tell you that there will not be many. If there are, the gown will be ready on the third day. In another week, we will also have a few more of the gowns and undergarments completed."

"Thank you for your time, Madame Dumas," Mama said. "We look forward to seeing your creations."

"Once we finish Lady Philippa's wardrobe, Your Grace, we will start on yours, Her Grace's, and Lady Georgina's."

"We will return to town fulltime at the beginning of February, Madame Dumas," Mama informed the modiste. "I will also be bringing out another daughter and two of my nieces. They, and Lady Mathilda, will also need complete wardrobes."

"I see I have my work cut out for me, Your Grace."

Mama smiled. "If you need to hire additional help, just let me know. I can help pay the salary of another seamstress or two if that would be helpful."

They left the modiste's shop, having been there three hours, and returned home. Mama cautioned them not to mention what Pippa's wedding gown looked like, saying it was considered bad luck for a groom to see the gown or even know about it."

She laughed. "You sound like the crew Seth sailed with, Mama. Seth has told me about some of their superstitions."

Pippa shared several of those superstitions and had the three laughing about them when Seth and James returned.

"The marriage settlements are done," James declared. "Seth and I had already sent word to Peabody what we wanted in them.

We went to his office and agreed upon the details. Peabody will write up everything and have his clerks make copies of the contracts. We will return to his offices tomorrow afternoon and sign them."

"And the license?" she asked.

Seth pulled it from his pocket and handed it to Pippa. "As you can see, it is official. We simply need the vicar to marry us."

"We can talk to him when we return to Kent," Mama said. "Pippa said she wishes for you to wed in the Shadowcrest chapel."

Seth took Pippa's hand. "Whatever my betrothed wants."

"Then let us talk about the wedding breakfast," her mother said, and they did so over tea, deciding all the dishes which would be served after the ceremony.

Pippa smiled so much, her face began to hurt. But she was the happiest she had ever been.

Nothing would ever change that.

CHAPTER TWENTY-TWO

SETH LEFT HIS tailor's, pleased with what he would wear to his upcoming wedding. Everything was falling into place. He and James had signed the copies of the marriage settlements Peabody had drawn up. Pippa had her final fitting for her wedding gown yesterday and had told him how happy she was with how it had turned out. She was going back to Madame Dumas' shop this afternoon to try on three other gowns which the modiste and her assistants had completed.

For him, the last piece of the puzzle would be taken care of now. James had recommended a jeweler to Seth, and he was on his way there in order to select Pippa's wedding ring.

When he arrived at the jeweler's shop, he disembarked from his carriage, eager to see what the man had to offer. He entered and saw a lone occupant sitting behind a long, glass case. Numerous items were on display, from rings and earrings to necklaces and bracelets.

"Good afternoon," he said. "I am Lord Hopewell. I was sent here by the Duke of Seaton."

The man set down the tools he had been using to polish a gemstone and bowed.

"It is good to meet a friend of His Grace's. I am grateful for the business."

"I am a fellow seaman, as His Grace was, and so I will need your guidance in the finer aspects of selecting a wedding ring for my betrothed."

Seth's eyes fell to the display case again, where gems of all kinds sparkled. He frowned, thinking none of them looked like Pippa.

"You don't see anything that appeals to you, my lord?"

He met the jeweler's gaze. "My intended may be from the *ton*, but she is a country girl at heart. She likes nothing better than to be atop a horse galloping in the meadow. Frankly, I cannot see her wearing anything so flashy or fancy."

The man nodded sagely. "Every now and then, I get a customer such as yourself. One whose bride-to-be has good taste, but they are simple tastes. I believe an elegant, gold band would be what you might wish to view, my lord."

The jeweler went to a drawer behind him and opened it, removing a tray of rings and bringing it close for Seth's inspection. He perused the lot, and then he chose two, lifting them from the black velvet they rested upon.

"One of these would be nice, I think. Can you tell me the difference between these two?"

"Of course. It is all in the quality of the gold which was used."

He explained karats to Seth and then recommended one wedding ring over the other, saying it would be more durable and still look beautiful.

"I will take that one then," he declared, happy that he had come to a decision so quickly. Then he thought a moment. "You have quite an array of earrings on display, but I am looking for something as this wedding band. Simple yet elegant. Might you carry a pair of gold hooped earrings?"

"Ah, you truly are a sailing man if you wish to give a pair of these to your bride. I get a few of them in here from time to time."

Seth nodded. "I have told her about various superstitions which sailors hold fast to, but I have also shared with her things they believe bring good fortune. She has wanted to travel the world her entire life, and I plan to make that dream come true for her. When we are wed, I wish to give them to her as my wedding gift."

"One moment, my lord."

The jeweler walked to a set of curtains and parted them, vanishing for a few moments. When he returned, one hand was fisted. He rested his arm upon the counter and opened his fist. Inside his palm lay a pair of shining gold hooped earrings, exactly the size Seth could picture Pippa wearing.

"This is what I want to purchase. I will take both the wedding band and these earrings, and I will sing your praises if I ever meet a man in need of a jeweler," he promised.

He watched as the jeweler placed the items in a small, velvet pouch, pulling the strings tight and handing the pouch over to Seth.

"How much do I owe you?"

The man named his price, which Seth believed more than fair, and he placed several gold sovereigns on the counter.

"This is too much, my lord," trying to hand him coins back.

"No, keep it. You've earned it this day."

The jeweler beamed at him. "You are a generous soul, Lord Hopewell. Your betrothed is a most lucky woman."

Seth smiled. "I'd like to think we are both very fortunate in having found one another."

He slipped the velvet pouch into an inner pocket of his coat and returned to his carriage, telling the coachman to drive directly to the Duke of Seaton's townhouse.

When he arrived, it was still half an hour before tea was to begin. If Georgie had not accompanied her sister and mother to the modiste's shop, this would be the perfect time to speak with her regarding the honeymoon.

Forrester admitted Seth and told Seth, "Her Grace and Lady Philippa have not yet returned from Madame Dumas' shop, my lord. Would you care to wait in the drawing room until tea is served?"

"I would like to have a brief word with Lady Georgina if she is not otherwise engaged," he told the butler.

"Lady Georgina is practicing the pianoforte in the music room, my lord."

"I can see myself there, Forrester. Thank you."

He had been in the music room two days ago when Georgie had played and Pippa and Seth had sung duets together. He enjoyed how well their voices blended and couldn't wait to teach her various sailing songs, some rather risqué.

The door to the music room was slightly ajar, and he slipped through it, leaving it the way he found it. Across the room, Georgie played with great passion. She might not be able to sing well, but her fingers were magical when dancing along a keyboard. He waited until she finished playing her piece, and then he applauded her effort, moving toward her.

"I did not hear you come in, Seth. I find I have a tendency to lose myself in my music when I play."

"I enjoyed listening to you play, Georgie. Could we sit a few minutes before we go to tea? I have something I wish to discuss with you."

She rose and went to a settee, indicating for him to take the seat beside her.

He did so, and then he said, "I know how very close you and Pippa are. I want to assure you that I never want to come between the two of you. You will always be welcome anytime, day or night, at Hopewood, as well as our townhouse here in London. I want you to think of our homes as second homes to you."

"That is very sweet of you, Seth. Yes, Pippa and I have worried previously about how marriage could change things between us. Our loyalties will need to lie with our husbands and not one another."

"I would never, ever ask Pippa to make a choice between you and me," Seth said fervently. "In many ways, I believe you will remain the closest person to her throughout her life. I do have something to discuss with you, however. A delicate matter."

"Your honeymoon, I suppose," Georgie guessed.

When he started to speak, she raised a hand, and he fell silent.

"Pippa has always desired to see the world, especially now that she has found love with you. I will not prevent you from taking her on that special journey, Seth. You are fortunate to have found one another, and you deserve the honeymoon of your choosing."

"I know Pippa was supposed to come to town and help you decide which man you should accept a marriage offer from, Georgie. If we stay here during the Season and then leave once you have wed, would that be acceptable?"

"No," she said firmly, surprising him. "What I want you to do, Seth, is leave as soon as possible on your honeymoon."

He shook his head in disagreement. "Georgie, we could not get anywhere and back in time for the start of the Season."

She placed her hand atop his. "I know this, Seth. I have changed my mind about needing Pippa's help in this decision. I have seen her lead by example. She did not need to ask my opinion about you. She listened to her heart—and that is what I plan to do. I intend to trust my heart in helping me find a man I love, one I might spend the rest of my life with.

"I believe in love, Seth. I have seen it with James and Sophie, and now I see it with you and Pippa. I may find a husband this Season, or it may take more than one Season to do so. Whatever the case may be, I trust that my heart will guide me where I am supposed to be and who I am to share it with. I *will* pick the right man, Seth—and he will be one such as you—not worried about sharing me with Pippa. In fact, I hope that the four of us will become quite good friends."

His heart swelled with love for Pippa's twin. Seth embraced Georgie, kissing her cheek, quietly saying, "Thank you. You have allayed all my fears."

He released her and reached inside his coat pocket. "I want to share something with you."

Pulling open the pouch, he tilted it so that the jewelry inside fell into his palm.

"Oh, Pippa's wedding band! She will love this, Seth. And earrings? These are quite lovely."

He slid the items into their pouch again, sealing it and slipping it inside his pocket once more.

"I told Pippa how there are sailors who wear gold hooped earrings for good luck when they sail. I plan to give her these when we set out on our voyage together."

Georgie squeezed his hand. "You are a very thoughtful man, Seth. I hope that I will find a man just as generous and kindhearted as you are."

The clock chimed four times, and she said, "Goodness. We are late for tea. I am surprised no one came to fetch us."

They made their way to the drawing room, which was already boisterous with chatter. Seth felt blessed he was marrying into such a large, happy family.

He spied Pippa standing by the window gazing out, a forlorn look upon her face. Moving toward her, he slipped an arm about her waist, surprised when she tensed up.

"Come have a seat, love. It is time for tea."

She turned away without a word, moving to the only open settee and seating herself. Seth followed her, wondering what was wrong to have her so out of sorts. Perhaps one of the gowns had not turned out to her liking, but he couldn't see Pippa being worried or bothered by something so trivial.

Sophie and Dinah poured out for their large group, and Dinah handed him a saucer and cup, which he passed to Pippa. She brought the cup to her lips immediately without putting in her usual sugar and cream. Now, he knew something was wrong.

He accepted a second saucer from the duchess and then looked at his betrothed.

"Something is bothering you, Pippa," he said quietly. "You cannot hide it from me."

She turned to him, and he saw anger sparking in her eyes. "But *you* can hide things from me, Seth?"

Confusion filled him. "I have not hidden anything from you, Pippa," he said earnestly. If you feel I have wronged you in some way, please let me address it. Remedy it."

Her gaze turned wintry. "You would like that, wouldn't you? Poor, foolish little Pippa. Never aware of anything going on about her, doing everything her mama—and now her betrothed—tells her to do."

Her words caused anger to surge through him. "Pippa," he said quietly but firmly, "we need to talk. Now. I won't let this misunderstanding go any further, and I would like to hope you would feel the same."

Tears welled her eyes. "Oh, Seth, I love you so much. I thought it was a miracle that someone like you loved me in return. I realize now what a fool I have been. What a fool you have made of me."

She slammed her saucer on the table in front of her. Her abrupt action caused all conversation to cease.

Pippa stood, gazing at her family and then said, "The marriage is off. I will not be wedding Lord Hopewell."

Chapter Twenty-Three

Pippa wanted to walk slowly and gracefully from the room, proving she had dignity and maturity. Instead, cowardice won out.

She fled the drawing room before anyone could stop her. As she reached the corridor, she heard a cacophony of voices break out, causing her to stumble. She feared Seth would follow her. No, she knew he would. Because of that, she had to make it to her bedchamber and throw the lock. If she had to, she would stay inside the room until the Second Coming occurred.

But she could not look at him. Not after what she had seen.

Hiking up her gown, she raced down the hallway, reaching the bedchamber she had been given. The one she had let stay empty while she shared that of her twin.

The traitorous Georgie.

Entering the room, she slammed the door and threw the lock. Out of breath, she leaned her back against the door and then slowly slid down it, landing on her rump. Pippa cursed under her breath, something which she had never done before. Mama would have been appalled.

But she had good reason to use foul language.

Her life had changed in an instant. She and Mama had arrived home from their appointment with the modiste, bringing along three new gowns with them. Wearing a gown created by Madame Dumas had made Pippa feel very feminine. She wanted to look pretty for Seth. Yes, he understood she was more comfortable wearing her breeches and tailcoat, but she wanted to be a wife he could be proud of.

Forrester had told her that Seth was already here, having gone to the music room to see Georgie. Pippa had sent a footman to carry the boxes with her new gowns to her bedchamber. Glancing over, she saw them sitting on the bed. She tamped down the urge to go and rip her wedding gown into shreds as hot tears fell from her cheeks, landing on the bodice of her dress.

Mama had told her it was almost time for tea, and Pippa had said she would fetch Georgie and Seth. She had been so eager to see her betrothed. Every time she laid eyes upon him, her heart raced and the blood coursing through her veins sang a song of love.

And hope. Hope for the future, which had now been dashed.

She found the door to the music room ajar and leaned inside, not hearing Georgie playing. Instead, she had seen Seth embrace her twin—and kiss Georgie.

Nausea filled her, and Pippa had fled, running blindly down the hall. She had vomited in an urn and was so ashamed, she did not say anything to any of the servants. Instead, she ducked into the library, her heart hammering wildly in her chest.

Betrayed. By her betrothed. And her sister. She didn't know which hurt worse and decided they were equally hurtful.

How long had they been together? Laughing behind her back?

She heard a muffled voice and placed her ear to the door, thinking she heard, "This is it." Then a loud pounding sounded.

Oh, that was definitely Seth.

Pippa sat with her cheek against the door, tears dropping onto her bodice, wishing she could crawl in a hole and never come out.

"Open this door now, Pippa!" roared Seth.

Somehow, she managed to push herself to her feet. "You may pound on the door until Doomsday, my lord. I have no plans to open it to you."

"Pippa!" he shouted, beating on the door again, and she almost found the amusement in the situation.

Almost.

When the beating stopped, she shouted, "You may knock until your fingers are bloody and your pecker falls off, my lord, but I am not opening this door. Now, go away and leave me in peace."

She didn't want to be this close to Seth—even with a door between them—and so she pushed herself to her feet and crossed the room, sitting in the chair by the window. She waited and heard nothing. More hot tears fell as she realized he had listened to her and walked away. Pippa was so angry at herself. Why would she still want him after what he and Georgie had done to her.

Yet she did.

She wanted his kiss. His touch. She didn't know how she could take one more breath without him in her life.

Then suddenly, a loud crash sounded. The door flew open, Seth falling through it, dropping to his knees. Pippa shot to her feet as he stood. Instead of coming toward her, though, he walked away. When he closed the door he had just broken through, he faced her, a grim expression on his face.

"Do not touch me," she warned. "I will scream to the bloody high heavens if you do. And don't think James won't come and take your head off because he will."

"He won't," Seth said smugly, a tight smile on his handsome face, and she wanted to slap it off.

"James is my family," she said. "*You* are not."

Seth started toward her, but Pippa was not going to back down. Instead, she raised her chin a notch, daring him to come closer.

Which he did.

When he reached her, his face softened, as did his voice. "Pippa, love, you saw something you misinterpreted."

Her hands shot out, slamming against his chest, causing him to stumble back a pace.

Narrowing her eyes, she said, "You do not get to tell me what I saw. I *know* what I saw, you rotten scoundrel. You. Betraying me. With my sister."

Collapsing into the chair, she rested her elbows on her knees, pushing the heels of her hands against her forehead.

"I know Georgie is prettier than I am. She has wonderful curves and beautiful breasts. She is graceful and sweet—when she is not betraying me. I know I am too lean. My breasts are too small. My—"

Seth's hands touched her shoulders. "You sister is pretty, Pippa. But you are beautiful to me."

She knocked his hands away, her gaze still upon the ground. "Just go, Seth. Please. I am humiliated enough to know the two people I love most in the world have humiliated me."

His fingers caught her chin, forcing it up, their gazes meeting.

"I love you. You. Not Georgie."

She bit her lip. "That makes it even worse then, you dallying with her while you are betrothed to me."

"Pippa, I want you to listen to me."

He caught her waist and brought her to her feet. She tried to get away, but Seth held tight.

"Now, I want you to look at me, as well. I want you to see my eyes. I have nothing to hide from you. Neither does Georgie."

She raised her gaze, meeting his defiantly.

"I went to talk to your twin about our honeymoon. I offered for us to stay through the Season. Through her wedding, if she decided she would wed. Then I said we would leave. I know how close the two of you are and how much Georgie was counting upon you to help her decide about a husband.

"She told me to take you on the honeymoon after our wedding."

Pippa blinked, not expecting to hear this.

"Your twin saw us fall in love. You didn't need Georgie to tell you that you loved me or that I loved you. She understands now that you could talk about her suitors until you were blue in the face, but in the end? Her heart must be the one who speaks to her. Georgie knows how important it is for us to go away together. For you to see the places you have always longed to see. For us to do this together. She told me her heart will tell her when she has found the right man for her. The man she wishes to be her husband."

Tears blinded her, and she could barely see Seth now. "But you were embracing. You kissed her. I saw it!"

"I did give her a brotherly hug. As a thanks for her being so understanding. She knows I would never do anything to come between the two of you, and she hopes when she finds true love, the four of us can be good friends and share in many good times. Yes, I kissed her cheek."

His hands released her, coming to cradle her face. "But you are the one I love, Pippa. You are the woman I cannot live without. My life is better each day—because you are in it."

He and Georgie had not made a fool of her. Pippa had done that all on her own.

"Oh, Seth," she moaned, her head falling against his broad chest, her tears soaking his coat.

He smoothed her hair, uttering nonsense to her, calming her. She might not have understood his words, but she did understand their meaning.

She was loved. By this man.

Pippa lifted her tearstained face, her mouth seeking his and finding it. Their kiss was tender, full of promises of the life to come. A life shared.

Seth broke the kiss and gazed down at her. "I love you, Philippa Strong. And I will love you more tomorrow and even more so the day after that."

"I love you, too, Seth. I am sorry I was such a featherhead. I should have known you—and Georgie—would never betray me. I will never doubt you for as long as we live."

His response was to kiss her again, long and deep, causing desire to flood her. Pippa clung to him, pressing her body against his, wanting to make things right between them.

He lifted his head, her lips feeling bruised. "We should rejoin the others."

She winced. "Did they think my behavior appalling?"

"Georgie was the one who quickly figured it out. Our innocent hug and my kissing her cheek in gratitude was quickly explained to the others. James gave me permission to follow you to your bedchamber." He kissed her quickly. "But we should rejoin them now. They will be worried."

"Not as worried as I am that I have caused a rift between you and me—and Georgie and me."

"Your sister will understand. You have that special connection."

He went to release her, but Pippa held tight to him.

"I don't wish to rejoin the others. I want to stay here with you."

Seth smiled wryly. "That would not be the ideal thing to do, love. I am already in no condition to return to the drawing room and may have to actually send you there by yourself."

"Why not?" she asked, pressing against him—and discovering why. "What on earth?"

"It is what you do to me, love. When I want you, my pecker—as you so delightfully called it a few minutes ago—rises. It is an indication of how much I want you."

Pippa giggled. "I had Mama explain things to Georgie and me. In regard to a wedding night. She made the marital act sound most unappealing, but I know whenever you touch me, I feel as if fire ripples through me."

"Your mother wed a man many years older than she was. There was no desire between them. Seaton did the absolute minimum to try and get sons off her."

"I know what you did to me in the cottage that day was most appealing," she said, her voice low and tantalizing.

Seth grinned. "Are you trying to seduce me, Lady Philippa?"

"Is it working, Lord Hopewell?"

"Yes, but I am going to show far more willpower than you are. Seriously, Pippa. I simply can't make love to you with your entire family waiting downstairs for you to appear and let them know all is right between us. Besides, we aren't even wed yet."

She pretended to pout. "All right, Lord Stick-In-The-Mud. Just remember that I was willing to couple with you. Even before we wed."

He kissed her hard, laughing as he did so. "Oh, Pippa, my darling love. I cannot wait to speak our vows and make you truly mine."

Seth kissed her a final time, for so long that she lost track of time. When he released her, she wobbled a bit, and he caught her elbows to steady her.

"Shall we return to the drawing room?" he asked. "We have been absent far too long."

"Yes," she agreed. "Wait a moment."

Going to her hand mirror, she saw a few stray strands had escaped and took the time to re-pin the errant locks.

"Now, I am ready, my lord," she told him. "And I won't even touch your arm on our way there. Hopefully, you will recover by the time we reach the others."

They went to the drawing room, and as they entered, she heard the lively conversation come to a complete halt. Ten pairs of eyes focused on her. James frowned deeply. Sophie and Mama looked concerned. Aunt Matty shrugged. Georgie's gaze searched hers. Her other sisters and cousins sat on the edge of their seats, worry on their faces.

"All is well," Pippa declared, and a collective sigh filled the room.

She and Seth returned to where they had been sitting before her announcement. She looked at her relatives, knowing how much each of them loved her.

Especially Georgie.

"I leaped to a very rash conclusion," she admitted. "It was wrong of me to think the worst of the two people I love most." She looked to her twin. "Forgive me?"

Georgie came toward her, and Pippa rose.

"You are my other half, Pippa," her sister said. "I love you dearly, just as Seth loves you. Together, you will have a marriage filled with love and light."

The twins embraced, and Pippa vowed never to fight with her sister again.

They pulled apart and retook their seats, and Effie asked, "How many times did you kiss? When you were making up?"

"Effie!" she said. "That is a very personal question. One which I am never going to answer." Then Pippa smiled smugly. "But kissing did play a part in helping me clear my head."

"We need a number, Pippa," Lyric said. "How many kisses did you share?"

"Why is that so important?"

Everyone laughed, and Mirella said, "We all bet on the outcome, Pippa. We knew Seth would be able to explain things to you. We simply wagered on the number of kisses it took to convince you that he loved you."

Pippa roared with laughter and told them, "Neither Seth nor I will ever tell."

CHAPTER TWENTY-FOUR

IT WAS HER wedding day.

Pippa lay in bed, Georgie still snoring lightly beside her. Tomorrow when she awoke, it would be Seth by her side instead of her twin. Would he snore? Did she? She had no idea if she did or not. Georgie had never told her if she did so, but then again, her sister slept like the dead.

She rose and went to the window, looking out. It looked as if the rains from yesterday had finally ended. She remembered an old saying—happy is the bride the sun shines upon—and wondered if there would be sun this morning for the ceremony. She didn't think it really mattered. What was important was that she and Seth would be starting their lives together.

"What are you thinking about?" Georgie asked sleepily, stacking pillows behind her as she came to a sitting position.

Pippa returned to the bed and crawled in next to her twin. "A little bit of everything. It is so hard to believe that this time tomorrow, I will be a married lady. Viscountess Hopewell."

"You will make for a wonderful one, Pippa," her sister declared. "You have a good head on your shoulders, and Mama has taught you enough about how to run a household. You will handle your duties with ease."

She chuckled. "I won't be running my own household for a

good, long while. Seth believes we will be gone at least a year and a half, possibly longer."

Georgie threw her arms around Pippa, squeezing her tightly. "You are going to have the most amazing time seeing the world with the man you love by your side."

"You know I have always wanted to travel, but the opportunity to do so in Seth's company will make it all the more special. Promise me that you will write and tell me what happens during the Season. It is hard for me to imagine I will mostly likely come home and find you wed to a man whom I have never even met!"

"It will be fine, Pippa. I have seen how things are between you and Seth. James and Sophie, too. I will settle for nothing less than love. If it takes one Season or five of them, I am determined to find love."

She smiled, smoothing her twin's hair. "Or love might actually find *you*. That is what happened to me. I was merely sitting by the lake one day when Seth approached, carrying Felix."

"You will need to teach your husband to fish once you finally return home. I cannot believe he is a sailor, and he has never gone fishing."

The twins giggled, and then a knock sounded at the door. It was Millie and Kitty with trays of food. Mama accompanied them and once the servants left, they had a private breakfast together, just the three of them.

"Do you have any more questions about married life?" her mother asked.

Pippa shook her head, thinking she already knew far more than Mama did about the intimacies between a man and wife—and she wasn't even wed yet.

"Seth has the experience to show me the way, and we both have plenty of love in our hearts, Mama. I only hope Georgie *and* you can find a man as good as Seth."

Mama brushed Pippa's cheek with the backs of her fingers. "Not only is Seth a good man, he lives in a most convenient place.

We will never be far apart, my darling. Even once Effie makes her come-out and is wed and settled, I most likely will move to Crestridge. It is still close to Shadowcrest and Hopewood, and it will give James and Sophie the privacy they need as they create their own family."

Her mother turned to Georgie. "If only we could find a husband for you in this vicinity, my dearest Georgina."

"I can see myself now, going about the ballrooms of London, being introduced to titled gentlemen and my first question being, 'Where do you live, my lord? If it is not Kent, then you will simply not do.'"

The three of them laughed together.

A knock sounded at the door, and Mama said, "That will be the hot water for your bath, Pippa. I am going to dress myself now. Georgina, you must also dress so that we can be free to assist your sister prepare."

An hour later, Pippa was bathed and dressed, wearing her wedding gown, which everyone was seeing for the first time, oohing over it. It was of soft pink wool and flattered her figure. By now, her other sisters and cousins had gathered inside the bedchamber, each one trying to help ready her and give her advice.

"I will need you to exercise Starlight for me, Effie. I will be gone a long time, and I want to make certain she is cared for properly."

"That will not be a problem, Pippa. It only means I will get to ride twice as much. Caleb is teaching me many things about the estate, and I will ride Starlight every other day as we go about Shadowcrest. I will also ride for fun, so Starlight will do estate business some days and simply enjoy being out and about on others. Starlight will be waiting for you when you return, though. I know she is your pride and joy."

"Seth was telling us some of the places you will call upon during your voyage," Mirella said. "He suggested each of us write letters and send them to those ports of call, so that you might receive mail and news from home every time you come ashore."

"Some of the news will be dreadfully out of date," Allegra pointed out. "But you can count on us to write to you."

"You may all write to Pippa," Lyric declared. "I am going to write to Seth since he has no other relatives to do so. I think he would appreciate having correspondence of his own to read. Not that you won't share your letters with him, Pippa."

"That is a lovely idea," Georgie told her cousin.

A knock sounded at the door, and Mirella answered it.

"Might I come in?" Caleb asked. He smiled at her. "Ah, you make a lovely bride, Pippa." He looked to the others. "It is time for you to make your way to the chapel. I am here to escort you there. Aunt Dinah, Sophie says you are to remain behind and ride with Pippa and James. She has been at the chapel all morning, making certain everything has been taken care of. I just came from there, and the chapel looks as beautiful as our bride here."

She knew Lyric and Sophie had supervised the servants in taking many plants to the chapel and couldn't wait to see how festive it would be.

"I want to check with Cook on how the wedding breakfast is coming," Mama said. "I will meet you downstairs in the foyer, Pippa. Come along, girls."

Everyone left the room except for Georgie. Her twin came and gave Pippa a final embrace.

"The next time I see you, I will be waiting at the altar to witness your vows to Seth. Oh, Pippa, I am so very happy for you. You are the first of the Strong women to wed. You and James have set a high standard for the spouses brought into our family. I pray the rest of us will all make love matches. Even Mama and Caleb."

"I love you so much, Georgie. While I do regret that I will miss out on your come-out Season—and most likely your wedding—I want you to know that I am always with you in spirit."

Georgie clasped Pippa's hands. "And I will carry you in my

heart."

The twins went downstairs to the foyer, and Pippa told Georgie goodbye. Her sister left to catch up to the others, walking the short distance to the chapel on Shadowcrest lands.

James entered from outside, giving her a smile. "The others have headed for the chapel, and the carriage is waiting to take the bride and her mother to the ceremony."

"Thank you for walking me down the aisle, James, and for standing up with Seth as we speak our vows."

"I'm only glad you were wise enough to marry a fellow ship's captain, Pippa. You have made a very wise choice in selecting Seth Atwell to be your husband."

Mama arrived. "Cook has everything well in hand. I think most of the other servants are already at the chapel."

"Then it is time for us to make our way there," James declared, offering his arms to her and Mama.

They went to the waiting carriage and were soon at the chapel. James and Sophie had wed here at short time ago, and Pippa hoped her ceremony to Seth would be just as beautiful and meaningful as that one had been. The fact that it occurred at Christmastime added a special flavor to the event, and as they stepped inside now, her eyes swept over the place, seeing the holly hanging everywhere and the loops of ivy along the pews. The scent of pine hung in the air.

She and James lingered at the door while Mama went to take her place on the first row of the pews.

Pippa's heart leaped when she met Seth's gaze. He awaited her now at the altar, and she fought from pushing her brother away and racing down the aisle to jump into her groom's arms.

Georgie was seated at the pianoforte, and she played as James walked Pippa down the aisle. Her gaze never left Seth's, and her brother handed her over to her soon-to-be husband. As they joined hands, Georgie left the pianoforte and came to stand on Pippa's other side, while James went to Seth's right.

"We should look at the vicar," Seth whispered, his gaze pinning hers. "But I will admit I am having trouble dragging my eyes from you, love."

She beamed at him. "Well, the sooner you look at him, the sooner we may begin—and the sooner we will become husband and wife."

Seth laughed aloud. "Then let us begin," he proclaimed, looking to the clergyman. "Make it quick. I am ready to start my life with Lady Philippa."

Chuckles were heard throughout the chapel at his bold words.

Pippa felt Seth's hand take hers, threading their fingers together. They spoke their vows, their voices clear and strong. When her groom slid the wedding band on her third finger, she thought it absolutely perfect.

Once they had been pronounced as man and wife, she gazed up at the man she had pledged her eternal love to.

"I am going to kiss you now, Lady Hopewell," Seth said in his low rumble.

Hearing her new title gave her a bit of a thrill, and she replied, "I am eagerly awaiting that kiss, Lord Hopewell."

His lips touched hers, and a deep warmth filled Pippa, a glow that started from within and spread throughout her limbs.

She could kiss this man forever.

The vicar cleared his throat, and Seth broke the kiss.

"It is time to sign the marriage license, my lord," the clergyman said. "We must make things official, you know."

James and Georgie accompanied them to the vestibule just off the front of the chapel, where the four of them placed their names on the certificate, and the vicar recorded the ceremony in the chapel's registry. Someday, she would return here with her children—even her grandchildren—and find their names listed here, remembering this day.

It was official now. Pippa was wed to Seth.

"Take the carriage back," James told them. "And take your time. We will be waiting for you at Shadowcrest whenever you finish here."

James and Georgie left the vestibule, along with the vicar, and Seth wrapped his arms about her again.

"I do believe His Grace was giving us permission to kiss for a bit," her new husband said, a wicked grin upon his sensual lips.

"Why, I think you are correct in that assumption, my lord," she said playfully.

Pippa slipped her hands behind Seth's nape and pulled him down to her, where they exchanged a good number of kisses.

She was the one who ended things, saying, "We should head back before the wedding breakfast grows cold and my relatives get tired of waiting for us."

Her new husband escorted her to the ducal carriage for the short ride back to Shadowcrest. They entered and went to the dining room, where the wedding breakfast would be held, finding everyone seated. Mama had asked what Seth's favorite dishes were and made certain Cook prepared them, along with the ones Pippa had asked for.

They dined and talked as champagne flowed freely. Aunt Matty had said champagne was a must for a wedding breakfast, and tasting it now, Pippa agreed. She made a special point of thanking Sophie and Lyric for how lovely the chapel's decorations had been.

"It was fun to do this for you," her sister-in-law said. "All the Strongs pitched in to make my wedding to James come off perfectly. I wanted the same for you. I only wonder who the next bride in the family will be."

Pippa could tell that Seth was eager to leave, and so she went to Mama and hugged and kissed her goodbye.

Seth joined them, slipping an arm about Pippa's waist, and said, "We will return in two days' time for Christmas dinner, Dinah." Then he smiled wolfishly. "Until then, we will neither expect nor entertain callers."

Mama laughed. "I know you will take good care of my darling girl, Seth."

"She will take just as good of care of me, Your Grace."

They went outside to where Seth's carriage awaited them, and she hugged and kissed all her relatives goodbye, promising she would see them in two days.

Seth handed her into the carriage and climbed in after her. They kissed the entire way to Hopewood, and her body began thrumming with anticipation of what was yet to come.

CHAPTER TWENTY-FIVE

IT WAS ONLY a little after noon when they arrived at her new home. Pippa thought since she had visited the estate many times and been inside the house a few times over the years, it might become home to her more quickly than if she entered a strange abode for the first time. Then again, they were making plans to leave England soon after the new year came, so her home would be on a sailing vessel during the foreseeable future.

The Robbs greeted them as they stepped from the carriage, and Pippa saw that all the other Hopewood servants were standing outside, divided into two lines, facing the carriage. It was a bit overwhelming to see so many of them and think she was now the lady of the house and responsible for all of them.

Robb said, "The servants wished to be here when Lady Hopewell arrived."

Mrs. Robb added, "They are all very happy you have come to Hopewood, my lady."

"Might I address them?" she asked Seth, who nodded.

Stepping toward the group, she said, "I want to thank you for the warm welcome you have extended to me this day. I know it takes a great many servants to keep a large household such as Hopewood running like clockwork. Please know that I appreciate all your efforts, and I will do my best to learn your names as quickly as I can."

She then took the time to go down each line, allowing Robb to introduce everyone present, from scullery and house maids to grooms from the stables.

When she had spoken to the last one, Pippa said, "Please, go back inside. The day is chilly."

Seth stepped to her, taking her elbow and guiding her inside to the foyer.

Mrs. Robb said, "Your trunks arrived earlier today, my lady. I had them placed in your rooms. You have a sitting room and a bedchamber, which are located next to his lordship's rooms."

"Lady Hopewell will store her things there, but she will spend her nights with me," Seth let the housekeeper know, causing Pippa to blush at his frankness.

"Of course, my lord," Mrs. Robb said smoothly, unaffected by the declaration. "It will be good for her ladyship to have a place to bathe and dress separately from you." She turned to Pippa. "No maid came with your trunks, my lady."

"I did not bring one from Shadowcrest," she told the older woman. "With his lordship having us take such a lengthy honeymoon, I thought it best to wait and hire one after we return from our travels."

"Then I will help you myself during the short time you are here," the housekeeper assured Pippa.

"What of Tompkins, my lord?" the butler asked. "Will you take your valet with you?"

Pippa and Seth had discussed whether to bring any servants or not, and they had decided they simply wished for it to be the two of them. Seth assured her he could play lady's maid to her, and they could always find a sailor or two anxious to make a few extra coins that might help them with laundry aboard the ship.

"I will need to give him his release," Seth said. "We won't return for some time."

He waved Tompkins over. The valet had been lingering at a distance.

"You have heard of our plans to take an extended honeymoon?"

The valet nodded. "I have, my lord."

"I am going to give you six months' pay. You will be free to seek another position in a different household. It would be unfair to ask you to wait here at Hopewood until our return."

Tompkins frowned. "I would prefer working for you, my lord."

"We will be gone far too long. You can't sit around, wasting your time."

"My brother is a tailor in London, my lord. He can always use an extra hand, especially when the Season comes around. If I went to work for him, would you send for me when you do return?"

"I would be happy to have you back, Tompkins," Seth said. "I will notify you when we make our way back to England. Just leave me the name of the shop if you would."

"Thank you, my lord," the valet said, looking relieved.

Her husband turned to her. "Shall we go upstairs, my dear?"

She slipped her hand through the crook of his arm, and he led them to his bedchamber.

"I thought we were going to the drawing room," she said. "If the servants know we are . . . *here* . . . they . . . they will know what we are up to!"

He laughed, rich and deep. "I would hope they would know that I am ready to make my bride mine." Seth pulled her into his arms. "I have been waiting for this very moment, Pippa."

She bit her lip. "Mama said . . . well, she said you do this kind of thing at night. When it's dark."

He smiled wryly. "And did your mama have a happy marriage? Was she worshipped by your father?"

"No," Pippa said slowly.

"Well, you are going to be the most happily wed woman you will ever meet," he assured her. And I plan to worship every inch of you, love. It is going to be a most thorough exploration.

Now—and each time I make love to you."

Her face flamed, which only caused Seth to laugh even more. His lips sought hers, and soon the heated kisses they shared caused all thoughts of impropriety to flee. She only wanted to love and be loved by this amazing man.

Seth began peeling the layers of clothing from her, kissing her as each piece fell to the ground. He eased off her slippers, untying the ribbons that held her stockings, rolling those down as his tongue followed along her calf, causing desire to shoot through her.

Finally, she stood before him, bare, and he unpinned her abundant, dark brown hair. It fell to her waist in waves.

Cradling her face in his large hands, he said, "I think I fell in love with you the first time I saw you and your wonderful cornflower blue eyes."

"The Strong eyes," she murmured, leaning in and running her lips along his jawline, her fingers untying his cravat and pulling it from him. "Let me return the favor, my lord, and get you out of these clothes."

"You think to replace Tompkins?" he teased, his fingers moving through her hair as she pushed his coat from his shoulders and down his arms.

Pippa kissed him as she unbuttoned his waistcoat, removing it, then undoing the buttons of his shirt. Pulling it over his head caused her to have to break the kiss, and when the shirt floated to the ground, she was already ensnared in his arms again, their lips fusing.

She placed her palms on his chest, feeling the heat in him, pushing back and studying him.

"I have wanted to see your North Star tattoo ever since you mentioned it. It's an unusual shape for a star," she said, admiring both the tattoo and the chest it rested upon.

"It is called Polaris by some," he told her. "It roughly stays in the same place in the night sky, which makes it a reliable way to gauge north if you don't have a compass. It isn't the brightest star in the sky, but it is easy to spot, especially when you are out at sea."

"How do you find it?" she asked, her natural curiosity feeding her interest.

"Have you heard of the Big Dipper?"

"Yes, I have seen it in the sky. It is much easier to spot in the country than in town."

"Once you find the Big Dipper, the two stars on the end of its cup point the way to Polaris. The Big Dipper always points to the North Star at any time of night on any day of the year. I liked knowing that. The steadiness. The consistency. I wanted to be that kind of man."

"And that is why you chose this tattoo."

She traced it with her fingers and then boldly pressed her mouth to his muscular chest, allowing her tongue to trace it a second time.

Seth growled, yanking her to him, devouring her. She loved his masculine scent. The feel of his hard body. The power contained within him.

"Boots off," he managed to get out, stumbling back to the bed and sitting upon it.

"Aye-aye, Captain," Pippa said, helping to pull each of them from his feet.

She then took his hands, pulling so that he stood, and she worked his trousers down his legs. His manhood jutted straight out from a thick thatch of dark hair, fascinating her. Once he stepped from the last of his clothes, she grasped it in her hand.

"It is hard as steel and yet feels so smooth," she marveled, her thumb caressing its head.

He groaned. "You'll be the death of me, woman. But what a sweet death it will be."

Somehow, they wound up on the bed, Seth hovering over her, his lips trailing down her throat and to her breasts. He kissed them. Sucked them. Laved them. Kneaded them. She never knew how sensitive they were until his touch.

As his hands and lips wandered her body, she did the same, touching, kissing, tasting him. Pippa knew he liked what she did by the noises he made. She made similar ones herself. For a moment, she pitied Mama for never having experienced the passion of true love.

Seth kissed her everywhere, finding spots on her which were sensitive to his touch. He straddled her now, hovering over her, kissing her deeply.

Lifting his mouth from hers, he said, "This hurts a woman the first time, love. But it's quick—and it will never hurt again."

"I don't care," she proclaimed. "I want to be yours, Seth. All yours."

His hands framed her face. "And so you shall be, my dearest love."

He kissed her again, distracting her, but Pippa felt his manhood began to press against her core. His fingers parted her, and he pushed inside, filling her.

The kiss ended, and he looked puzzled.

"What's wrong? It didn't hurt me, Seth. Not like Mama and you said would happen."

"I should have broken through your maidenhead," he said. "Ah. I think I know why. You have ridden for many years, Pippa. I have heard tell of some women who feel no pain when they couple the first time because of the strenuous exercise they have undergone when riding."

She locked her fingers behind his head, pulling him down to her. "Then I suppose riding is a good thing," she told him before their lips met.

As they kissed, Seth withdrew from her and pushed inside her again, in and out. She caught his rhythm and began moving, as well, her hips meeting each thrust. His fingers also teased her, and she felt that familiar pressure building inside her. He had called it an orgasm, and she knew it was about to erupt, like a volcano spewing lava.

"Yes! Yes! Yes!" she cried into his mouth as the warmth enveloped her and she bucked beneath him.

For his part, Seth continued to drive into her and then he, too, was shouting his own pleasure. Pippa felt a warmth fill her, deciding it must be the seed he filled her with that Mama had mentioned.

Collapsing atop her, she hugged him to her, loving the feel of his body atop hers.

Seth rolled, and then she was atop him. He smiled lazily at her.

"How was that, Viscountess Hopewell?"

She pillowed her hands against his chest, resting her chin atop them. "It was even better than I imagined, Captain." Smiling, she added, "Georgie always is saying she plays so well because of all the practicing she does. Well, my lord, I believe I have found something I wish to practice at so that I will become superb at it."

"I love you, Pippa Atwell," her husband declared. "And I will make myself available to practice daily with you. Multiple times a day."

"You can do this more than once a day?" she asked.

He pushed his fingers into her hair, massaging her scalp. "I will have to rest between rounds of practice, but it can be done more than once." Grinning wickedly, he added, "And in more than one way. I cannot wait to teach you all those ways, love."

"Could I be on top as you were?" she asked.

"Of course."

"Oh, I think that would be like riding a horse!" she declared.

"On top. Side-by-side. From the rear. Sitting. Standing," Seth rattled off. "We have many ways to go about lovemaking."

Pippa smiled at her husband, the love of her life. "When can we practice again?"

EPILOGUE

London—July 1811

PIPPA SAT WITH her eyes closed, feeling the pull of Adam at her breast. Her nine-month-old son had been a good nurser from birth. She never felt closer to her baby than the times she nursed him. She smiled to herself, wondering what Polite Society would think of a viscountess who chose not to have a wet nurse but instead nursed her own baby.

She didn't care. She and Seth had blazed their own trail around the world, experiencing life together as a married couple in a most unique way. Her husband had introduced her to different peoples and their cultures. She had grown quite adventurous and eaten unique foods, including octopus and witchetty grubs. They had spent the first six months of their honeymoon in North America, visiting Canada and the United States. She fell in love with Boston and Baltimore, in particular.

They had gone down the coast of South America, rounding the Cape Horn, making their way across the Pacific to Cook's Sandwich Islands. They had stayed there longer than they had anticipated, allowing Pippa to give birth on the island of O'ahu, known as The Gathering Place. She had enjoyed those lazy days spent on the beach before Adam's arrival, her skirts hiked up to her knees, sitting in the sand, wading in the surf, picnicking as the warm sun shone on them.

Thankfully, she had recovered quickly from her firstborn's birth, allowing them to head to Australia. From there, they had traveled to India, then Egypt, and down to Madagascar, rounding the Cape of Good Hope and heading north toward Portugal.

And now England.

Thankfully, letters awaited them in various ports of call, ones sent by her family to both Seth and her. They had been written months before they were received, so she knew the news within them was terribly out of date, but she could hear the voices of her relatives in her head as she read these over and over.

She had written home of Adam's birth, so everyone would know they were coming home with an extra family member. Seth said since she was nursing, it was most likely the reason she had yet to become with child again. She would continue to nurse Adam until he turned a year old, and then she would see if any more children were in their future. She and Seth made love frequently, and she would miss the motion of the ship, which added a new dimension to their lovemaking.

Adam stopped sucking, and Pippa saw he had fallen asleep. She rose and rested him in the hammock, dressing since they would soon be arriving at their final destination.

Seth bounded into the cabin, his hair windblown, his clear blue eyes standing out in his tanned face. She, too, was tan from spending so much time in the sun, something else that would horrify the *ton*. They would be arriving with the Season still having a month to go, and Pippa had no desire to attend any of the events this year. She and Seth had discussed matters, and all they wanted to do was be at Hopewood until next spring, when he would take his seat in the House of Lords and they would make their debut into Polite Society as Lord and Lady Hopewell.

"We are so close, Pippa," he said excitedly, pulling her into his arms and giving her a searing kiss. Oh, the man did know how to kiss.

"It is hard to believe we are almost home and will be seeing everyone," she said. "Just think—we will be meeting Georgie's husband for the first time! I hope he likes me. Us."

Her husband kissed her again, hard and swift. "He will. Georgie listened to her heart. She chose the right man for her. It will be good to get to know him. And meet the other new spouses, as well." He smiled. "Who knows? Perhaps more marriages have occurred and more children are expected that we don't even know about yet."

She cupped his face, her thumbs caressing his cheeks. "If I haven't told you enough, thank you. For marrying me. For this incredible trip. For giving us Adam." She smiled. "And for my gold hooped earrings. I have earned the right to wear them now since I have crossed the Equator and am a seasoned traveler."

Pippa kissed Seth softly. "But my wanderlust is gone, my love. All I want to do the rest of our lives is be at home, whether at Hopewood or in town. Or visiting relatives. There truly is no place like home. We have traveled far and wide, and I believe England is the best place of all."

Her husband kissed her tenderly. "The best place to be is when I am with you, Pippa. And Adam. Here is to the next chapter in our lives—and all the memories yet to be made."

"I love you so much."

Seth smiled. "And I love you even more."

He released her and scooped up the sleeping babe. "I promise I won't awaken Adam until we anchor in London's harbor, but I do want him to get his first glimpse of home from sitting on the Thames."

His fingers found hers, and Seth led them to the deck. Minutes later, the ship maneuvered into its slip and dropped anchor.

Pippa's eyes found Georgie, and she begin waving madly, just as her twin did back at her. Then Georgie took the hand of the large man next to her and pointed at him, grinning like a fool, letting her twin know that this was her husband. He cradled a babe in one arm, and tears flooded Pippa's eyes at the sight.

She saw others on the dock, waiting to greet them. Mama was blowing her kisses, and Pippa realized her mother was heavy with child. Her smile widened even more, pleased that her mother had found the love of a good man and would soon be a mother once again. James and Sophie were also there, James holding their son George in his arms. She hoped George and Adam would be not only cousins but good friends.

Others were waving and shouting, and she saw Mirella with a handsome man at her side. This past spring would have been her sister's come-out Season, and she wondered if Mirella stood with her betrothed—or if the pair had already wed. Effie was also jumping up and down, and Caleb wore a broad smile on his face. This homecoming was incredible, flooding her with emotions.

Pippa decided a house party would be in order, with all her relatives attending, so she and Seth could spend time with everyone and find out everything that had occurred since they had been gone. It would be good for Adam, too, to meet all his relatives, especially cousins he would grow up with.

She turned to her husband, who now held a wide-awake Adam in his arms. Seth leaned down and kissed her.

Oh, it was so good to finally be home.

About the Author

Award-winning and internationally bestselling author Alexa Aston's historical romances use history as a backdrop to place her characters in extraordinary circumstances, where their intense desire for one another grows into the treasured gift of love.

She is the author of Regency and Medieval romance, including: Dukes of Distinction; Soldiers & Soulmates; The St. Clairs; The King's Cousins; and The Knights of Honor.

A native Texan, Alexa lives with her husband in a Dallas suburb, where she eats her fair share of dark chocolate and plots out stories while she walks every morning. She enjoys a good Netflix binge; travel; seafood; and can't get enough of *Survivor* or *The Crown*.

Milton Keynes UK
Ingram Content Group UK Ltd.
UKHW020640040324
438885UK00016B/845